A
SHOWER
OF PASSION

Sara Landers moved to stand before the fire, and she held her hands and arms out toward it, shivering as she did so. Mike Flynn looked at her, and saw that her dress was soaked clear through. It was so wet that it clung to every curve and crevice of her body, causing her nipples to stand out in bold relief.

Sara suddenly felt a heat in her body that wasn't caused by the fire, and she looked over to see Mike staring pointedly at her. His intent was clear. She glanced down at herself and saw why.

Mike turned away, then walked over toward the bed removing a blanket. "You'd better get out of those clothes," he said.

"What?"

Mike held up the blanket. "You can wrap yourself in this," he said. "I'll step out front."

Mike walked outside to stand under the eaves. He was aware of the fact that she was undressing behind him, and his blood raced and his pulse pounded as he thought of it, but he was determined to control his impulses. He wanted to go to her now, more than he had ever wanted any woman in the world. But he would not do so . . . unless she asked him. It was very important to Mike that Sara want it as much as he.

The door to the shack opened, but Mike didn't hear it. Not until Sara softly called his name did Mike know she was there , . .

Paula Fairman

VALLEY OF THE PASSIONS

PINNACLE BOOKS   NEW YORK

VALLEY OF THE PASSIONS

Copyright © 1982 by Script Representatives, Inc.

An original Pinnacle Books edition, published for the first time anywhere.

First printing, July 1982

ISBN: 0-523-41749-7

Cover illustration by John Solie

Printed in the United States of America

PINNACLE BOOKS, INC.
1430 Broadway
New York, New York 10018

VALLEY
OF THE
PASSIONS

Chapter One

Sara Landers was a pretty girl. She was tall and slender, though certainly rounded enough so that no one could doubt her sex, even from a distance. Her skin was fair, her cheekbones high and her eyes brown. Despite the brown eyes, she was blonde. In fact, her hair was so bright a gold that her father called her "Ra," after the Egyptian god of the sun, because, in his words, "She has stolen a bit of brightness from old Ra himself." Sara's father was a former college professor, and thus given to such erudite analogies.

It was perhaps because her father was possessed of a great respect for education that he allowed his daughter to take part in a unique experiment. Franklin Landers allowed Sara to return to the east to study at Swanhope

1

University, where Landers himself had taught. The only field of study open to women was Liberal Arts, and though Franklin would have preferred a more vocationally oriented curriculum, he sent Sara to school anyway, because it was 1881, and time for women to assert themselves.

Franklin kissed Sara goodbye, told her how proud he would be when she returned with her degree in hand, and sent her off to college. She was returning home now, three and one half years later, but there was no degree in her hand.

Sara shifted in her seat, trying for the thousandth time to find some way to get comfortable. It was impossible. Though she had been on the train for only five days, she felt as if her journey had no beginning and would have no end. It seemed she had always been on the train, and she could scarcely remember a time when her legs weren't cramped and her bottom didn't hurt. She was dirty from smoke and soot and hot and sticky from five days without a bath.

There was a time before the train, though, and when Sara thought of it, her face grew deeply crimson, even now, five days after the fact. She was certain that the others in the car could read her thoughts and knew of her shame. She tried not to think of it but the terrible images popped into her mind unbidden, and her sin was as fresh and her shame as great as it was the moment it happened.

2

While attending school, Sara lived with a former associate of her father's, a professor, John Barnes, and his wife, Ann. There were no dormitories available for women, and it was necessary for Sara to make such an arrangement if she wanted to attend the college.

Professor Barnes was a very handsome man in his late forties. His hair was still dark, though now brindled with silver. He wore a small, neatly trimmed moustache, and his dark eyes flashed with an inner light. He was a man of great humor, and he found much to laugh about, so that Sara greatly enjoyed being in his presence.

Sara liked Professor Barnes very much, and when he told her she should think of him as her uncle, she accepted the suggestion enthusiastically. Ann Barnes, the professor's wife, was a different story, however. Ann was small and plump, and though Sara knew that Ann was younger than Professor Barnes, she looked and acted years older. Ann tolerated Sara, but never seemed to show the young girl any genuine friendliness. Sara was so naive that she didn't realize that her beauty had caused the animosity which the older woman exhibited toward her. She didn't understand that Ann was jealous of her.

Sara had developed into the lovely flower of womanhood, with an innocent joy over the effect she had on men. She had discovered that it was exciting to cause the blood of the young male students to run hot, and she was an outra-

3

geous flirt, leading the young men on a merry chase, but knowing always that she was in full control. It was fun to proceed to the very brink of danger, then smile, and step cleanly away. It was exciting not only for the risk involved, but also in another way, for Sara had learned that she was a woman of passions and desires which needed some innocent way of release. This game provided Sara with that way.

Sara's flirtatious ways didn't end with the boys in school, however, and it was this that caused her difficulty. She discovered that her flirtatiousness also had an effect on Professor Barnes, and she found it particularly exciting to be able to cause a man as handsome and important as a college professor to be aware of her. It was a game, and she played it well, never realizing the possible consequences. Then, during a moment of indiscretion, in a spontaneous bit of gaiety, Sara went into his arms to allow him to embrace her in a bear hug. The bear hug lasted much longer than she expected, and then, as she felt his body full length against hers, she felt something which was both tantalizing and frightening. She felt a bulge in the front of the professor's pants and, as a victim is hypnotized by a snake, Sara felt powerless against the urge that caused her to lean into it.

Barnes's hands went to the back of her thighs, where he let them linger. He kneaded and massaged her through the folds of her dress, and though his hands didn't touch her flesh, her skin burned just the same. Her knees

4

grew weak and a bewildering heat flashed through her body.

"So!" Ann's voice suddenly said, the words falling in the stillness of the room like frigid blocks of ice. "This is how I am repaid for having taken you into my home, is it? You are a vixen—a harlot—a viper I have taken to my bosom!"

"No," Sara gasped. "No, you don't understand. I'm just—"

"Please," Ann sobbed. "Please, just go away. Get out of my sight!"

Sara turned and ran in fear and humiliation. Her bedroom was just down the hall from the library, where the indiscretion had taken place, and she went inside and threw herself on the bed, crying bitter tears of remorse for what she had done. She could hear angry voices from the library, and finally the slam of the front door as Professor Barnes left the house.

The house was quiet for several moments after that, and finally, summoning all her courage, Sara went to Ann's room. She knocked lightly on the door, and when Ann didn't answer, she called out to her. She pushed the door open and stepped inside.

Ann was sitting at her dresser, holding a tear-stained handkerchief to her puffy eyes. She saw Sara in the mirror, and she held the young girl in a penetrating gaze which reflected betrayal and anger.

"What are you doing here?" Ann asked.

"I have come to apologize," Sara said. "And

to tell you that . . . I am so sorry and so ashamed. Nothing like this has ever happened before . . . I—I can't explain why it happened now."

"I can explain it," Ann said. "I have seen it coming for some time. Sara, don't tell me you don't know what you have been doing. Don't say you don't know what you have become?"

"What I have become?"

"A vixen," Ann said.

"But I've only been playing," Sara explained. "Please, believe me, Mrs. Barnes. I meant no harm. It was just a game."

"A game, was it? You throw yourself at men and you lure them with your wantonness, and yet you call that a game? I've seen you with the young men of the university, and now with my own husband. You are as dangerous as the sirens of the *Odyssey*."

"I didn't mean for it to go so far," Sara explained weakly. "I couldn't stop it."

"Of course you couldn't stop it. You have gone beyond your ability to control such things. When you act thus, you are inviting the devil to take command of your very body and soul."

"Mrs. Barnes, I'm so sorry," Sara said. "Please, don't be too harsh with Uncle John. It wasn't his fault."

"How well I know it wasn't his fault," Ann replied. "All men are powerless when faced with such wantonness. Oh, that I had perceived the danger and acted sooner! Why didn't I say something? I knew it. I knew all

6

along that it would come to something like this."

"I'll leave your house," Sara offered. "I'll seek residence somewhere else. I won't disturb your home any longer."

"No," Ann said. "It isn't enough that you leave this house."

"It isn't enough?" Sara asked. "I don't understand. What else would you require of me? Ask, and I shall do it."

"I want you to leave the school as well. I don't want you anywhere around my husband, ever again."

"Leave the school?" Sara's heart fell. She was so close to graduation, so close to achieving her father's dream. Surely Mrs. Barnes wouldn't be so vindictive as to make her leave the college.

"Yes," Ann said resolutely.

"But no, please, I have such a short time to go before I receive my degree. I can't leave. Not now."

"You must leave the school," Ann said resolutely. "Only if you are gone will I be satisfied that my husband is spared the evil which threatens to destroy his soul as well as your own."

"Mrs. Barnes, please, I beg of you. Do not make me leave the school."

"Leave," Ann said coldly. "Leave, or I shall inform the dean of your sinful behavior and insist that you be expelled."

"Very well," Sara finally agreed. "I'll leave.

7

I'll tell Uncle John that I must go because my father needs me to help with—"

"You will say nothing to my husband," Ann said. "I want you out of here now, before he comes back. Take your things and go directly to the depot. You may withdraw from the college by letter. Do you have enough money to return?"

"Yes," Ann said. "I just received the allowance for the final semester."

"Good," Ann said. "Then I suggest that you depart for Oregon at once."

Ann turned back toward the mirror, and though she wasn't looking at Sara, Sara could see the woman's reflection in the mirror, and she studied it for a long moment before she slowly turned and left the room, leaving the angry woman behind her.

That had all been five days ago. Since that terrible day, Sara had spoken to no one, other than the ticket agents and conductors. Now, sitting on the hard seat of the train, she tried to force that awful memory out of her mind.

The train began slowing, and Sara, thankful for anything that would interrupt her thoughts, looked out the window. A handful of small, weatherbeaten buildings slid by, then a station platform, and finally a depot. There were half a dozen horses and as many buckboards around the depot. It was just one of the many typical trackside towns along the western reaches of the railroad. Sara knew there would be many more before she reached Butte Valley, Oregon, where her father published the *Valley Monitor*, a weekly newspaper.

"Ma'am, this here is Twin Falls," the conductor said. "You'll be wantin' to get off here, if you're goin' on to Oregon."

"Thank you," Sara said. She stood up as the train squealed to a stop, then walked stiffly on legs sore from days of sitting. When she stepped down from the train her one piece of baggage was already on the platform, colorful now with the destination tags of the several railroads she had thus far ridden on.

Sara walked into the small, wooden depot building. A potbellied stove sat in the middle of the room, and though there was no fire now, it was black from the soot of long use. There was a wooden bench near the stove, and a highly polished brass spittoon near the bench. Despite the spittoon, a cigar had been thoughtlessly ground out on the wide plank boards of the floor.

The wall of the depot sported a calendar, with all the days crossed off until today's date: June 15, 1881. The picture on the calendar was of a night train crossing a trestle between two pine tree-covered mountains. The train's headlight speared forward in the darkness, and the tiny windows of the cars glowed golden. Sara laughed at the romanticized painting. The cars would be dark inside, she knew, and the people would be trying to sleep. Unsuccessfully, she added, with the experience of four such nights behind her.

9

Beside the calendar a clock ticked loudly, and beside the clock there was a printed time schedule. There were two ticket sales windows, but they were both closed. Despite the activity on the platform outside, the depot was empty, so Sara sat on the bench to wait.

Sara heard the conductor call "All aboard," then the rush of steam and the clatter of slack being jerked out of the cars as the train started. She looked through the window and watched the train leave. Only after it was gone, did the stationmaster come in. He looked surprised to see her sitting there.

"Somethin' I can do for you, ma'am?" the stationmaster asked.

"Yes," Sara said. "I'd like a ticket to Butte Valley, Oregon, please." Sara began to open her purse.

"Ma'am, they ain't nothin' I can do about that," he said. "The fact is, they ain't no trains a'goin' to Butte Valley, Oregon."

"What?" Sara asked, surprised. "But I don't understand. The Cascade Line tracks pass right through Butte Valley."

"Yes'm, the tracks pass through Butte Valley, but the trains don't."

"Of course they do. I rode a train when I left Butte Valley three years ago."

"Lots has happened in that three years, ma'am. Most of it bad. The Cascade Line fell on hard times. None of their trains is runnin' anywhere now."

"But . . . what about the railroad I was

10

just on?" Sara asked. "Couldn't they run one of their trains on the Cascade Line tracks?"

The stationmaster laughed. "No, ma'am. In the first place the track gauge is different, so's their trains wouldn't fit on Cascade tracks. In the second place the tracks don't belong to 'em, so they couldn't use 'em, even iffen they fit, 'n in the third place, they like as not wouldn't do such a thing for one passenger, even if they could."

"Maybe they'd make an exception for someone as pretty as this young lady," a new voice suddenly said.

Sara turned toward the sound of the voice. It was a man, tall, rawboned, and with a thick head of chestnut hair. He had an easy, engaging smile, and as he studied Sara, she saw the same look of appreciation in his eyes that she had seen in so many men who looked at her. Until the episode with Professor Barnes, that look pleased and even excited her. Now, she found it frightening, for she equated it with her own ability to maintain control.

The man bowed slightly, not stiffly or formally, but gracefully.

"I'm Michael Flynn, ma'am," the tall stranger said. "I'm with the Cascade Line. Is there something I can do for you?"

"I must go to Butte Valley, Oregon," Sara said. "I know the Cascade line trains used to go through there. When did they stop? And why did they stop?"

"They stopped about three months ago,"

Mike said. "And as to the why, they stopped when the cost of operation became greater than the gross income. Of course, I don't want to bore someone as pretty as you with the details of the business. You aren't supposed to understand such things."

"Mr. Flynn, I have had three years of business and accounting, as well as corporation law, at Swanhope University. I can read a profit and loss statement as well as anyone."

Mike Flynn smiled at Sara's haughty reply. "I'm sorry," he said easily. "I didn't mean to imply that you were not smart enough or anything. It's just that women don't normally. . ."

Now it was Sara's turn to smile and apologize.

"Please forgive me," she said. "It's just that I have had to deal with this same sort of thing for the last three years, and I'm somewhat defensive about being a woman."

"Miss, if you ask me, you have nothing at all to be defensive about." Mike rubbed his chin with his hand and studied Sara for a moment. Sara felt a strange heat building in her under the steady power of his gaze. She had never reacted quite like this to the sight of a man. It had always been she who enflamed the men, not the other way around. She tried to hold his gaze with one of her own, but she couldn't.

"Perhaps I am too hasty," Sara finally managed to mumble.

"Did you say you wanted to go to Butte Valley?"

"Yes."

"I might be able to help you."

"You can get me to Butte Valley?"

"I can't get you to Butte Valley, but I can get you to a place where you can take a train to Portland. From there you can get to Butte Valley by stage," Mike said.

"How?" Sara asked. "I mean, what do you have in mind?"

"I have to take an engine to Boise," Mike said. "From there, you could catch a train to Portland. It's roundabout, but it's about the only thing you can do under the circumstances. You could go with me, if you don't mind riding in the engine cab."

"Ride in the engine cab?" Sara asked. "Why, I wouldn't know what to do."

Mike laughed. "You wouldn't have to do anything at all," he said. "I'd do all the work. I even have to fire the boiler myself, because right now I don't have the money to hire crews, so there won't be a fireman."

"Flynn, you can't let a passenger ride in the engine cab," the stationmaster said. "It's against company policy."

Mike laughed. "You forget, Eb, that *I'm* the company now, so I make the rules. And the rules are that if a beautiful young woman in distress needs a ride to Boise, she can ride in the engine cab with me. Now, how about it, miss, what do you say? Do you want to come along?"

All the common sense Sara could muster screamed at her to say no! How could she possibly think of going on such a journey with a strange man? And yet, the thrill and excitement of riding in the cab of a locomotive was stronger than the warning voices that shouted in her mind. Besides, there was some justification to accepting the offer. She did need to get home, and this appeared to be the only way.

Sara smiled at Mike.

"Yes," she said. "I accept your kind offer."

Chapter Two

Mike grabbed Sara's suitcase and started across the tracks to a side-track, where a single, steam-blowing engine sat waiting.

"I've already fired her up," he said. "So we can get going right away."

As Sara approached the big engine, the thought of what she was doing began to sink in. As it sunk in, it became more frightening to her.

"I know it's supposed to be ladies first," Mike said. "But you'd better let me climb up first, then I'll help you."

"All right," Sara said. She was standing by the wheels, marveling at the size and power of the locomotive. The wheels were taller than she was, and she had to look up to see the top of the rim. The wheel rims were white; the engine itself was green, with red and brass trim.

Mike saw her looking at the engine, and he paused for just a moment before he climbed up.

"Isn't she beautiful?"

"I beg your pardon?"

"The engine," Mike said. "She was the most beautiful engine we had on the line. I'm glad I was able to save it."

"Yes," Sara said. She hadn't really looked at it in that way, but there was a sense of beauty in all the awesome power the engine showed.

Mike climbed into the cab, then stretched his hand down toward Sara's. "All aboard for the . . . what's your name, miss?"

"Sara Landers."

"All aboard for the Sara Landers Special."

Sara took Mike's hand, and as their hands touched she felt something jump between them, like the electric spark of a telegrapher's key. She knew that Mike felt it as well, for he smiled broadly as he pulled her up into the cab.

As Sara strained to climb, the action forced her dress tightly against her body, and her curves were well accented. Mike noticed them with obvious delight, but he refrained from saying anything, thus sparing Sara increased embarrassment.

Inside the engine, there was a maze of pipes, valves, switches, and gauges. There was a small, cushioned seat on one side of the engine cab, and an iron seat, like the seat of a bicycle, on the other side. Mike moved to the bicycle seat and began twisting a valve, as if turning on water.

"Have a seat," he invited generously, pointing to the cushioned bench.

Sara sat down gratefully, and watched as Mike twisted the valves. There were so many that she had no idea how anyone would know where to start.

"Are you an engineer?" she asked.

"Yes," Mike said. He turned a valve, and there was a sudden puff of steam. Mike jumped, then started twisting it frantically, until the steam stopped.

"Wrong valve," he said sheepishly.

"Haven't you ever driven this engine before?" Sara asked.

"Nope," Mike replied easily. He twisted another valve, and this time the steam was vented into the right place. The train began to roll. "Ah, that's the one I need," he said. He looked at Sara and smiled proudly, and to Sara, he had the look of a little boy who had just done something right.

"Isn't it amazing," she said, "that turning that one valve could make this big engine move?"

"Yes, isn't it?"

"Which valve stops it?" Sara asked.

"Which valve stops it?" Mike replied, looking puzzled by the question. "You know, that's a good question. I guess we really should know

17

that, shouldn't we? I mean, in case we want to stop."

Sara laughed nervously. "You are teasing, aren't you?"

"No, I'm quite serious," Mike said. "We really should know how to stop this thing. I mean, what if we had to apply the brakes suddenly? Wouldn't it be to our advantage to know how to do it?"

"What are you talking about?" Sara asked, now more nervous than before.

"Look around, will you? It's probably shaped like a long lever, or handle, or something."

By now the train was rolling along at a pretty good clip, and Sara was becoming quite apprehensive about the whole thing. Had she placed her life in the hands of an incompetent?

"Why are you asking me?" she asked. "Where is the brake on the other engines? Aren't they pretty much alike?"

"I don't know," Mike admitted. "This is the only engine I've ever driven."

"What? I thought you said you'd never driven *this* engine."

"I haven't," Mike said. "Until right now."

"You mean you've never driven *any* engine before this?" Sara gasped.

"Nope," Mike said.

"But . . . but you said you were an engineer?"

"I am."

"An engineer who has never driven a train?"

"Oh," Mike said easily. "Did you mean *that*

18

kind of an engineer? Oh, no, I'm not a train engineer, I'm a construction engineer. I built this railroad."

"A construction engineer?" Sara asked in a weak voice.

"Ah," Mike said, putting his hand on a lever and smiling broadly in pride of accomplishment. "Here it is. We're all set now."

"Oh," Sara said. She had a hollow feeling in the pit of her stomach. She was with a madman. "We are going to be killed."

"No, we'll be all right," Mike insisted. He laughed. "One thing for sure, we can't get lost, can we? What's there to driving this thing? All I have to do is follow the tracks."

"You're crazy," Sara said.

"*I'm* crazy?" Mike said. "I didn't trust *my* life to someone who had never driven one of these things before."

Sara looked at Mike as if he were raving. Then suddenly the outrageously bizarre humor of the situation struck her, and she began to laugh. She laughed so long and so hard that tears came to her eyes, and her side hurt, and she had to hold her arms across her stomach.

Mike laughed with her, and he jerked on the whistle cord, so that the very engine seemed to join in.

"You're quite a girl, Sara Landers," he finally said, wiping his own eyes with his finger. "And 'tis proud I am to be havin' your company on this trip."

" 'Tis proud I am to be along," Sara said, giving a good impression of Mike's brogue.

Mike worked hard at keeping the fire stocked, throwing chunks of wood into blazing flames in the firebox. He kept the throttle open all the way, and though Sara had no way of knowing, they were running nearly sixty miles an hour. She did realize that it was much faster than any of the trains she had been on before. A few times she grew brave enough to stick her head out the window, peering ahead along the long, gracefully curved boiler, letting the wind blow through her hair and force her eyes into narrow slits. It was fascinating, watching the twin rails, so slender in the distance that they seemed to touch, yet opening wider and wider until they seemed to pass to either side of them as they raced by. The engine pounded across a bridge, and she could hear the thunder of their crossing. Then the track swept around a sharp curve, hemmed in by rocky bluffs to either side.

When the train came out of the narrow gorge, the valley opened up wide, with grassy fields, sparkling water, and large, beautiful trees. Mike began twisting valves, and finally he pulled the brake lever, to bring the engine to a halt.

"What are we doing?" Sara asked. "Why did you stop?"

"Raise the cushion, and look inside," Mike ordered.

Sara opened the cushion, and saw that the bench she had been sitting on was actually a storage chest. Inside the chest, she saw a picnic basket.

"A picnic basket?"

"We have to eat something," Mike said. "And I didn't bother to attach a dining car. Come on, there's a nice place over there, by the water."

Mike took the basket and started to climb down.

"Is it safe to leave the train here?" Sara asked.

Mike laughed. "No one is going to come along and hit it," he said. "This is the only engine on the line."

"Yes, but no better than you are at operating it, who's to say the engine won't run away and leave us stranded?"

"Touché, my girl, touché," Mike replied, laughing. "But I'm pretty sure we'll be all right."

Mike helped Sara down, then he walked to the rear of the wood tender, and reached down inside a burlap bag.

"What's that?" Sara asked.

"It's a trick I learned," Mike said. "You soak a burlap bag in water, then hang it out and let the wind blow across it. As the wind causes the water to evaporate, it cools . . . ah, here it is," Mike pulled out a bottle of wine. "It cools the wine. Feel this. It's just as cold as if it had been buried in a snow bank."

Sara felt the bottle, and was amazed at how cold it really was.

"What do we have for lunch?" Sara asked.

"Are you hungry?"

"Yes."

Mike laughed. "Good. I like a woman who isn't afraid to admit that she has an appetite for food. An appetite for food means you also have an appetite for life." Mike looked inside. "I don't know what we have, really. I paid Mrs. Minerva at the boardinghouse to prepare a picnic lunch for me."

"Oh, I wouldn't want to take any of your lunch," Sara said. "If she prepared for only one . . ."

Mike laughed again. "You don't understand how Mrs. Minerva does things," he said. "She was married for forty years to Big Paul, who weighed about 300 pounds, and stood about six feet seven. She thinks every man eats the way Big Paul used to eat, so she fixes the lunches accordingly. Then, God forbid you shouldn't get hungry later, so she puts enough in for a snack."

This time it was Sara's turn to laugh. "Is Big Paul still around?"

"No, he died about five years ago. Mrs. Minerva is sure it was because he was hungry. I just hope it wasn't acute indigestion. Ah, we have cold chicken and roast beef, potato salad, sliced cucumbers, baked bread, and a whole cake."

Mike found a flat rock, and spread out the red and white checkered tablecloth which Mrs. Minerva had folded in the basket, then set out the food. There was a glass and a cup in the basket, and these he filled with wine. He gave Sara the glass.

"Thank you," Sara said. "Oh, everything looks so good," she said. She took a swallow of wine and looked out across the valley. The field before them waved with flowers of every hue and description. There were the white and yellow oxeye daisies, the slender white and blue columbines, and the brilliant red Indian paintbrushes. Beyond the valley, a great range of snow-capped mountains rose.

"I had almost forgotten how beautiful our part of the country was," she said.

"Are you just coming back from school?" Mike asked.

"Yes," Sara said. "I hope Dad will be happy enough to see me that he won't be disappointed that I didn't get my degree." Sara stopped suddenly, then took a drink of wine to hide her embarrassment. She had said more than she intended, and she hoped Mike would not press her for more information.

"I'm certain he will," Mike said diplomatically. "Were you born out here?" he asked, graciously changing the subject.

"No, I was born in Baltimore. My father was a college professor there, but it had long been his ambition to go west and begin a newspaper, so, when I was ten years old, he did just that. He now publishes the *Valley Monitor*, of Butte Valley, Oregon."

"I have heard of the paper," Mike said. "It enjoys an excellent reputation."

"How nice of you to say so," Sara said.

"I am merely speaking the truth," Mike said. "I too, am from the east, by the way. I'm from Boston."

"Boston is a lovely city," Sara said. "My father has many colleagues in the universities there."

Mike laughed, self-deprecatingly. "I'm sure that your father's colleagues and my family have never crossed paths. My father was a policeman, Irish born, and my mother a charwoman. Sure 'n 'twas to escape such a life that I left the city as a boy of sixteen, lured by promises of adventure and glory in 'Custer's Own'."

"Custer's Own?"

"The Seventh Cavalry," Mike said. "'Twas a fine military organization, composed in the main of Irishmen like myself." Mike rolled his *r*'s, and Sara laughed.

"Sometimes you have a terrible brogue, and sometimes you have none. I never know if you are putting on an act or not."

"Sure, 'n you've discovered my secret, darlin'," Mike said. "For the truth is, I learned long ago that a brogue was not always the best thing to have, so I worked at discarding it. I can still use it if it comes in handy, such as working with a hard-headed bunch of Irish gandy dancers."

"What's a gandy dancer?"

Mike discarded the chicken bone, then made

24

himself a thick roast beef sandwich before he went on.

"A gandy dancer is a railroad worker," he said. "A track layer. Before I became president of the Cascade Line, I was a construction foreman."

Sara looked up in surprise. "You? You are the president of the Cascade Line?"

"That I am," Mike said.

"But you are so young. I thought railroad presidents were all old, and fat, and wore a monocule and a goatee."

"Well now, my girl, you have just described the presidents of *successful* lines."

"But even so, to be the president of a railroad. My, that's very impressive. Of course, it would be even more impressive if it were a line that had regular train service. I would love to see the trains running in Butte Valley again."

"Perhaps they will," Mike said.

"You mean there's a chance train service will start again?"

"Yes. I'm going to Boise now to meet with the board of directors of the Great Western Bank. If I am successful, you'll have your train service."

"Do you have a plan?" Sara asked. "I read in one of my business courses that banks don't like to lend money, unless there is a plan with a chance of success."

"I'll verify that your book is correct on that one point," Mike said. "But the truth is, I do have a plan. The problem is that the bank

25

thinks much as you were thinking a moment ago. They aren't certain that someone my age and with my lack of experience can run a railroad. I have to convince them that I can do it."

"How did you become the president of the railroad?" Sara asked.

"I elected myself," Mike replied, smiling broadly.

"You elected yourself?"

"Sure. I am the major stockholder, so I held a stockholders' convention of one, nominated myself, and elected myself as president."

"How did you go from being a soldier in Custer's army, to being a major stockholder in the Cascade Line?" Sara asked.

"I found little glory in the army," Mike said. "So when my enlistment was up, I left. Lucky for me, too, as you know what happened to Custer at the Little Big Horn. After that, I served on a ship for a while, carrying tea from China. Then I drove a stagecoach some, punched a few cows, followed my father's line of work and served as a lawman. I even did some gold mining."

"Oh, did you find any gold?"

Mike pulled out a rawhide cord that hung around his neck under his shirt. A nugget was suspended from the cord. "This is all the gold I found," he said. "I call it my lucky nugget, because I swore to stick with mining until I found gold. It wasn't much, but it satisfied my vow and let me get out of there."

"Then you went into the railroad business?"

"Yes," Mike said. "I learned a lot about construction and engineering while I was mining. When I quit that business, I took a job as construction engineer for the Cascade Line. By the time the railroad went broke, I had advanced to chief engineer. Construction, not the kind who drives trains."

"That I well know," Sara said. They had finished their lunch, and Sara was cleaning up, putting things back in the picnic hamper. "But how did you wind up as the major stockholder?"

"As the railroad began to run out of money, they started paying off in shares. I took on several projects for them, and so received several bonus shares. Then, when the other men didn't want their shares, they sold them to me at rock-bottom prices."

"I see," Sara said. "Do you think it was wise to buy them?"

"That we shall soon find out," Mike said. "If I can convince the bank to go with me, it was wise of me to buy the shares. If I can't, it was most unwise, for I'll wind up with nothing."

They returned to the engine and Mike climbed aboard, then helped Sara up. She took the basket from him and put it back in the chest, while he threw several chunks of wood into the firebox.

Sara watched him, enjoying the easy grace of his motion and the restrained strength of his arms and shoulders.

"Mr. Flynn?"

"Yes?" Mike said, looking over toward her as he poked at the roaring fire.

"You'll make it," Sara said. "I know you will."

"Well, I thank you for your vote of confidence," Mike said. He opened the throttle, and the train started forward again.

Sara leaned back on her seat and watched the rails rush toward them. She listened to the clack of the rail joints and the powerful throb of the engine, and before she knew it she was asleep.

"We're here," Mike said.

Sara had been sleeping, and she was startled by Mike's hand on her shoulder.

"What is it?" Sara asked. "What's wrong?"

"Nothing's wrong," Mike replied. "I just thought you might want to know that we are here."

Sara rubbed her eyes and looked out the window. She saw a depot building, a platform, and a freight warehouse, and knew she was at a rail yard, though the train was not where it would normally be when one arrived at a station.

"I'm not a scheduled operation," Mike explained, seeing the look of confusion on Sara's face. "I had to come through the switches to the most out-of-the-way track. The depot is over there." He pointed.

Sara stood up and stretched, and again her dress pressed tightly against her body, accent-

28

ing her curves. Again Mike stared, and this time she saw another look in his eyes, more frightening than the look she had seen in Twin Falls, for this one was deeper in intensity, as she were seeing the hunger which burned into his very soul.

"I appreciate the ride more than I can say," Sara said, speaking to break the tension of the moment.

The sound of Sara's voice seemed to bring Mike back, and he smiled at her. The light was still in his eyes, only now it was under control.

"What about the fare?" Mike asked.

"The fare? Oh, of course," Sara said. She was a little hurt by the request. Mike had not mentioned a fare when he invited her, and now she thought it was small of him. She began fishing around in her bag. "How much will it be?" she asked.

"About this much," Mike said, reaching for her and putting his arms around her. He pulled her close, holding her so tightly that she could feel the hard, rippling muscles under his shirt. His lips pressed against hers, amazing her by the sensations they evoked. The pleasure she had felt when in the arms of Professor Barnes was but a faintly glowing spark, compared to the roaring inferno Mike had just ignited in her body. Sara's head started spinning. She felt his tongue, first brushing across her lips, then forcing her lips open and thrusting inside.

Sara had been so surprised when Mike first grabbed her that she didn't struggle against

29

it. Now, all struggle was impossible, as the pleasureable sensations overwhelmed her. Mike slipped one big hand to her bodice, opened the buttons easily, then covered her breast and gently massaged and caressed it until it ached in sweet agony.

Finally, Mike broke off the kiss and withdrew his hand, leaving Sara standing there as limp as a rag doll. He laughed lightly. "I hate to disappoint you, but this is neither the time nor the place for us to go any further," he said easily.

Suddenly the spinning sensations stopped, and Sara realized what she had just allowed Mike to do, and the implications of what he just said. *What did he think she was?*

"Go farther?" Sara gasped. She slapped him as hard as she could. "And just what makes you think I wanted to go this far? You took advantage of me, sir!"

Mike put his hand to his face and held his fingers to his cheek, pinkened now from the force of the blow. He smiled sadly.

"I'm sorry," he said. "I was behaving like a boor, and it was most presumptuous of me to assume that you were responsive to such behavior."

"Presumptuous? That is the understatement of the year. Now, if you would, please show me the way to the depot."

"Let me walk you there," Mike invited. "The tracks may be dangerous."

"How can I be in more danger out there than I am in here?" Sara asked.

"I'm sorry," Mike said again.

Sara reached for her suitcase and started to climb down the ladder. "I hope I never see you again, sir."

"Sara, before you go?" Mike said.

Sara looked at him with her eyes snapping angrily. "Yes, what is it?"

"Perhaps you'd better . . ." he started, then he paused and pointed.

Sara looked in the direction Mike was pointing, then she gasped. Several buttons of the bodice of her dress were still undone. The breast that Mike had so adroitly fondled was exposed. Sara's anger and humiliation had been such that she wasn't even aware of it until Mike called it to her attention.

"Oh," she said, when she noticed it. "Oh, you are a horrible, horrible man!"

Sara repaired the damage, then walked across the tracks toward the depot with her face flaming so red, she thought it could be mistaken as a railroad signal.

Chapter Three

Lee Coulter sat on a fallen tree trunk, eating beans and bacon from his mess skillet. There were half a dozen other men sitting around, enjoying the same fare. In the middle of the group a campfire blazed, pushing back the night. Out in the darkness a frightened calf bawled for its mother, and was answered with a reassuring call. The same fire that had cooked the beans and bacon now warmed a pot of coffee, suspended from a rod which was strung out over the fire.

"Tell me, boss," Meechum said, wiping up the last of the bean juice with his fingers and a small piece of bread. "When you was a 'dandyin' around in San Francisco 'n all over the place, did you ever eat this well?"

The others laughed at Meechum, and Lee

laughed with them as he picked up some sand to clean his plate.

"I never did, Meechum," he replied. "I tried to get some beans and bacon at the Mark Hopkins Hotel, but they only wanted to serve pheasant under glass."

"Don't that glass get in your teeth?" Meechum asked seriously.

The others laughed at Meechum, then one of them asked, "Is they lots of pretty girls in them fancy hotels?"

"If they was, it's my guess the boss had his share," Meechum said.

"Yeah, I've seen the way pretty girls acts when the boss gets near 'em. You take Jennie Adams, for example."

"Jennie Adams?" Lee said.

"Sure. Don't tell me you've never noticed how she gets all calf-eyed when you come around her."

Lee walked over to slide his mess skillet in his saddlebag. He was twenty-eight, dark and handsome, in a fine-featured way. Until a year ago, he had been a wealthy playboy, spending the generous allowance his father provided for him in the gaming halls and pleasure palaces of San Francisco and Seattle. It was to this life that the cowboys had been referring.

That was all behind Lee now. His father had died during the winter, and Lee had inherited Broken Lance Ranch, the largest and most productive ranch in the entire valley. The energy Lee had once invested in having a good time was now invested in running his ranch. His father had correctly guessed that letting Lee "sow a few wild oats in his youth" would settle him for the serious days ahead.

"I can't say as I have noticed," Lee answered. "Jennie is a very pretty girl, but she's running her father's ranch, and she's been all business every time I've been around her."

"You're blind, then, boss."

"You're all blind iffin you haven't taken no notice of Professor Landers's daughter. You know the one I'm a'talkin' about? She's just come back from the east. I think she was goin' to school out there or somethin'. That's about the prettiest girl I ever seen anywhere."

"Do you mean Sara Landers?" Lee asked. He laughed. "I didn't know you were into robbing the craddle, Pomeroy. Sara Landers is just a little girl."

"She's the same age as Jennie Adams," Pomeroy said. "She might'a been a little girl when she left to go to that school, but she's a woman full growed now, and you ain't never seen one prettier. She's helpin' her pa put out the newspaper."

"That's right," Lee said. "She is about the same age as Jennie, isn't she? Maybe I'd better ride into town and check on my newspaper subscription. I sure wouldn't want it to run out."

"That's a good idea, boss," Meechum said. "Maybe I'd better check on mine, too."

"What the, hell for?" Pomeroy said. "You can't read."

The others laughed.

"Just the same, I hope she shows up at the Cowboys' Dance come this Saturday, 'cause I pure-dee plan to get myself into whatever square she's dancin' in. That way I can dosey-do her a bit myself," Meechum said.

There was the sound or an approaching horse, and the men looked up to see a rider coming into the golden bubble of light cast by the campfire.

"Hello, Purkee," Lee said. "There are some beans and bacon left."

Purkee pulled the saddle off his horse, then took out his mess skillet. He carried it over to ladle some beans up from the pot. He tore off a piece of bread, then walked over and sat down to eat before he said a word. He had been riding night-hawk, a title given the riders who watched over the herd at night.

"It's a fine thing, us sittin' here eatin' beans," Purkee finally said. "When there's a squatter somewhere who's eatin' Broken Lance beef."

"Eating Broken Lance beef? What do you mean?" Lee asked.

"I found one of our steers," Purkee said. Purkee, like all the cowboys, took a proprietary point of view about everything belonging to the Broken Lance, so saying "our steer" came easily for him.

"You found one of our steers on squatter

land?" Pomeroy asked. "Did you bring him back?"

"Weren't nothin' to bring back," Purkee said. "He'd been slaughtered, 'n there wasn't nothin' left but head and hide. The meat was all took."

"Damn it," Lee said, striking his hand with his fist.

"I tracked whoever done it," Purkee went on. "The tracks led across Durbin Creek, 'n onto the railroad grant land. You know what that means."

"Boss, they ain't nobody but squatters livin' on the railroad grant land," Pomeroy said.

"If you ask me, we need to pay them folks a little visit," Meechum said.

"Yeah," Pomeroy added. "And we can take a couple of torches along too. You know, as sort of a callin' card?"

"No," Lee said. "We aren't going to do anything like that."

"But, boss, we can't let them get away with butcherin' our beef," Pomeroy insisted. "If they tell other squatters they butchered one of our beeves 'n got away with it, the first thing you know we'll be feedin' all the sodbusters in the whole valley."

"They aren't going to get away with it," Lee said. "I'll go see the sheriff tomorrow. Butchering someone else's steer is grand larceny."

"Grand larceny, yeah," Meechum said. "Maybe the law will hang the son-of-a-bitch. It's been a long time since I was to a public hangin'. They're more fun than a county fair."

37

"You ain't gonna see no hangin'," Pomeroy said. "The sheriff couldn't find his ass with both hands and a map."

"They's fences too," Purkee said.

"Fences? What do you mean?" Lee asked.

"Them sodbusters have put up fences, all along this side of the creek. Our cows can't even get to the water."

"Damn it!" Lee said. "That's railroad grant land. It's still in dispute. The squatters have no right to fence it off."

"That's what I was thinkin'," Purkee said. "But they claim our cattle get into their fields and destroy their crops. Leastwise, that's what the fella said who was standin' guard by the fence."

"You mean there was someone standing guard?" Lee asked.

"Yep. He seen me drop a rope over one of the poles, commencin' to jerk the fence out, 'n he come out there with a scattergun 'n ask me to leave."

"What'd you do?" Pomeroy asked.

"I left," Purkee said easily. "Any more coffee?"

Meechum nodded and Purkee got up and poured a cup of the steaming black liquid into his cup. He sucked it through extended lips and looked at the others. "What would you have done?" Purkee asked.

"Iffen a fella come up to me with a scattergun 'n asked me to leave, why, I reckon I'd leave," Meechum said in a voice which let it be known that no one blamed Purkee. "But that still don't give that squatter the right to be there in the first place. Boss, we ain't gonna let 'em get away with this, are we?"

"The wheat field, down by the breaks," Lee said. "It isn't fenced, is it?"

"No," Purkee said. "Our cows don't generally wander down there. I guess the sodbusters figured there was no need for it."

"They figured wrong," Lee said. "Saddle up, men. We're going to move our herd."

"Now you're a'talkin', boss," Pomeroy said.

"You'd think they'd learn, wouldn't you?" Meechum asked. "You'd think they'd learn that this here valley is cow country. Them sodbusters got the whole rest of the state. They got no business in here. No sir, they got no business at all."

There was a quiet, almost a hesitant knock on Mike's door at the Fairmont Hotel in Boise.

Mike was in bed, covered by the bedclothes to his waist, naked from the waist up. Around his neck hung the gold nugget, nestling in the thatch of chestnut hair on his chest. The hair gleamed almost red in the glow of the bedside lantern.

"It's open," Mike said.

The door was pushed open and a woman came inside. She had long, red hair. The color came from a bottle, but had the effect the woman wanted. She touched her hair nervously, almost shyly, and smiled at the man who was in bed.

"Did, uh, you ask to see me?"

"Yes," Mike said. He patted the side of his bed and invited the girl over to him. "Set down."

The girl looked at the bedside table and saw a bottle of whiskey and a glass. The whiskey had caught a ray of light from the lantern, and glowed brilliant amber, as if it had captured a bit of the lantern's fire. There was an empty glass beside the bottle.

"Would you offer a girl a drink?" she asked. Her voice wasn't shy now she knew she was in the right room. It was husky and deep with the promise of what she could do.

Mike pulled the cork from the bottle with his teeth, then poured the whiskey, never taking his eyes away from her. She was pretty, in a garish sort of way. Perhaps she could dull the terrible, aching desire he had felt, ever since leaving the engine he had shared with Sara Landers.

"What's your name?" Mike asked.

"Laura."

Mike looked at Laura, trying to make her over in his mind, trying to make her a surrogate for Sara Landers. After he gave the glass to her, he took a long drink straight from the bottle. Perhaps senses dulled by drink would help.

Mike wiped the back of his hand across his mouth, recorked the bottle, then set it down. He felt a need now, which couldn't be denied, and he reached up and put his hand to the bodice of the woman's dress. He could feel her warm, heavy breast through the red cloth.

"I know what you want," Laura taunted, looking at Mike through bright, blue-green eyes. She undid the buttons of her bodice, then pulled her dress off, over her head. She was dressed for her profession, and she wore nothing beneath her dress so that Mike was treated to the sight of her naked body, perhaps older than her years, though still firm and inviting.

The woman folded her dress carefully and placed it on a chest by the wall, then turned to face Mike once more. Her body was subtly lighted by the lantern beside the bed, and the area at the junction of her legs was darkened by the shadows and by a tangle of dark hair which belied the red of her head, and which curled invitingly at her thighs.

Mike turned down the covers, inviting the girl into bed with him, and as he did so, Laura saw that he, too, was naked. Mike's own need for her was already evident.

"Oh," Laura sighed when she saw him. "Oh, honey, you *do* know how to make a girl feel wanted, don't you?"

Mike pulled her to him, kissing her open mouth with his own, feeling her darting tongue probe against his lips. He moved over her.

The woman warmed as quickly as Mike, and she received him happily, wrapping her legs around him, meeting his lunges by pushing against him. She lost herself in the pleasure of the moment, and Mike could feel her exploding around him as he jerked and thrust in savage fury, spraying his seed into her and finally collapsing across her.

Later, when their rapid breathing had stilled and Laura lay back with her dyed-red hair spread out, fanlike, on the pillow, Mike reached for the whiskey bottle and pulled the cork again. Laura looked at him, studying him for a long moment through the blue-green eyes which seemed so penetrating.

Mike held the glass toward her, offering her a drink, but with a nod of her head she declined. Mike made a little move toward her with the bottle, as if toasting her, then he turned it up and took a deep drink.

"Is she pretty?" the woman finally asked. It was the first sound since the murmurings and exclamations of passion a few moments earlier, and the words sounded almost foreign to the quiet of the room.

Mike looked at her.

"Is who pretty?"

Laura raised herself on one elbow, and the cover fell down, exposing her breasts.

"The one who drove you to me."

Mike got out of bed with a creaking of springs, then padded, naked, over to the window. He pulled the dark green shade to one side with his finger, and peered down the street toward the depot. It was there he had last seen Sara Landers.

"You are a very pretty woman," Mike finally

said. "What makes you think I would need someone else to drive me to you?"

"I am a whore," the woman said easily, and without shame. "When a whore is with a man she discovers many things about him, things the man doesn't want her to know."

"You mean you have what the Indians call medicine?" Mike asked. "You know what I am thinking?"

"Perhaps it is a type of medicine, yes," Laura said.

Mike chuckled again, then padded back toward the bed.

"How would you like to spend the night here, with me?" he asked.

Laura grinned broadly. "I would like that," she said. "I would like that very much."

Mike rubbed his gold nugget. "Maybe you will bring me luck," he said. "I have a meeting tomorrow."

"A big meeting?" Laura asked.

"A *very* big meeting," Mike said.

Chapter Four

The late afternoon sun speared through the window, illuminating millions of dust motes, and splashing pools of light on the highly polished conference table. Four men sat on one side of the table, and Mike Flynn sat on the other side. He fingered his gold nugget as he studied the board members. Each of the four men had a folder of papers, and they shuffled through them importantly. One, a large man with heavy white muttonchop whiskers, polished his glasses, then put them on and stared across the table at Mike. His name was Potter, and he was the chairman of the board.

"Mr. Flynn, our final figures have been compiled," he said. He cleared his throat. "The cash we received from the sale of all moveable stock, plus the sale of the office buildings here in

Boise, and the sale of the buildings and furnishings in Portland, came to a grand total of $458,384.17. We have applied that to the debt the Cascade Line owes this bank, leaving a balance due of $41,615.83. The current value of your holdings, to include all non-moveable fixtures such as track, bridges, grading, etcetera, and the single engine and ten passenger cars, five freight cars and 25 cattle cars you have insisted upon retaining, comes to a little over $100,000. Technically, Mr. Flynn, your assets are now greater than your liabilities."

Mike grinned broadly. "Then I'm in business?"

"Not exactly," Potter said. "We have looked over your plan of operation, and we find one rather substantial flaw."

"What flaw have you found?" Mike asked.

"It's the land grant property, Mr. Flynn. You are planning to use it to improve the position of the railroad, but the land has not officially been transferred into your hands."

"It will be on June 30th," Mike said.

"Only if railroad service is re-established by that time," Potter said. "If you don't have regular service on a scheduled basis by June 30th, the land reverts to the United States government."

"I'm aware of that," Mike said. "Service will be re-established by June 30th."

"Mr. Flynn," Potter said. He rubbed his hand through his hair and looked at Mike, as if forced to explain something to a child. "This is June 23rd. What makes you think you can have scheduled service established by the 30th?"

"I will do it," Mike said simply. "Provided I get the support I need from you gentlemen."

Potter cleared his throat. "You have asked for one hundred thousand dollars . . ."

"Yes," Mike said.

"That's quite impossible. The government grant land cannot be used as collateral, and you don't have $100,000 worth of property."

"I don't understand," Mike said. "You just said my total worth was $100,000."

"From that, you must subtract the nearly $42,000 you owe. And you must also consider that much of that is nonrecoverable. The only thing that can be converted to cash is the . . ." Potter looked at the folder in front of him. "The Sara Landers Special."

"No," Mike said. "That is the only train I have. Without it, I have no business at all."

"We realize that," Potter said. "So we are willing to make this proposition to you. We will accept the Sara Landers Special as collateral for a loan of $10,000."

"Ten thousand dollars?" Mike said. He sighed. "That's not much money, is it?"

"It depends on how you look at it," Potter said. "If you have to raise it, it's a great deal of money. If you are going to try to operate a railroad on it, it's very little."

"Ten thousand dollars," Mike said again. He

sighed, and fingered his gold nugget for a moment. "All right, I'll do it. When you get right down to it, I really don't have any choice."

"Mr. Flynn, I do hope you fully understand the provisions of this loan," Potter said. "You must repay one-fourth of the loan within three months from the time you accept it, and the next installment is due three months later. If you miss one payment, the Sara Landers Special can be taken away from you."

"Yes," Mike said. "I understand. Where do I sign?"

Potter slid a paper across the table and showed Mike where to sign. Attached to the paper was a bank draft for ten thousand dollars, made out to Mike Flynn, president of the Cascade Railroad Line.

Mike signed the paper, then took the draft. He put the draft in his pocket and stood up, then shook the hand of each of the board members.

"Gentlemen, it has been a pleasure doing business with you," he said.

"I hope our next meeting is just as pleasant," Potter replied.

Sara stepped back and looked at the page-plate. She had taken all morning to set the type, but now it was finished, and needed only to be put on the press to print the paper. The type was set backwards, but Sara's eye was so practiced that she could read it easily, and she proofed the dateline: *June 27, 1881, Butte Valley, Oregon.*

Behind Sara her father worked on the press, making adjustments here, wiping it with a cleaning rag there. He pampered it and treated it almost as if it were a living thing. Though the big-city dailies had steam-operated presses which could turn out thousands of copies an hour, the *Valley Monitor* still depended upon a hand-operated, flat-plate printing press. It was adequate for their needs.

"Ra, did you read the Polecat column?" Franklin asked his daughter.

"I read it as I was setting the copy," Sara replied.

"That's no way to read an editorial," Franklin chided. "It should be read slowly, so that every word has meaning."

Sara laughed. "Dad, you act as if the Polecat column is a work of art."

"It is, Ra," Franklin replied seriously. "On, not the writing itself, mind you. I make no bones about my writing ability. I'm just a simple country newspaper man. But the *art*, Ra, is in the fact that it exists at all. I've attacked the United States government for not being more decisive with the railroad grant lands. I feel they should either turn title over to the railroad, so the railroad could sell the land to raise much needed revenue, or they should take the lands back so the cattlemen could buy them. They definitely should *not* leave the lands in limbo, so the squatters can move in."

"Do you think the government will listen?" Sara asked.

"I don't know," Franklin admitted. "But it's a wonderful country, where a citizen can attack his own government in print, and not fear reprisals."

"Who are the squatters, Dad?" Sara asked. "How did they get out there on the railroad land?"

"They came here by wagon train," Franklin said. "Two years ago a wagon train bound for Portland was snowed in here, and had to spend the winter. The folks hereabout took pity on them. They supplied them with food, shared their water, even sponsored a dance to raise money for them. But when the snows cleared, the wagon train didn't move on. The squatters learned that the land they were on was in dispute, and they figured they had the right to stay as long as they wanted."

"What's wrong with that?" Sara asked.

"Well, to begin with, it's not legal," Franklin said. "No one can settle there until after the 30th of this month, when the railroad loses title."

Sara thought of Mike Flynn, and his plans to save the railroad. She had not mentioned him to her father, and now she wondered if losing the land would make his task more difficult.

"Do you think the railroad will lose the land?" she asked.

"Oh, I'm certain of it," Franklin said.

"If they lose the land, they really will be out of business, won't they?"

"They are already out of business."

"But I thought someone was trying to save the railroad."

Franklin chuckled. "There's a fella named Flynn . . . Michael Flynn, I believe. I've heard he is trying to save it, but I also know that he didn't get as much money from the bank as he had hoped."

"Oh," Sara said sadly. "That's too bad."

"Are you feeling sorry for Mr. Flynn?" Franklin asked in surprise.

"No," Sara said quickly, not wanting her father to ferret out any more information. "I was just thinking of how nice it would be to have rail service here in the valley."

"Oh, it'll come," Franklin assured her. "No one is going to dig up the tracks, and as long as they are here, someone will come along and use them. Perhaps another, more established railroad, which can afford to absorb the loss of revenue, until it becomes a paying operation."

"Dad, what will happen to the lands if the railroad loses them?"

"The cattlemen have first claim on them," Franklin said. "You see, every one of the ranchers are now running more cattle than they can actually support with the grass and water that they own. So, they have had to resort to using the railroad grant lands. Now that's worked out just fine, because there has been enough to go around. But the squatters have moved in, and they have cut off the water and the grass. This is a ranching valley, as you well know, and anything that hurts the ranchers, hurts the economy of all of us. That's why I think the government should run the squatters off."

"Where would they go?" Sara asked.

"Well, they could go to wherever they were headed for in the first place," another voice said, and startled, Sara and Franklin looked around to see a man standing just on the other side of the counter.

"Lee," Franklin said. "I didn't hear you come in."

"Hello, Professor," Lee said. He took off his hat and smiled engagingly at Sara. "You can't be Sara?"

"Hello, Lee," Sara replied. Lee was as handsome as he had always been; as handsome as he was when Sara was a young girl with a large but secret crush on the wealthy playboy she saw only occasionally.

"What do you think of Ra now?" Franklin asked proudly, as he saw the unabashed way Lee was looking at her.

"Professor, I've never seen anyone more beautiful," Lee said. "And that is truly a fact."

Sara smiled and blushed at the compliment.

"Well, you didn't come to the newspaper office just to look, did you?" Franklin teased. "Or did you?"

"Could you blame me if I had?" Lee replied. "But the truth is, I have come for something."

"What can I do for you?" Franklin asked.

"I want some posters printed, Professor. You know the kind, like the wanted posters the law puts out when they offer a reward for someone."

"Wanted posters? Are you putting out a reward on someone?"

"No," Lee said. "I just want that kind of a poster. I want it to say: 'Warning. This is cattle range land. Fences or any other obstruction to water and grass will be removed by force.' I want it big enough so that a fellow can read it from quite a distance."

"Do you think that will have any effect on the squatters?" Franklin asked.

"I really don't know," Lee said. "But I've got to try."

"Are they giving you any more trouble?"

"They butchered one of my beeves last night. I was going to report it to the sheriff, but I decided to let it go this time. I really don't know who took it. Besides, they only took one, and they didn't take it to sell, because they took the meat. I guess they were hungry."

"If you ask me, Lee, you are just too good to them. They have no business out there in the first place."

"I'm hoping these posters will do the trick," Lee said. "I'm going to post them everywhere, then I'm going to tear down every fence, gate, water-flume, and grain storage building I see."

"I'll have them ready by tomorrow morning," Franklin promised. "Is that soon enough?"

"Yes," Lee said. "I can have them all posted

by tomorrow afternoon, and still have time for the Cowboys' Dance tomorrow night. You remember those, don't you, Sara?"

"How could I forget the dances at the Star Hotel?" Sara replied. "Dad used to let me go, but he wouldn't let me dance because he said I was too young."

"You aren't too young now, are you?" Lee asked. "I would be awfully pleased if you would let me escort you tomorrow night."

"I don't know," Sara started, but Franklin interrupted.

"Ra would be happy to go with you, Lee. What time will you call for her?" Franklin asked.

"I'll be here at seven," Lee said. He put his hat back on, smiled, then left. Sara waited until he was gone before she spoke.

"Why didn't you let me speak for myself?" Sara asked.

"I didn't know what you would say," Franklin admitted. "I wanted you to say yes, so I just said it for you."

"How did you know I would want to go?"

Franklin chuckled. "Ra, do you think I don't know what kind of a crush you used to have on Lee Coulter?"

"You knew?" Sara gasped. "But that's impossible. I never told anyone. How could you have known?"

"Fathers have ways of knowing such things," Franklin said. "Besides, he's not only handsome, he's the wealthiest and most successful

54

rancher in the entire valley. You'd have to go a long way before you landed a better catch than Lee Coulter."

"Landed a better catch? You make it sound as if he were a fish."

"A *big* fish," Franklin said. He laughed, then grew more serious. "Listen, Ra, I certainly don't intend to push you into anything. If you'd rather not go to the dance tomorrow night, just say so. I'll find some excuse for you."

"Oh? Just try and keep me away," Sara teased. "Those summer dances are about the closest thing to a social life we have in Butte Valley. I'm going, all right. It's just that in the future, Dad, let me arrange my own dates, all right?"

"I'll try to remember that," Franklin promised.

Jennie Adams raised up from the smell of burnt hair and flesh, and looked down at the calf she had just branded. She rubbed her soft brown hair away from her forehead, and glanced toward the holding pen with flashing blue eyes. She was a very pretty young woman, though she insisted on wearing the same jeans and shirt outfits that the cowboys on her ranch wore, so that one had to look at the gentle curves and soft features to see the femininity she possessed.

Jennie Adams was twenty-three, and it was legend among not only her ranch hands, but the ranch hands of the entire valley, that she could rope and brand as well as any man, and ride better than anyone. For the last six years, Jennie had won the Independence Day horse race, and the odds were strongly in favor of her winning again this year.

"Miss Jennie, there's only about three more of the little critters that need a mark," Curly, her foreman, said. "If you want to take a break, I can finish up for you."

"No, thank you, Curly," Jennie said. "I'll finish." Jennie put the branding iron back in the fire. Then she saw a rider approaching. She shielded her eyes from the sun and stared for a moment, then she smiled broadly. "On second thought, if you don't mind, I will let you finish."

Curly looked up, surprised at Jennie's sudden change of mind. Then he saw the rider too, and he understood. Lee Coulter was dropping by for a visit.

Lee Coulter's father and Jennie's father had settled the valley years before. Lee's father had died a few years earlier, and Jennie's father had been injured in an accident, though he was still alive and as active as he could be, although he had to use a cane.

Stump Adams had also seen Lee approaching, and by the time Jennie was out of the cattle pen, Stump had hobbled down from the house, and father and daughter met their visitor by the outside well.

Lee swung down from his horse, greeted

both of them, and took a drink of water before he spoke.

"Well, Lee, what brings you to the ranch?" Stump asked.

"I've come to ask you if you'll throw your weight behind a campaign I'm starting," Lee said, flinging the last few drops of water from the dipper, then replacing the dipper on the nail.

"What kind of campaign?"

"I'm having some posters printed," Lee said. "It's a warning to all squatters that the railroad grant land is cattle range land. The poster tells how we're going to tear down all fences and the like which would interfere with cattle getting to water or grass."

"By damn, it's about time," Stump said. "You're mighty right. I'll back you."

"Good," Lee said. "That's good, Mr. Adams. When the others hear you are behind it too, we'll have one hundred percent cooperation in the valley."

"Are you going into town on the Fourth of July?" Jennie asked Lee.

"On the Fourth? I don't know, why?" Lee asked.

"Oh, no reason," Jennie said, her face reflected a little disappointment.

Lee smiled. "Oh, you must mean for your race," he said. "I guess I might as well. After all, I have bet one hundred dollars on you to win."

"Really?" Jennie said, smiling brightly. Then she frowned. "Oh, Lee, I hope I don't let you down."

"You won't let me down. Oh, by the way, guess who I'm taking to the dance tomorrow night?"

"Who?" Jennie asked, brushing the hair from her forehead with a nervous gesture.

"An old friend of yours," Lee said.

"An old friend of mine?"

"Yes," Lee said. "You remember Sara Landers, don't you? It seems to me that I remember the two of you being very close."

"Oh, yes," Jennie said easily. "We were very good friends, and I feel just terrible for not getting in town to see her before now. I've been so busy with the ranch . . ."

"Jennie is practically running it for me now," Stump put in. "I've been worthless as a plug mule ever since I smashed up my leg."

"Nonsense," Jennie said. "I'm helping you, but I'm certainly not running the ranch."

Lee smiled. "That's not what I hear," he said. "I hear you are the best rancher in the valley."

"That's the truth," Stump said. "That's the absolute truth."

"Well, if you haven't seen Sara since she returned, maybe you'll get a chance to see her tomorrow night," Lee suggested.

"Tomorrow night?"

"At the dance."

"Oh. Well, I probably won't be going to the

dance," Jennie said. "I've got so much to do here, and I really don't care much for those silly things. You know how it is."

"Why, Jennie Adams, I've heard you say two or three times this week how you were looking forward to going," Stump said.

"Well, not really the dance part," Jennie said. "I was just looking forward to getting into town."

"If you get into town, try and make it to the dance," Lee said.

"I'll try," Jennie promised.

Lee swung back onto his horse. "And, Mr. Adams, it's good to hear that you'll support my poster campaign." He touched the brim of his hat. "Goodbye."

Stump and Jennie watched him ride off, then Stump spoke.

"You know, when George was alive, he and I use to think that maybe . . ." He let his voice trail off.

"Maybe what, Dad?"

Stump laughed. "Oh, you'll probably think it's the silly notion of a silly old man," he said. "But we used to think that some day you and Lee might get married. We thought it would be nice to combine the Broken Lance and the Rocking A."

"You and Lee's father thought we would get married?"

"Yeah," Stump said. "I guess it was silly, huh?"

"Yeah," Jennie said, laughing. "That was very silly."

Jennie hoped that her father couldn't tell that the laughter was forced . . . forced to prevent tears from coming to her eyes.

Chapter Five

The Morning Star Hotel was the biggest hotel in Butte Valley. In fact, if one didn't count the Widow Murphy's house, which she converted into a small hotel after her husband died, the Morning Star was the only hotel in Butte Valley. It was three stories high, with fifteen rooms on each of the top two floors, and a restaurant and ballroom on the ground floor.

Every Saturday night during the summer, the ballroom was taken over by the Valley Cattlemen's Association for the Cowboys' Dance. The dance was free to all comers, and it was, as Sara had told her father, the biggest social event in Butte Valley.

Excitement would begin to build Saturday morning, when the stagecoach would arrive with the band. The children of the town would start gathering around the stage depot about half an hour before the stage was due, laughing, pulling each other's hair, sometimes breaking into a dance of their own. They pretended to be the band, strumming imaginary guitars and playing phantom fiddles and accordions.

A few of the cowboys would drift by casually, as if they had other business to attend to and just happened to be in the area. The young women would drop into the general store, just next door to the depot, where they would buy brightly colored ribbons or notions, pretending an innocence of the fact that the band was at that very moment unloading their instruments. On many such mornings last minute adjustments to dance cards were arranged by the "chance" meetings.

The arrival of the stage would first be announced by the driver's trumpet. He would sound it as soon as the stage crossed the bridge, far down in the valley, and its clear, brassy tone would carry into town, alerting everyone, so that by the time the coach and six rolled down Main Street, nearly half the town had turned out.

Sara stood in the window of the newspaper office, watching as the stage stopped, and the four men of the band climbed out, then began taking their instruments down. They realized they were the center of much attention, and they moved importantly, engrossed in the work of unloading, seemingly taking no notice of the excitement their arrival had caused.

"How do they look?" Franklin called from the press. He was preparing it for the printing of the posters Lee had ordered.

"Who?" Sara asked.

Franklin laughed. "The band, of course. Do you think I didn't know why you were looking out the window?"

Sara smiled and came away from the window. She picked up the poster stock and put it in place for the printing. "The band looks fine," she said. "It'll be a nice dance."

"Good, good," Franklin said. "Your first dance after returning home should be a nice dance. If I thought the prettiest girl in the valley would save at least one dance for her father, I might even be persuaded to go."

"Oh, I'm terribly sorry, Father, but my dance card is filled with big fish," Sara teased. Franklin laughed, then twisted the handle of the press, and the first poster was done.

The wagon drew to a stop by the edge of the wheat field. There were two men in the wagon, one very large man with a full beard, and the other, a younger version of the large man. The men were Arnold Penrake, and his seventeen-year-old son, Caleb.

"Jumpin' jeehosifat, Pop, what happened to our wheat?" Caleb asked.

The field before them was mashed flat, with the just budding heads trampled in the ground. Arnold had seen fields like this before, after a hail storm, and once, back east, during the Civil War, when an army moved through.

"I don't know, boy," he said.

Arnold got down from the wagon and walked over to the edge of the field. He bent to one knee and picked up a handful of dirt and straw. Ten acres of wheat, totally destroyed! It was a mystery, until he saw the cow droppings and hoof marks.

Arnold stood up and stuck his hands deep into his bib coverall pockets, and looked out across the valley. Far in the distance, he could see the herds staying near the grass and water. The question was, what brought them up here to the wheat field? There was no water for them. They wouldn't have come unless . . . Suddenly Arnold realized what had happened and he spit angrily upon the ground.

"They was drove," he said resolutely.

"What'd you say, Pop?" Caleb asked.

"Them cows was drove into our wheat fields," Arnold said. "Now what'd they wanna go 'n do that for? This part of the valley over here ain't even in dispute."

"I don't know, Pop, them cattlemen do some things just for pure meanness," Caleb said.

Arnold started back toward the wagon, when he noticed something he hadn't seen before. A white poster was attached to a nearby tree. He walked over and pulled it down, then read it.

"They got no right," he said angrily.

"What is that, Pop?"

Arnold held the poster up for his son to see.

"The cattlemen say they are going to tear down all our construction in the grant lands. They got no right to do that."

"They don't need right on their side," Caleb said. "This here is cow country 'n ever'body seems to be on the cowman's side."

Arnold folded the poster up and put it in his pocket.

"I know what we could do," Caleb said. "We could butcher a cow ever'time they tear down one of our fences."

"No," Arnold said emphatically. "That'd put the law on their side for sure. Butcherin' a steer is a jailin' offense. Tearin' down a fence is just like spittin' on the street. 'Bout the most can happen is a fine, 'n then the fine goes to the gov'ment, 'n not the fella who got his fence torn down. If they caught us butcherin' a steer, they could shoot us dead, and no one would blame 'em. It's too dangerous."

"It ain't dangerous at all," Caleb said. "I kilt one yesterday mornin', and never heard a word about it."

"What?" Arnold asked, looking at his son in shock. "Did you just say you kilt a steer yesterday?"

"Kilt 'im, skint 'im, and took the meat," Caleb said proudly.

"Then it was you!" Arnold said angrily. He swung his hand, bringing the back of it sharply across Caleb's face. There was a resounding smack, and Caleb's head perked under the impact of the blow. "It was you that brung this on us," he said.

Caleb looked at his father with seething anger smoldering deep in his eyes. A thin trinkle of blood dripped down from his nose.

"I'm goin' into town tonight," Arnold said. "And I'm gonna pay for the steer you butchered. It'll take ever'thin' we have left."

"Pop, what are you gonna do that for?" Caleb asked. "We *deserve* that meat, after all they've put us through."

"Boy, I guess I just been flappin' my gums around you twenty years for nothin'," Arnold said as he urged the team on. "You ain't learned nothin', have you?"

By dusk, the excitement which had been growing for the entire day in Butte Valley was full blown. The sound of the practicing musicians could be heard all up and down Main Street. Children gathered around the glowing, yellow windows, and peered inside. The dance floor was cleared of all tables and chairs, and the musicians had been installed on the platform at the front of the room.

The band started two or three numbers, "Buffalo Gals," "The Gandy Dancers' Ball," and "Little Joe the Wrangler" being the most popular. Horses and buckboards began arriving and soon every hitching rail on Main Street was full. Men and women streamed along the boardwalks toward the hotel, the women in colorful ginghams, the men in clean, blue denims and brightly decorated vests.

"Lee arrived at the Landers' house, which was located at the opposite end of Main Street from the newspaper office, promptly at seven. He was wearing a tan suit and highly polished boots, with a dark silk vest covering a white frilled shirt.

"Lee, you do know how to turn out," Franklin said, as Lee stepped into the house.

Lee smiled. "I haven't worn this suit since San Francisco." He looked up as Sara came into the room. Sara was wearing a bright blue gingham dress, trimmed in white faille. A wide white sash was around her waist, accenting her figure beautifully, and Lee took in a sharp breath as he saw her.

Sara returned Lee's look with her own appraising stare. If anyone else in the valley had attempted to dress as Lee was dressed, they would have been considered, vain, a dandy. Lee Coulter could bring it off because he was handsome enough to do justice to the clothes, and virile enough to falsify the charge of dandyism.

As Sara examined Lee, she felt a slow building heat in her body, and she wondered what it would be like in his arms. Then, as quickly as the thought surfaced, she submerged it. What was there about her that made her react so to men? First there was Professor Barnes, then there was Mike Flynn. Now there was Lee

Coulter. Was Ann Barnes right? Had the devil taken possession of her body and soul?

As Sara thought of Mike Flynn, she recalled the wild trip on the engine, and the rapture of his passionate kiss and embrace at the trip's end. Would Mike Flynn come to the dance—alone? If so, would he ask her to dance? What would it be like to see Mike Flynn and Lee Coulter, each one vying for her attention?

"Is there something wrong?" Lee asked. "You didn't answer."

"What?" Sara replied. "Did you speak to me?"

"I asked if you are ready to go," Lee said. "The dance is starting."

"I'm sorry," Sara said. "I must have been thinking of something else." She dare not mention Mike Flynn to Lee. "I must warn you that some of my dances are promised," she added with a smile.

"Oh?" Lee replied. The expression on his face showed that he didn't like that idea.

"To my father," Sara added with a small laugh.

Lee smiled broadly. "Oh, your *father*. Well, as long as your father is the *only* other person on your dance card."

Sara walked between Lee and her father, as they went to the hotel. Even before they arrived, they were able to feel some of the excitement, for the hotel was aglow with light, and bubbling over with conversation and laughter.

The high skirling of the fiddle could be heard, even from a block away.

' Once inside, the excitement was all it promised to be. Girls in butterfly bright dresses and men in denim and leather laughed and talked. To one side of the dance floor there was a large punchbowl on a table. Sara watched one of the cowboys walk over to the punchbowl and, unobtrusively, pour whiskey into the punch from a bottle he had concealed beneath his vest. A moment later another cowboy did the same thing, and Sara smiled as she thought of the potency of the punch.

The music was playing, but as yet no one was dancing. Then the music stopped, and one of the players lifted a megaphone.

"Choose up your squares!" the caller shouted.

The cowboys started toward the young women, who giggling and turning their faces away shyly, accepted their invitations. In a moment there were three squares formed and waiting. Sara and Lee were in the square nearest the band, and as she looked across the square she saw Jennie Adams.

"Jennie!" Sara squealed, and the two women rushed together and embraced quickly.

"I was wondering when you were going to see me," Jennie said. "I saw you the moment you walked in. Of course, everyone saw you. You look simply wonderful."

"Oh, don't be silly," Sara said. "Jennie, you must come to see me."

"I will," Jennie promised, and as the caller

raised his megaphone, Jennie and Sara moved back to their positions in the square.

The music began, with the fiddles loud and clear, the guitars carrying the rhythm, the accordion providing the counterpoint, and the dobro singing over everything. The caller began to shout, and he clapped his hands and stomped his feet and danced around on the platform in compliance with his own calls, bowing and whirling as if he had a girl and was in one of the squares himself. The dancers moved and swirled to the caller's commands.

Around the dance floor sat those who were without partners, looking on wistfully; those who were too old, holding back those who were too young. At the punchbowl table, cowboys continued to add their own ingredients, and though many drank from the punchbowl, the contents of the bowl never seemed to diminish.

When Sara danced with her father, she noticed that Lee was dancing with Jennie. If Sara had a best friend in the valley, it would be Jennie, for the two girls, both single children, had grown nearly as close as sisters over the years. And yet, not even Jennie had known of Sara's childhood crush on Lee.

The dance went on into the night, and though a couple of the cowboys who had drunk too much punch got into an argument over the favors of one of the young women, the ruckus was quickly and quietly settled so that nothing disturbed the dancers. But that peace was disturbed around 10:30, when a large, bearded man, carrying a pitchfork, walked into the ball-room.

"You can't come in here, sodbuster," one of the cowboys called, and started toward him, bent on throwing him out.

The big man shoved the cowboy back with such amazing strength that the cowboy hit the punchbowl table, and knocked the bowl onto the floor. It broke with a crashing tinkle of glass, and some of the women let out small shouts of fear and surprise.

"What do you want?" Franklin asked the man. "Why have you come in here to disturb decent folks?"

"I want to see Lee Coulter," the man said calmly. He spoke in a quiet voice, but it was a deep and rumbling voice which sounded loud in the sudden quiet of the room.

The man was in his mid-to-late forties. He was wearing bibbed overalls and a red shirt. His hat, unlike the stylish, blocked hats of the cowboys, was misshapen and tattered, sweat-stained and dirty. He had a full gray beard, and his eyes reflected the light of dozens of lanterns and candles, giving them a demonic glow. His forearms, exposed by the rolled-back shirt, bulged with muscle.

Lee was standing right beside Sara when the man spoke his name. Sara felt Lee tense, then start toward the middle of the dance floor to confront him.

"Here I am, Mr. Penrake," Lee said calmly. "What do you want?"

"Justice," Penrake said.

"Justice?"

Penrake pulled a dirty wad of bills from his bib pocket.

"Here is twenty dollars," he said. "They tell me that's what one head will bring in Portland. I'm payin' for the steer my boy Caleb kilt yesterday mornin'."

There was a buzz of excitement through the room, but then it stopped, as Lee made no effort to retrieve the money.

"What's the matter?" Penrake asked. "Ain't squatter money good enough for you?"

"Where'd you steal that money, Penrake?" one of the cowboys jeered, and the others laughed and made catcalls.

"Well, now, Mr. Penrake," Lee said. "It's one thing for you to come up and ask me if you could buy one of my beeves, but it's quite another for you to take it first, and pay afterward."

"Yeah," one of the other cowboys called. "That's called rustlin' in this territory."

"I think we oughtta string 'im up!" another shouted, and Penrake looked around nervously, but he didn't make any effort to leave.

"There's another matter I'd like to discuss with you," Penrake said. "You ran your cows over my wheat."

"Yes, sir," Lee said. "I'll confess to doing that."

"I figure I would have made about thirty bushels an acre on that ten acres," Penrake said. "At thirty cents a bushel, that comes to ninety dollars. I'll deduct this here twenty dollars, 'n you'll owe me seventy."

"Mr. Penrake, your wheatfield was on grazing land," Lee said.

"My wheatfield was on the railroad grant land, Coulter," Penrake said. "And that means that I have as much right there as you or any of your cows."

"Mr. Penrake, if you have a few head of cattle, or a few horses you would like to turn out on that land, I don't think anyone in the valley would begrudge you. The cows and horses eat a little grass, drink a little water, then they move on, leaving the land and the grass and the water for others. When you plant crops, Mr. Penrake, you fence off the grasslands and the water, and you plough up what you don't fence off. You are taking it all for yourself, and you leave nothing for anyone else."

"I have as much right to that land as anyone, until the gov'ment decides what to do with it," Penrake said. "And not you nor nobody else can stop me. And as for these things," Penrake pulled a crumpled poster from his bib pocket and Sara recognized it as one of the posters she and her father had printed for Lee. "You know what you can do with these things?" Penrake shouted angrily.

"I'm glad you noticed them," Lee said calmly. "Now there will be no question when we start taking down your fences."

"You aren't taking down any fences of mine,

sir!" Penrake shouted. He lunged at Lee with the pitchfork, and Sara, frightened that Lee would be killed, screamed, "Lee, look out!"

Lee saw Penrake lunge toward him, and, at the last second, he managed to lean away just as the tines of the pitchfork slipped by. He grabbed for the handle of the pitchfork, but Penrake was a powerful bull of a man and he managed to jerk the pitchfork back, pulling it free from Lee's hands. Penrake laughed evilly and lunged again, but again Lee managed to dance lightly to one side.

"Stop them!" Sara called. "Somebody please stop them!" But even as she yelled, she knew that Lee was on his own, and she bit her lips and hung on the edge of stark terror as she watched the angry giant try to kill the man who had brought her to the dance.

Penrake had the advantage in strength, but Lee was more agile, and this time, instead of trying to grab the handle, Lee hit Penrake in the face with his fist. He was well set, and he put a lot of power behind his swing. Penrake, who was concentrating on thrusting the pitchfork, didn't see the blow coming, and Lee caught him squarely on the nose.

Penrake let out a bellow of pain, and a small trickle of blood began oozing from his nose. Lee felt the nose go under his fist, and he knew he had broken it. And yet, amazingly, Penrake didn't go down. Instead, with a roar which exposed his teeth, now stained red with the blood which ran across his mouth and into his beard, Penrake made still another lunge.

"Knock him down, Lee!" one of the cowboys shouted in a lusty cheer, and Lee, wondering just what it would take to knock him down, caught Penrake with another solid blow, this time aimed for the Adam's apple. That one did the trick, and Penrake dropped the pitchfork, then grabbed his neck and fell to his knees, gagging and choking and trying to breathe.

"You've got 'im, Lee!" someone else shouted. "Now finish him off!"

Lee stepped up to Penrake and drew back his fist for one more blow, then he held it for a moment and finally let his arms drop to his side.

"Mr. Johnson?" Lee called quietly.

"Yes, Lee?"

"I'm going to write out a draft to Mr. Penrake for seventy dollars. When he brings it to the bank Monday morning, I would like you to honor it without question."

"Very well, Lee," the banker said.

"Now, Mr. Penrake, you have recovered the loss of your wheat, sir. Now, if you would, please leave, as you are disturbing folks who just want to have a good time."

Penrake stood up, still clutching his neck. He looked at Lee with a face red from the struggle and his anger. Lee finished writing out the draft and handed it to the big man. Penrake took it sullenly, and put it in his pocket without saying a word.

"Don't bother to thank me," Lee said easily. "But be prepared, Mr. Penrake, because your fences *are* coming down."

Penrake started to reach for his pitchfork, but Lee put his foot over the handle. "You can pick it up Monday, when you come to the bank," he said. "Good evening, Mr. Penrake."

Penrake scowled at Lee, then at the others. Finally he left the room and the men and women in the room cheered for Lee.

"Music!" Lee called. "We have more dancing yet."

About half an hour before the dance was over Professor Landers said that he was tired, and he left. When the dance finally did end, Sara and Lee walked home alone. It was a beautiful evening and the moon was in a quarter phase, so that the stars were even more brilliant.

"I certainly missed our starry evening skies when I was away," Sara said.

"You had the same stars back east," Lee teased.

"No, I think not," Sara said. "They were but pale imitations of these. See how they glisten? It's almost as if the taller trees are holding them in place, they seem that close."

"I'm glad you like them so," Lee said. "Perhaps it will keep you here."

"Lee, that was a nice thing you did back there at the dance," Sara said. "Other, lesser men would have beaten him and thrown him out without a thing. You paid for his crop."

"I wish he would leave the valley with that money," Lee said. "But never mind. In just a few more days the railroad is going to default on its land, and we'll get control. Then we'll have the law on our side."

"What if the railroad doesn't default?" Sara asked. "What if they begin service?"

Lee laughed. "In three more days? There hasn't been a train through here in six months, so there isn't likely to be one through in three days."

"But what if there is?"

Lee sighed. "I hear there's a guy named Flynn in charge now. I also hear he's an incompetent fool who thinks he can do singlehandedly what an entire corporation couldn't do. He'll make some puny effort, then he'll give up and the land will be available. In fact, I wouldn't be surprised if Flynn hasn't already given up."

"If I know Mike Flynn, you shouldn't count him out yet," Sara said. Then she wanted to bite her tongue, for she would have preferred never to have spoken the words. She had never mentioned her strange meeting with the impertinent Mr. Flynn, not even to her father.

"If you know Mike Flynn?" Lee said, surprised by her statement. "What do you mean? Do you know him?"

"No, not really," Sara said quickly. "I did meet him, quite by accident, on the way out here."

"Evidently he made quite an impression on

you," Lee said. "At least, enough of an impression to lead you to think he may succeed."

"I have nothing to base that on," Sara said. "He just impressed me as a most aggressive young man, that's all."

Lee chuckled. "It will take more than aggressiveness to save this railroad," he said. "It will take money. It will take a great deal of money, and I know that Mr. Flynn is in short supply of that particular commodity. But, enough of that. Did you enjoy the evening?"

"Yes," Sara answered. She looked at Lee and smiled broadly. "I can't tell you how *much* I enjoyed the evening."

"I hope you will allow me to provide you with many more such evenings," Lee said.

Lee leaned toward her then and kissed her. He did so quickly and easily that Sara didn't expect it, and was in the middle of it before she even realized what was going on.

The kiss was not as demanding as Mike's kiss had been, but it was overpowering in the sensations it evoked. It was a skillful kiss, from one who was obviously experienced in such things, and because of that was intensely stimulating. It left Sara's senses reeling and her mind spinning. Finally, Lee pulled his lips from hers, though he continued to hold her and look into her eyes with his lips less than a breath's distance away.

"You shouldn't have done that," Sara said.

"I wanted to," Lee said easily.

"Do you always do just what you want to?"

"When I can," Lee said. He smiled. "I hope you aren't going to tell me you didn't enjoy it."

"No," Sara admitted. "I won't lie to you. I did enjoy it. But I shouldn't, don't you understand?"

Lee laughed. "Sara, let the other silly young women say such things. You know better. Now, kiss me again, and this time, let yourself enjoy it as you know it can be enjoyed."

They kissed a second time and Sara met his lips with her own, not retreating, but moving into the kiss, testing to see how far it could carry her. She closed her eyes and drifted with the sensations evoked by the kiss. Then, suddenly, she thought of the kiss she had shared in the engine cab with Mike Flynn and her breasts ached with that same, sweet agony. She longed for the thrilling caress that had so enflamed her then, and she strained against Lee, mashing her breasts against his chest. Suddenly, she realized what she was doing, and, abruptly she pulled back.

"No!" Sara said in a voice that was almost a sob. "Please, stop!"

Lee looked at her, confused by her sudden action, but he didn't press the matter.

"All right," he said easily. "I'll stop . . . this time."

Sara turned and ran into the house. What was wrong with her? Was she so wanton that her passions had finally gained control over her reason?

Chapter Six

"Oh, Christ, hear us," the vicar of St. Paul's Episcopal Church intoned.

"Oh, Christ, hear us," Sara, and the other parishioners responded.

"*Kyrie eleison.*"

"*Christe eleison.*"

"*Kyrie eleison.*"

Sara was particularly attentive to the prayers of the Holy Eucharist on the Sunday morning immediately after the dance. She was praying for forgiveness, not for a sin of the flesh, for as yet, Sara had committed no such sin, but for a sin of the spirit.

"*We acknowledge and bewail our manifold sins and wickedness, which we from time to time most grievously have committed, by*

*thought, word, and deed, against thy divine
Majesty."*

By thought. And if by thought, also by
dream, for it was for Sara's dream that she was
asking particular forgiveness.

Sara had dreamed the night before. It had
been a frightening and shameful dream, and
yet, despite the fear and the shame, there had
been an unwanted and bewilderingly pleasant
side to it as well. In her dream those passions
which she tried so desperately to keep in check
gained control of her subconscious, and played
upon her hidden desires.

In her dream she had been with Lee Coulter.
She had kissed him, just as she had last night
on her father's front porch. The kiss in her
dream, like the kiss in real life, deepened, and
in her dream Sara closed her eyes so she could
no longer see Lee Coulter, but she could still
feel him, as the kiss spread fire through her
body.

Her lover's lips lingered for a long moment
on her lips, then they moved down to the hollow of her throat. Sara's arms rose slowly, as
things move in dreams, and they circled
around his broad, *naked* shoulders. How had
he become naked?

Now, they were no longer standing in front
of her house, but were in a bed . . . her bed,
naked flesh against naked flesh. His hands
caressed her, moving gently across her breasts,
lingering for a moment to fondle sensitive

nipples, then dipping down to more exciting areas. Sara's legs parted, and she felt a gentle stroking. It was a caress which was tender, but persistent.

Sara felt waves of heat emanating from her loins as the fingers plucked upon the soul-strings of her sensitivity. She had a faint notion that she should resist, and yet a part of her realized that this was just a dream . . . and she asked herself, what harm could there be in giving in to the yearnings of a dream?

Then, in the midst of her dream the face of her phantom lover became very clear and she gasped, for it was the face of Mike Flynn! At the very moment Sara realized that her lover was Mike Flynn, the sweet tenderness which had been building inside gave way to a mounting sensation of urgency, bursting over her like a cascade of fire, searing her with its all-consuming wonder. Then, as the wave of passion receded, she saw Mike's face growing more and more indistinct, slipping away until it was gone—and she was awake.

With her pulse pounding and her skin tingling with the last currents of pleasure, Sara pulled her own hands away. Her face flamed in embarrassment as she realized her sin, and shame pulled at her, diluting the edges of her slowly receding passion and pleasure.

Sara had lain in bed until it was light, not daring to go to sleep again for fear of repeating the shame that had awakened her before.

* * *

"Ra," Sara's father whispered. "Aren't you going to take communion?"

Sara looked around, startled by the fact that the people were already proceeding to the altar rail for communion. She had been on her knees for the entire service, praying for forgiveness for the passionate nature of her body.

Sara moved to the altar with the others, received the bread and wine, then returned, feeling now that she had done all she could do. If she were going to stand condemned for her passions, then she would stand condemned.

Father Percy stood on the front steps of the church, telling everyone goodbye as they left. He held Sara's hand in his for a long moment, and looked at her with eyes shining with pride.

"It does my heart good to see a young woman display such piety," he said to Sara. "I saw that you were on your knees for the entire service, and I know your spiritual rewards will be great because of it."

"Thank you, Father Percy," Sara replied.

"Child, have you ever considered the possibility of becoming a nun of the Episcopal Church? It is a rich and fulfilling life," Father Percy said.

"A nun?" Sara replied.

"You could devote your life to our Lord," Father Percy said. "A lifetime of piety and reflective meditation."

Why not? Sara thought. She could live a life of repentance, and if Satan actually had gained control of her soul, as Ann Barnes claimed, then he would be denied whatever evil purpose he had in store for her. And yet, even as she considered the proposal, she knew she could never live such a life. She smiled graciously.

"No," she said. "I don't think I could do that."

"It's a pity," said Father Percy.

Suddenly their conversation, and the conversations of the others who were visiting after church, were interrupted by the sound of a train whistle. For just a moment everyone looked at each other in surprise, for there had been no train through Butte Valley for nearly six months.

"It's a train," Mr. Johnson, the banker, said, as if everyone didn't know. Somehow, putting it in words seemed to galvanize the others to action.

"A train!" someone else yelled, and the call was passed on, so that within a minute not only the parishioners of St. Paul's, but the congregations of the Baptist and Methodist churches, as well as those who hadn't gone to church at all, knew that a train was coming to Butte Valley.

Everyone began moving toward the depot, slowly and hesitantly at first, as if unsure of themselves. Then, as the train grew closer, they could hear the venting of steam and the puff of smoke. The long, lonesome-sounding whistle blew again, and its sound hurried the people on. Soon, the townspeople were gathered on the platform of the boarded-up depot.

"Here she comes," someone called, though

his shout was hardly necessary, for everyone watched as the train came around the curve and into the town itself. It was pulling a string of empty cars. Already some of the children were running alongside, shouting and jumping with glee.

"My, have you ever seen anything so beautiful?" Franklin asked, as the train drew up alongside the station platform.

Sara recognized the green and red brass-trimmed engine as the same one she had ridden in going to Boise with Mike Flynn. Then, leaning out the cab window behind the engineer, she saw the smiling face of Mike Flynn.

And something else!

Painted under the cab window in bright gold, with red filigree, was the name: *Sara Landers Special.*

"Look!" someone shouted. "Hey, look at the name! Miss Landers, have you noticed? The train is named after you!"

"Ra, what is this?" Franklin asked. "What is all this about? Did you know this train was to be named after you?"

Sara gasped.

"I . . . I didn't know anything at all about this," she said. "Why did he do such a thing?"

"Why did *who* do such a thing?" Franklin asked, clearly confused by the turn of events.

"Mike Flynn," Sara replied.

"Ra, do you *know* Mike Flynn?"

"I can't talk now," Sara said. She turned, and

86

with tears of anger burning her eyes, pushed her way back through the crowd.

"Aren't you going to stay, Miss Landers?" someone else shouted. "Look, this train is named after you!"

Sara started to go home; then she changed her mind and started for the newspaper office. It was closed on Sunday, and she would be alone there.

How could he? she thought. *How could he humiliate me so?*

The train rolled to a majestic stop, then squirted steam from the driver-wheel cylinder. The great puff of steam first frightened, then amused those who were too close when they realized there was no danger. Mike climbed down from the engine, where he was immediately surrounded by the citizens of the town.

"Who are you?" someone shouted.

"I'm Mike Flynn, president of the Cascade Line Railroad," Mike answered.

"Have we got train service now?"

"You see her sitting here, don't you?" Mike answered with a broad grin.

"Why is Miss Landers's name on your engine?"

"Can I buy a ticket now?"

"What about the grant land? Does it belong to you now?"

Mike laughed and held up his hands, begging for some quiet.

"Ladies and gentlemen, I am going to hold a

town meeting this afternoon, right here in this depot," he said. He looked toward it. "As soon as I can get it clean enough for people to go in," he added.

The people laughed.

"What's the meeting for?" someone asked.

"It's to answer any questions that any of you may have concerning the Cascade Line," Mike said.

"What time?"

"Two-thirty," Mike said. He smiled. "Provided you quit asking me questions now so I can get to work."

Reluctantly, the crowd began to break up, then drifted away, talking among themselves as they speculated about the possibility of railroad service being restored.

"Mike, I'm going to vent all the steam and bank the fire," the engineer called down from the cab.

"All right, Sollie. Then you, Carl and Burke come and help me with the depot."

"Right," Sollie replied.

Mike looked at the engine proudly, then he wiped away an imaginary spot from the shining green paint with his handkerchief.

"I am Professor Franklin Landers, sir," a voice said from behind him, and Mike turned quickly toward him. The professor was not quite as tall as Mike, though he was a good-sized man, and handsome enough that Mike saw easily why Sara was so pretty.

Mike stuck out his hand. "I'm very glad to meet you, sir. I'm Mike Flynn."

"Would you mind explaining this?" Professor Landers asked, pointing to the name on the engine cab.

"Isn't she beautiful, though?" Mike asked. "She's a 4-4-2, tall, wide and handsome. And look at the size of the driver wheels."

"I don't mean the engine, sir, I mean the name," Franklin said. "My daughter seemed quite upset when she saw it, and I am most concerned about it."

"Sara was upset?" Mike asked. "Professor, I'm sorry. I had no idea she would be upset. I certainly wouldn't have done it, had I known that."

"Why did you do it? And how do you know her? I had no idea the two of you had ever met."

Mike laughed, a small, friendly laugh.

"I really don't know her, Professor," he said. "I did meet her briefly, and I was struck with her beauty. Then, when it came time to name the engine, I wanted a name worthy of such a beautiful engine, and the beauty of your daughter came to mind. So I named it the Sara Landers Special. Where is Sara? Perhaps if I talked to her," Mike suggested.

"No," Franklin said. "Let me talk to her first. If she is willing to talk to you, I'll send her over to the depot."

"Thank you," Mike said.

Franklin looked at the engine and the long

line of cars. "And now, Mr. Flynn, I want to ask you a few questions, not as a father, but as a newspaperman. Are you serious about restoring rail service to the valley?"

"Yes," Mike said.

"You sound awfully sure of yourself," Franklin said.

"I am."

"Mr. Flynn, while I am inordinately proud of this valley, I am the first to admit that the economics don't justify rail service. Except for a few shipments of cattle during the shipping season, what will be your customer base? Surely you don't expect to make it on passenger service?"

"No," Mike said. "I have another plan."

"Another plan?"

"Yes," Mike said. "But it isn't one I care to discuss yet. I must first establish rail service before this plan has any chance of succeeding."

Franklin smiled. "Would I be missing my guess if I suggested that you would have to establish rail service before the 30th?"

"You are an astute man," Mike said.

"Then it does have something to do with the grant lands?"

"Yes," Mike said.

"Mr. Flynn, it is no secret that you have been given a loan by the Great Western Bank. It is also no secret that they only advanced you ten thousand dollars. That hardly seems enough money to run a railroad."

Mike smiled, and pointed to the three men who were working in the depot.

"Do you see those three men?" he asked. "Sollie is the railroad engineer, Carl, his fireman, and Burke, his brakeman and conductor. They are the only three men I have on the payroll. I have no other encumbrances, other than the service debt owed to the Great Western. Ten thousand dollars *is* enough, as soon as I start bringing some money in."

"Well, Mr. Flynn," Franklin said. "I wish you every success on what seems to me an impossible venture. I must say we have sorely missed rail service here in the valley, and I am certain that everyone wishes you only the best."

"Good," Mike said. "I hope the valley and the railroad prosper mutually. By the way, you will speak with Sara, won't you? I'd like very much to talk to her."

"I'll speak with her," Franklin promised.

Chapter Seven

Franklin didn't find Sara at the house, so he walked down to the newspaper office. There he found her arranging type. It was just busy work, Franklin knew.

Franklin took off his hat and hung it on the hatrack. He rubbed his hand through his hair and looked at his daughter. She was pretending great concentration upon her task.

"Mr. Flynn says that rail service will be restored to the valley by tomorrow," Franklin said.

"I'm certain that is news which will be well received," Sara replied.

Franklin looked at his daughter, at the quick, nervous movements of her hands, and the set expression in her face. He waited, hoping she would volunteer some information, but she remained silent. Finally Franklin himself broke the silence.

"He calls you Sara."

No answer.

"He speaks as if he knows you, Ra. He says he wants to talk to you."

"I don't want to talk to him," Sara replied. She dropped a letter, and Franklin bent down to pick it up.

"Here," he said. He put his hand over her hand as he gave her the type-set letter, and that stopped her work. She stood there for a moment, without looking at him.

"Ra, honey, what is it?" Franklin finally asked. "Does this Mr. Flynn have anything to do with the reason you came home from school without finishing?"

Franklin's question surprised Sara. She had told him she came home to help with the paper, and he had expressed such pleasure over seeing her again that he never questioned her about it.

"What do you mean?" Sara asked.

"Ra, I wrote to the school. Your grades were excellent, and they were most surprised by your sudden withdrawal. That means it had to be some personal reason which drove you to quit school before receiving your degree. As it was personal, I haven't asked you before now, but the strange circumstances surrounding Mr. Flynn have me curious and I am violating the promise I made to myself not to ask you. Does Mr. Flynn have anything to do with your leaving school?"

"No," Sara said. She sighed. "At least, not directly, though it is all tied together."

"Do you want to tell me about it?"

"I can't," Sara said. "Oh, Dad, I'm so ashamed," she finally said, and she turned to her father, who took her in his arms. He patted her lightly on the shoulder and let her cry for several moments before he said anything. Finally he spoke.

"Ra, did this man, Flynn, did he . . . uh . . . compromise you in any way?"

"What do you mean?" Sara asked.

"Ra, you're a big girl, you've been away to college, I'm sure you know what I mean," Franklin said.

Sara was silent for a long moment.

"Did he seduce you?" Franklin finally asked, speaking very quietly.

"No," Sara answered.

Franklin smiled. "Well, then, what is the big . . ." he started to ask, but Sara interrupted him.

"I wanted him to," Sara said in a voice that was barely audible.

"I see," Franklin said.

"And last night," Sara went on. "Last night, when Lee brought me home from the dance, he kissed me goodnight, and during the kiss . . . I wanted him to seduce me as well."

"Did you tell this to Lee, or to Mr. Flynn?" Franklin asked.

"Did I tell them?" Sara asked. "No, of course not. I wouldn't . . . I couldn't tell them. But I had such strong . . . almost aching . . . desires," she said.

Franklin gave a little laugh, then pulled his daughter to him and hugged her.

"Ra, that's not anything to worry about," he said. "You are young, and that kind of urge is natural in the young."

"But not women, Dad. Women aren't supposed to feel like that," Sara said. "That's why I feel such shame."

"That's very interesting," Franklin said. "And tell me, did you learn that in one of your courses? Because if you did, the curriculum has been changed since I taught there."

"No," Sara said. "It's just something that I know."

"I see," Franklin said. "Then how do you explain all the evidence to the contrary?"

"I . . . I don't know what you mean," Sara said.

"Ra, I taught English and literature for a great number of years. I've read the stories, poems, essays and letters of every writer since the Elizabethan times, both men and women writers. These writers wrote beautifully of the same feelings you are talking about. Feeling them is natural, Ra. It is modern society's insistence upon submerging them that is unnatural."

"Ann Barnes said the devil has taken possession of my soul," Sara said.

"Ann Barnes is a frustrated old carp," Franklin said. "She always has been and she always will be. I've never known what John saw in her. Tell me, did Ann Barnes have anything to do with your leaving school?"

"Yes," Sara said.

"Say no more," Franklin said. "I don't know what her reason was, nor do I care. To think that she caused you to leave school short of receiving your degree!" Franklin looked into Sara's face, then kissed each tear-welled eye. "The truth is, Ra, now that you are back home, I'm *glad* you left school. I missed you much more than I ever thought I would, and I don't think I could give you up to allow you to return."

Sara smiled through her tears. "I'm glad," she said. "For now, I've no wish to return. I want to stay here with you, and help make the *Valley Monitor* the best newspaper in the world."

"We already are the best paper in the valley," Franklin teased, a reference to the fact that they were the only paper. "We are well on our way to conquering the world, I would say."

Franklin's joking had the desired effect, and Sara laughed.

"Are you going to speak with Mike Flynn?" Franklin asked.

"I don't know," Sara said.

"Where did he kiss you?"

"*What?*"

Franklin chuckled. "Lee Coulter kissed you last night on our front porch. Where did Mike Flynn kiss you? He did kiss you, didn't he?"

"Yes," Sara admitted, blushing under her father's questioning. "He gave me a ride from Twin Falls to Boise in the cab of his engine."

"The Sara Landers Special?" Franklin teased.

Sara smiled. "Yes. Only it wasn't the Sara Landers Special then, it was just an engine. Anyway, when we reached Boise, he grabbed me and kissed me before I knew what was happening."

"And now he is here, in the same valley as Lee Coulter," Franklin said. "It's going to be quite a battle."

"What is going to be quite a battle?" Sara asked.

"Watching the two of them square off against each other," Franklin said. "I wouldn't miss it for anything."

"What makes you think there will be a battle between them?"

"Ra, don't you think each of them believe they have some proprietary claim on you? I mean, after all, you allowed both of them to kiss you, did you not? That does give them some justification for thinking as they do."

"I didn't actually *allow* them to kiss me," Sara said. "They just kissed me, and . . ."

"And you allowed it," Franklin said.

Sara looked down in embarrassment. "Yes," she said. "I suppose I did."

"That's what I mean," Franklin said. He put his arms around her again. "Now, don't get me wrong, Ra, I'm not finding fault with you. I explained that your behavior has just been in accordance with the laws of nature. But it is a fact that there is going to be a battle. Mike Flynn and Lee Coulter are going to go after each other like two animals in the forest. It is going to be glorious to watch." Franklin pulled out his pocket watch and looked at it. "Oh, I nearly forgot the vestry meeting. I must hurry."

Sara watched her father leave, then she walked over to sit in the big chair behind his desk. She thought of what he had said about the two animals in the forest, and as she thought of it, she suddenly got a mental image that was too strong to put aside.

In the image, Sara saw herself as a doe in the forest, watching the battle between two magnificent stags. She imagined herself to be a beautiful, sleek female, standing in the dappled sunlight beneath the trees, watching as the males battled for her favors.

One male thrusts toward the other, and there is a flash of silver in the sun, as the antlers clash like the crashing of sabers. Then one of them, a beautiful creature with rippling sensual muscles, is victorious, and he trots toward her, with his head held proudly high, his nostrils distended, and his eyes flashing with haughty confidence.

The male rubs against her, finding that part of her which is responsive, playing skillfully upon the erotic glands which the mating season has made sensitive. She responds in the way nature intends, returning the nudging and rubbing until the stag's blood runs hot, and he consummates the coupling with a trumpeting bellow of joy.

Lee was sitting on the leather settee in the parlor of his house. He was fingering a rawhide quirt as he listened to Stump Adams. Several other ranch owners were also there, having come naturally to Lee's house as they heard of the arrival of the railroad.

"The way I look at it," Stump was saying, "this fella Flynn has got to have it in mind to sell us the land. I figure he's countin' on usin' it as a means of raisin' money to operate."

"That makes sense to me," one of the others said. "What do you think, Lee?"

"What you gentlemen are saying makes sense," Lee said. "But the question is, what price is Mr. Flynn aiming on putting on the land?"

"Well, whatever price he sets, he's pretty well got us over a barrel, doesn't he?" one of the ranchers suggested. "I mean, we need that land. There's not a one of us here who isn't runnin' more cattle than our own land can support."

"Perhaps so," Lee replied. "But does it seem fair to you gentlemen to have to pay an exorbitant rate for that which should rightfully be ours in the first place?"

"What do you mean?"

"Tell them, Stump."

"What Lee is talking about is the fact that his daddy and me could have filed on that land

100

years ago, back when we first come to the valley. We didn't neither one of us file on it, thinkin' at the time that it would be greedy to take more'n we could use. Besides, keepin' it open land sort of made it ever'body's land."

"Yeah, that was sort of how I looked at it too," one of the other, older ranchers said. "I didn't come here 'till after you 'n George Coulter had already settled most of your part of the valley, but I seen what you done with the range land and I did the same thing."

"It would have belonged to all of us, just as it was intended," Lee said. "Except for one problem. The government decided to use that land as incentive to get the railroad in here. Without consulting with us, they took claim to the land, and made a conditional grant to the railroad."

"Maybe this here Flynn fella won't meet the conditions," someone put in.

"All he has to do is start running the Sara Landers Special up and down that track, and he's met that condition," someone said.

"What?" Lee asked, looking up quickly. "What did you say?"

"I said all he has to do is run his train up and down the—"

"No, no, you said something about Sara Landers."

"I'm sorry, Lee," the rancher said, when he saw how the information affected him. "I thought you knew that Flynn had named his train the Sara Landers Special."

"No," Lee said. "She *said* she knew him," he added, almost as if speaking to himself. Then when he saw the others looking at him he grinned sheepishly. "Never mind," he said. "I was just recalling something the lady said. But you are right, Abel. All Flynn has to do to meet the conditions is start running his train. So we can assume that the land is his. Now, we must come up with a plan to buy it, but at a rate *we* consider fair."

"What would you say a fair rate might be?" Stump asked.

"There's one hundred thousand acres," Lee said. "Fifty cents an acre would be fifty thousand dollars. I would think that would be a lot of money to a man who is desperately in need of it. In fact, it's a lot of money for us to raise, but we can do it."

"You speak as if coming up with that much money is a cinch," Abel said. "It ain't that easy for me."

"Sure it is," Lee said, smiling broadly. "Any bank in the land would lend one dollar on the acre."

"I don't understand," one of the others said. "If *we* could get one dollar on the acre, why couldn't Flynn?"

"Because he is already overextended with his railroad," Lee said. "He would not be considered a good credit risk."

"You think he would be desperate enough to sell it to us for *half* its mortgage value?" Stump asked.

102

"Why not?" Lee replied. "He got it for nothing. And, like we already said, by rights it belongs to us anyway. I figure we're doing him a favor by paying him fifty thousand dollars."

"All right, Lee, I'll go along with you," one of the ranchers said. "And maybe all these other folks will too. But what about Flynn? Maybe he did get it for nothing. He can't be no fool. He has to know the real value of the land. What if he won't sell it to us?"

Lee got up from the chair and walked over to the roll-top desk. He pulled an envelope from one of the pigeon-holes.

"I got a letter from Washington, answering an inquiry I made about the Railroad Grants Act which gave the land to the Cascade. There's an interesting paragraph here I'd like to read to you."

Lee cleared his throat and began to read: ". . . Therefore, in order to take possession of the land known as the Butte Valley Railroad Grant land, the Cascade Line must begin operation on, or before, June 30th, 1881, and they must sustain that operation on a scheduled basis for at least six months."

Lee put the letter back in the envelope and looked at the others with a smile on his lips.

"So, what does that mean?" Abel asked. "He's going to start his service tomorrow."

"He must sustain regularly scheduled service for six months," Lee said. "Now I ask you, gentlemen. If we don't give him our business, how is he going to continue his operation?"

103

Abel smiled broadly. "Oh," he said. "I think I'm beginnin' to get the picture here. What you're sayin' is we'll tell the fella to sell us the land at our price . . . or he gets no business from us. Is that it?"

"That's it exactly," Lee said. "We'll organize a total boycott of his operation. He can only run his train up and down those tracks empty for so long, then he's going to have to do one of two things. He's either going to have to come to terms with us, or he's going to go out of business. In other words, gentlemen, we have just jerked a cinch into him."

Abel laughed. "You know, Lee, you are a sneaky son of a bitch. I'm sure glad we're on the same side."

Chapter Eight

Sara stood on the depot platform and looked up at the engine. Even cold and silent, it seemed alive to her, and she recalled that thrilling afternoon she had ridden in the cab from Twin Falls to Boise. And now this beautiful engine had her name. She had reacted badly when she first saw it, more out of shock than anything else. Now, though she still wouldn't admit it to anyone, she felt a sense of pride because of the distinction.

"Sara!" a voice called from the door of the depot. "Sara, you *did* come!"

Sara turned toward the voice, and for just an instant, seeing him, she felt a flash of warm recalled passion, though she was able to repress that quickly enough not to give herself away.

"So," Sara said, as Mike approached her. "I

see you have made good your promise to start rail service."

"Yes," Mike said. The smile left his face and he looked at Sara seriously for a moment. "Your father told me you were displeased at seeing your name on the engine. I meant no disrespect at all. If you wish, I'll remove your name."

"Why bother?" Sara said. "Everyone has seen it now. The damage has been done."

Mike smiled brightly. "You mean I can keep it on?"

"You may as well," Sara replied.

Mike grabbed Sara in his arms and swung her around. "Sure'n you've made me a happy man, girl!" he said.

"Put me down!" Sara said, pushing herself out of his arms.

"I'm sorry," Mike said. "I suppose I am being a bit rambunctious, aren't I? Come on, let me introduce you to the crew that'll be workin' the train."

"What? You mean you won't be the engineer?" Sara asked, with a teasing grin.

"You've a serpent's tongue about you, girl, for recallin' my difficulty with the beast. Come on, look over the depot . . . perhaps it could use a woman's touch. You might give me an idea as to how to make it a bit more attractive."

Sara followed Mike into the building, which had been boarded up for some time. Three men were working inside, sweeping the floor, picking up trash, and washing windows. Despite their efforts the building still had a dank, unattractive look and smell.

"The best thing you could do is tear it down and start all over," Sara said, wrinkling her nose in distaste.

"I'm inclined to agree with you," Mike said, looking around in despair. The partition around the ticket window was half torn down. "Unfortunately, this is the only thing we have, so we have to use it."

"Hey, Mike, I found the clock back there," Burke said. "And it still works. I just set it."

"Put it on the wall," Mike said. "We can't have a time schedule if we don't have a timepiece. Is that the right time?"

"Yep, five of two," Burke said, as he set the clock on a small shelf that protruded from the wall.

"The town meeting is scheduled in here at two-thirty," Mike said.

"Two-thirty?" Sara gasped. "You mean you are going to have the entire town in here a little over thirty minutes from now?"

"Yes," Mike said.

Sara sighed. "Give me a broom," she said, taking one from Sollie.

"Sara, girl, that's your church dress. I wouldn't want you workin' in your church dress," Mike said.

"I don't have time to go home and change," Sara said. "And if you are going to have the entire town in here, the least you can do is have the place clean."

"Right," Mike said happily, beaming proudly over the fact that Sara had pitched in to help them. "Oh, say, what about curtains? Do you think they would help?"

"I wouldn't put up curtains," Sara said. "They would just block out the light, and you should let as much light in as you can. Also, have the man who is cleaning the windows change the water. It's so dirty now that he's doing little more than spreading the dirt around."

"Good idea," Mike said. "Carl, you heard the lady. Go fetch some clean water."

By two-thirty the people of the town began coming toward the depot in twos, threes, and large groups. Entire families came, and even the babes in arms looked around curiously, sensing the excitement of the meeting. The older children ran around the train, looking up at it in open-mouthed wonder, ignoring the calls of their mothers to come away before they got run over.

The depot was clean, though some of the more obviously damaged areas still stood in need of repair. Mike stood just in front of the ticket window, watching, as the men and women came inside and settled on the benches of the waiting room. Finally the people stopped coming, and Mike assumed they were all present, so he started to talk.

"Folks, my name is Mike Flynn," he said. "I intend to set up an office right here in this building, and in that office conduct all the business of the Cascade Line. If any of you merchants, or ranchers, or anyone else, for that matter, have any freight shipments you want to arrange, I can take care of them."

"What about passenger service?" one man asked.

"Yes, sir," Mike said. "In fact, with the establishment of this service, it is now possible for a person to step on the train here at noon on Monday, and eat your noon meal in New York City, the following Sunday."

"Mister, do you know what you are saying? It took me nine months to get out here," someone said, and everyone else laughed.

"Did you come by wagon?"

"Sure did. Left from Saint Louis."

"I imagine you made about ten miles per day on the trip out," Mike said. "It might interest you to know that on this train, you can go further in *one hour* than it was possible to go in an entire week by wagon."

There were gasps and exclamations of wonder at the news.

"Yeah, but does this here train go all the way to New York?"

"No," Mike admitted. "It goes to Boise, Idaho. There, you can make connections to take you anywhere in the country."

"Is it safe?"

As that question was asked, the train whistle was blown, and Mike smiled.

"Ah, that's the signal that the engineer has the steam built back up. And now, sir, to answer your question as to whether it is safe or not, I'm going to demonstrate. If you would all step outside, please, Burke Carmody, our conductor, will help you board the train. I'm providing a free train ride for everyone."

At that announcement, the children, who had been paying attention to what was going on, let out a loud cheer. Some of the men also cheered, though reaction from most of the women seemed to be apprehension.

"How far are we goin'?" one of the men wanted to know.

"Just up to Butte Pass," Mike said. "As you know, the view of the valley from up there is quite beautiful."

"Just up to the pass? Mister, that's thirty miles from here."

"We'll be there in less than an hour," Mike promised. "In fact, I'll have you back here before six o'clock this evening. Now, who wants to go?"

"Me, me!" some of the children shouted, and they were through the doors and headed for the train before their nervous mothers could react.

"It's perfectly safe, believe me," Mike assured them.

Gradually people began to move toward the train, so that by the time the steam valve was open and the train moving, nearly half of the town had taken Mike's offer.

Sara stood in the door of the depot and waved to many of the passengers as the train began backing away. Only the engine was actually backing, having been disconnected, and then shunted around a switch to the opposite end of the train.

"Is he going to back all the way to the pass?" Sara asked Mike, who had stayed behind.

"Yes," Mike said. "A steam engine is just as efficient backing as it is going forward. Once up there, he can shunt around to the front of the train again. We have to do that because we don't have a roundhouse where the engine can be turned around. Why didn't you go?"

Sara smiled. "I just had a week on a train, remember?"

"I'll never forget," Mike said, and Sara knew he was referring to the kiss they had shared. She blushed. "Can you forget?" Mike asked.

"Yes," Sara said. "And I would advise you to forget as well, for it is not something that will occur again."

"All the more reason I should remember it," Mike said.

Sara started to respond to Mike's comment, but she stopped short when she saw a man getting off a horse near the hitching rail.

"It's Lee," she said. This was the first time she had seen Lee since telling him goodnight the evening before, and now, both Lee and Mike were to be together in her presence. Was this the presage of the battle her father had warned her about?

"Who?"

"Lee Coulter," Sara said.

111

"I've heard the name," Mike said. "He is a rancher, isn't he?"

"Yes."

"Hello, Sara," Lee said as he approached them. "Won't you introduce me to your friend?" Lee looked toward the receding train and its passengers, still waving gaily out the windows. "Since he named his train after you, he must be your friend."

"Lee, this is Mike Flynn," Sara said.

"Glad to meet you, Lee," Mike said, sticking his hand out.

Lee looked at Mike's hand for just a moment, then took it, but only perfunctorily.

"Flynn, let's get right down to business," Lee said. "I'm going to have a meeting out at my ranch tomorrow night. I'd like you to be there."

"Will the other cattlemen be there as well?" Mike asked.

"Every cowman in the valley," Lee said.

Mike smiled. "Then I'll be there. I think we have a little business to discuss."

"Yes," Lee agreed. "I think we do. Sara?" he said, looking at her, and offering her the crook of his arm. "Come along, and I'll walk you home."

Sara saw the two men exchange looks as Lee made his offer, and she was both thrilled and excited by it. Then, reason told her that the most prudent act on her part now would be to accept Lee's offer. That would at least separate them, before anything could happen.

112

"Thank you," she said, smiling and taking his arm. "That is very kind of you."

Mike smiled graciously as Sara nodded her head goodbye, then he watched them as they walked away.

"I'm going to beat you, Coulter," he said under his breath. "I'm going to beat you with Sara, and I'm going to beat you at your game, whatever your game happens to be. You can count on that, my friend."

Though Lee's meeting was billed as a ranchers' business meeting, any occasion for a large gathering of people was as much a social event as business. For that reason, the ranchers' wives and many of their children came to Lee's ranch that evening. They dressed up, and arrived in phaetons, broughams, landaulets and other elegant carriages, though there were also a sprinkling of the more pedestrian conveyances, such as buggies, buckboards, and wagons.

"I've laid the table," Jennie said, coming up to stand beside Lee and look out over the crowd of people who had gathered at his invitation. "I dare any of these galoots to leave the meeting hungry."

Lee looked at Jennie and smiled. "Jennie, if you set a table as well as you rope and brand, then I'll allow as how the ranchers will eat well tonight."

Stump, who had come up right behind his daughter, laughed at Lee's comment.

"I've told her, Lee, that when a man takes a

113

notion to find a woman to marry, he's generally a lot more interested in what she can do in the kitchen than what she can do out on the range," Stump said.

"Oh, pooh, what do I care about any man who is looking for a woman?" Jennie asked. "So far, I'd rather keep company with a steer, than with any man I've met."

Lee laughed. "That doesn't say very much for any of the men around here, does it? I certainly hope there's one woman who doesn't share your low opinion of men. At least one man in particular."

"What woman would that be?" Stump asked.

"Dad, that's none of your business," Jennie scolded.

"That's all right," Lee said. "Stump Adams is more like an uncle to me than any man I've ever known. If he doesn't have a right to know, I'd like to know who does? That woman is Sara Landers, Mr. Adams."

"My, you do work fast, don't you, Lee?" Jennie said, forcing a smile. "She has just returned from the east and you are already staking your claim."

"I have to," Lee said. "It seems this Flynn fella got a head start on me."

"Yes," Jennie said, and this time her smile was genuine. "I heard that the train was named after her."

"Well, all I can say is that Flynn won't know what happened by the time I get through with him," Lee said.

"Yes, well, I wish you luck. Oh, would you excuse me? I see Mrs. Petry has arrived. She has a mare which is about to foal, and I want to ask how the mother-to-be is doing."

Jennie actually used Mrs. Petry as an excuse to leave, for, in fact, she knew exactly how the mare was doing, having spoken with Mrs. Petry only this afternoon. But the conversation had grown too painful, for in truth, Jennie was in love with Lee. She had never admitted that to anyone, and had even discouraged her father from talking about it. But though unspoken, the love was there, as strong as it ever was, even though Lee had never given her the slightest indication that he returned it.

Jennie, like Sara, had developed a childhood crush on Lee. But now, Sara's feelings seemed to be reciprocated, and though Jennie's heart was broken by that prospect, she made a silent vow never to say or do anything that would interfere, because she valued her friendship with Sara as much as she did her love for Lee. To gain one at the expense of the other seemed no gain at all.

Lee and Stump watched Jennie as she moved through the crowd of people who had gathered in Lee's house.

"I wish she would take an interest in men," Stump said. "I'm not going to live forever, and it would be nice to know that she has someone to look out for her."

Lee laughed. "It seems to me, Mr. Adams, that Jennie Adams is one girl who will never need looking out for. She's as capable as any man I've ever known. She can ride faster, rope better, brand more surely—in fact, there's very little she can't do."

"Yes, I know," Stump said. "Everyone knows about that, and they speak of that as if it were all there was to the girl. But look at her, Lee. Just take a good look at her. I'm not blind. I know she's my daughter, but, by thunder, she's a pretty girl too, isn't she? I mean, I'm not just prejudiced, am I? Isn't she a pretty girl?"

Lee looked across the room at Jennie. Jennie was smiling at Mrs. Petry, and she moved her hand up to brush back a wave of hair. Her eyes were sparkling, and her teeth were bright behind the smile. As if for the first time in his life, Lee saw that she was, indeed, a beautiful girl. For just an instant, he felt a pang of . . . of what? Something missed? It was only a fleeting sensation, dismissed so quickly that his conscious mind wasn't aware it had occurred, one second afterward.

"Yes," Lee agreed. "She is a very pretty girl."

"And yet she seems condemned to a life of spinsterhood," Stump said. He sighed. "But it is her life, after all, and I suppose I should let her live it without my interference."

Jennie finished her conversation with Mrs. Petry, moved on to speak with a few other guests, then stepped outside, on the front porch.

Sara and her father were arriving at that moment. Their vehicle was a closed wagon with

116

the *Valley Monitor* logo painted on its side. It lacked the style and elegance of the other carriages, but the closed wooden body allowed them to transport papers in the worst weather, and insure their dryness.

"I hope they haven't started their discussions yet," Franklin said as he parked the wagon. "If only I hadn't dropped that plate just before we were to print the Emporium handbills."

"Don't worry, Dad. Even if Mike has arrived, the business hasn't begun yet, I'm sure. You know how this type of thing is. The people will visit and socialize for a long time before the business begins."

"Interesting," Franklin said.

"What?"

"You call him Mike, he calls you Sara, and yet until I met him this afternoon, I'd never seen the man in my life."

"It . . . it means nothing," Sara said. "He's just the kind of man one calls by his first name. Even his employees call him Mike."

"That's true," Franklin agreed, "for I heard them. Still, it doesn't seem proper, somehow."

"You don't seem to have any objections to my calling Lee Coulter by his first name," Sara said.

"That's different," Franklin explained. "You've known Lee ever since you were a very young girl. That lends some propriety to the situation. You've only known Mr. Flynn for a short while."

"I wonder if he is here yet," Sara asked, as

they walked across the lawn toward the front porch.

"I don't think so," Franklin said.

"Why not?"

"I hear no sounds of combat," he teased.

"Pooh," Sara said. "You are making a mountain out of a molehill."

As Sara and her father reached the porch, they saw Jennie Adams. She was leaning on the porch rail, looking out toward the tall fir trees on the opposite bank of the McCauley River, a swiftly flowing stream that cut through the middle of the valley, supplying water year-round and making the valley ideal for cattle ranching.

"Hi, Jennie, what are you doing out here?" Sara asked. "Did it get too loud inside?"

"The action hasn't started yet," Jennie said. "Mr. Flynn hasn't arrived. I just wanted to come outside and get a little fresh air, and listen to the river."

"It is nice out here," Sara agreed.

"Come on, Ra, let's get inside," Franklin insisted. "We're late as it is."

Sara smiled at Jennie, then followed her father into the house. The inside of the house glowed golden with the light of many candles and lanterns, and with the brilliance of the overhead chandelier. Even the gaily colored dresses of the women seemed to add to the brightness.

Sara saw Lee coming toward them. Lee shook Franklin's hand, then placed a proprietary kiss on Sara's cheek. She thought it better to accept the harmless kiss graciously than to protest the unwarranted liberty.

"I was getting worried," Lee said. "I was beginning to think that you might not come. It's going to be a very important meeting, and I think you should be here."

"I wouldn't have missed it for the world," Franklin said. "It's my fault we're late. Just as we were ready to print some handbills, I dropped the plate and scattered type everywhere. We had to reset the entire thing."

"Are you hungry?" Lee asked. "There's enough food to feed an army laid out on the dining room table."

"Lee, my boy, you do things grandly, don't you?" Franklin said. "I must confess that food sounds very good to me right now, as we had to work through dinner. Ra, won't you join me?"

"Not just now, Dad," Sara said. "I'll get something later. First I want to visit."

"Of all God's creatures, only the human female would rather visit than eat," Franklin said, as he started toward the dining room.

Sara was looking around the room, searching the faces of all the guests.

"He hasn't arrived yet," Lee said.

"Who hasn't arrived?"

"Mike Flynn. You are looking for him, aren't you?"

"Yes," Sara admitted. "After all, I am a news-

119

paper reporter, and he is the cause of this meeting, is he not?"

"Yes," Lee said. He looked at Sara for a long moment. "Are you going to tell me?"

"Tell you what?"

"Why Mike Flynn named his train for you."

"I don't know why he named his train for me, Lee," Sara said. "I gave him no encouragement to do such a thing."

"But you said the other night that you knew him."

"I met him as I was returning home from school," Sara said. "That's all."

Lee smiled broadly and sighed, a deep sigh of relief.

"Good," he finally said. He took her hand and held it. "It is good that I have nothing to worry about."

Chapter Nine

The Lee Coulter ranch was as easy to find as Mike had been told it would be. It was a huge house with cupolas, dormers, arches, scrollwork, and wrought-iron adornment, and Mike had the rather ungracious thought that it looked more like a wedding cake than a house. On this particular night it was well lighted, with a glow of gold spilling from every window. It was surrounded by horses and carriages.

As Mike tied his horse to the hitching rail he could hear the McCauley River rushing behind him. He looked around to take in the ranch, not only the main house, but the outhouses, barns, horse-lots, and the rest. This was an exceptionally well-maintained and affluent looking ranch. It appeared as if Mr. Lee Coulter had everything a man could want: money, position, a fine

121

house and a large ranch. He also wanted Sara Landers.

"I hate to disappoint you, Mr. Coulter," Mike said under his breath. "But you aren't going to get Sara Landers."

Mike walked up onto the porch and pulled the bell cord. The door was opened almost immediately by a very pretty woman with soft brown hair and flashing blue eyes. She laughed.

"Well, now, I *know* you must be Mr. Flynn," she said. "I know everyone else." She stuck out her hand. "I'm Jennie Adams."

"You're right about me," Mike replied, smiling at her friendliness. "I am Mike Flynn."

"You don't look like a monster, Mr. Flynn, despite what they're all saying," Jennie said.

"Oh? Am I supposed to be some kind of a monster?"

"To some, you are."

"Why? Doesn't the valley want rail service?"

"Oh, we want rail service all right," Jennie said. "But we also want the grazing land."

"I see," Mike said. "By grazing land, you're talking about the railroad grant land, are you not?"

"Yes," Jennie said. "They're in the library right now, trying to come up with a plan to keep the land."

"Why aren't you in there?" Mike asked. "Aren't you interested in what happens to the graze land?"

"I'm a woman," Jennie said.

"I noticed," Mike smiled. "I may not look like a monster, but you *do* look like a woman."

"I accept that as a compliment," Jennie said. "And I appreciate the thought. But the truth is, I'd much rather be in there with the men than in the parlor with the other women, carrying on all their foolish pratter-waller. I'm as good a rancher as any man in there, and I've got a right to know what's going on, seeing as it might affect my ranch."

Mike looked around the house. "Is Sara Landers here yet?" he asked.

Jennie smiled. "So, you too have fallen under her spell, have you? I don't guess I can fault you for that. She is a very beautiful woman. Yes, she's here. She's in the library with the men."

Mike looked at Jennie in surprise.

"In her case they made an exception, because she's a newspaper reporter. This meeting does pass as news, I suppose."

"Well," Mike cracked, "then you won't really miss anything, will you? You can always read about it in the newspaper."

"At least *you* don't have to read about it in the newspaper," Jennie said. "Go on in." She smiled. "I'm getting anxious to see what's going to happen anyway. I think I'll sneak on down and stand outside the library door and listen in, if you won't give me away."

"I won't breathe a word," Mike promised.

Mike followed Jennie down a wide hall toward the library. The hallway was furnished

123

with half a dozen hall-stands, tables, and a large grandfather's clock. The walls were hung with antler racks, Indian carpets, and a rather large painting of a stern-looking man in a heavy beard. A brass plate beneath the picture identified the man: *George W. Coulter: 1824–1879.*

"That's Uncle George," Jennie said.

"Uncle? You mean Lee Coulter is your cousin?"

Jennie laughed. "Not really, but Dad and Uncle George settled this valley together, so Mr. Coulter became sort of an honorary uncle. He was a good man. It was a sad day when he died."

The door to the library was open, and as they approached, they could hear someone speaking.

"That's Lee's voice," Jennie whispered.

". . . stick together, the railroad cannot dictate terms to a united group of ranchers. I say that Mr. Flynn will listen to our terms, or he can listen to the rattle of empty trains."

Mike stepped into the doorway just as the last words were spoken. He leaned against the door without announcing his presence. Jennie stayed just outside and out of sight.

"Lee, I need to get some cattle to market soon," one of the other ranchers said. "I had a hard winter, and I don't really have enough to make a trail drive practical. If I could ship some head on through to Denver, I could get a

124

good enough price to get me out of a jam. The railroad seems like a good deal to me."

"Carter, all I'm asking is that you pull your belt in and stick it out. It might get hard, but in the long run, it will guarantee us the grazing land that we need."

"I'm willing to listen to Lee Coulter," one of the other ranchers said. "After all, he's the biggest and wealthiest rancher in the valley. He must be doing something right."

"I chose the right daddy," Lee said, and the others laughed at his self-deprecating remark.

"No matter, I say we listen to him too," another put in. "When this fella Flynn comes, let's just tell him what we want. As far as I am concerned, we can just dictate our terms to him and he won't have any say in the matter at all."

"And just what *are* those terms?" Mike suddenly asked. His voice startled the others, and they all turned, as one, to see him standing in the door.

"Well, Mr. Flynn." Lee said. "I see you made it to our meeting."

"Just in time, it would appear," Mike said. He walked through the room to stand in the front, next to Lee. He pulled a cheroot from his inside jacket pocket and lit it, cupping his hand around the match and puffing out clouds of blue smoke before he waved the match out. "Now," he said. "Would someone care to tell me just what terms you are talking about?"

"It has to do with the railroad grant land," Lee said.

"What about it?"

"Well, it's no secret that you need money, Flynn. And it's no surprise where you're going to try to raise that money. You are going to try to sell the grant lands to us."

"I've considered that possibility," Mike admitted.

"We are willing to pay you fifty cents an acre for the land," Lee said.

"Fifty cents," one of the other ranchers shouted. "And not one penny more."

"I see," Mike said. "Gentlemen, I am sure you realize that I had the land appraised while I was putting together the financial package that allowed me to begin business with this railroad. The sale value of that land is at least two dollars an acre, and with aggressive marketing, even more. Why, you can borrow one dollar an acre on it. What makes you think I would sell it to you for fifty cents an acre?"

"The way I see it, Flynn, you don't have any choice," Lee said triumphantly. "Because if you don't sell to us at our price, we won't be using your railroad."

"Gentlemen, if you would just think about it for a moment, you would realize that you and the railroad have mutual interests. You depend upon a solvent railroad in order to have access to the best markets for your cattle, and the railroad depends upon solvent ranchers in order to have customers for our service. One hand washes the other, so to speak."

"Tell me, Flynn," Lee asked. "In this hand

washing operation, what did you plan to charge us for the graze land?"

"Nothing," Mike said.

There was a buzz of surprise and curiosity.

"Nothing? What do you mean, nothing?" Lee asked.

"I didn't intend to sell you the grant lands," Mike said.

"You aren't going to sell to us?" Stump asked. "Then what are you going to do with the land?"

"Nothing," Mike said. "For the time being, I am willing to let things stay as they are."

"You mean you are going to let the cattlemen continue to run their cows on the grant lands?" Franklin asked.

"Yes," Mike said. "Miss Landers, I hope you are getting all this down," he added, looking pointedly at Sara, who was sitting nearby with a pencil and tablet.

"Get this down too, Sara," Lee spoke up. "Flynn, what are you planning on charging us for the right to *use* the land?"

"Nothing," Mike said easily.

Again there was a buzz of surprise and excitement.

"I told you," Mike said, when the buzzing died down. "Our coexistence depends upon a mutuality of interest. One hand washes the other. I will allow your cattle to use the grant land, and you will ship your cattle on my railroad. Are we agreed?"

127

"You have to have our cattle to survive, right?" Lee asked.

"You are right on that score," Mike said. "I know you were planning on boycotting the railroad, and I have to confess to you that the prospects of a boycott sounded awfully bleak. If you had done it, I would have to try something else."

Lee laughed derisively. "Mr. Flynn, just what else could you have done?"

"Well, you know the old saying," Mike said. "If Mohammed can't go to the mountain, then the mountain will come to Mohammed."

"I think you have that just reversed," Franklin chuckled.

"Not in this case," Mike said mysteriously.

"Has your train service started yet?" Lee asked.

"I started it today," Mike said. "The train went to Boise, empty. There we will pick up ten cases of canned peaches for Miller's Emporium. That is not exactly revenue-producing freight, gentlemen, so as you can see, I am dependent upon your cooperation."

"How much will you charge us?" Carter asked.

"Fifty cents per head, per hundred miles," Mike said. "It will cost you two and a half dollars to get one cow to Boise."

"What's a head bringing in Boise right now?" Abel asked.

Mike cleared his throat. "I'll be honest with you, gentlemen," he said. "You won't get any

128

more for your cattle in Boise than you would if you drove them up to Portland and sold them there."

"What?" Carter asked. "What are you saying? Are you telling us we should pay you two dollars and fifty cents a head to ship our cattle to Boise, where we sell them for the same amount of money we can get in Portland? All things considered, we'd *lose* money if we did something that foolish, wouldn't we?"

"It would have been more honest, Flynn, if you had told us in the first place that you were going to charge us for using the land," Stump said.

"Believe me, I'm not trying to come up with some hidden charge," Mike said. "But I ask you to consider this. Denver is paying thirty-five dollars a head. You could ship them on to Denver for another two and a half dollars, and you would net thirty dollars a head."

"We would *net* thirty dollars a head?"

"That's right," Mike said.

"That all sounds fair, Flynn," Lee said. "But there are a few questions I'd like to ask.

"You go right ahead and ask them," Mike invited.

"Is it possible for us to contract with your railroad for a shipment all the way to Denver?"

"No," Mike replied. "My railroad goes only to Boise. But you can make further arrangements in Boise to take you on to Denver."

"I see," Lee said. "In other words, we have to switch railroads?"

"Yes."

"Isn't it true, Mr. Flynn, that during peak shipping times the cattle sometimes have to remain in feeder-lots until enough cars are available to ship them on?"

"Yes," Mike agreed. "But that is true only during peak shipping times. This isn't peak shipping times. That's why the prices for your cattle are so elevated."

"The price for keeping them in feeder-lots is also elevated right now, is it not? In fact, it's fifteen cents per animal. A stay of one month could add four and a half dollars to the cost, and there's no telling what the market for our cattle would be if we had a month's delay. The price might drop to twenty dollars a head, and if it does, we've lost money."

"See here, Flynn," one of the cattlemen sputtered. "Is that right? Could that happen?"

"That is highly unlikely," Mike said.

"Highly unlikely, but it could happen, right?" Stump asked.

"No," Mike said, as the group of men began to buzz angrily. "No, that isn't right. You would have to have a combination of highly unusual circumstances for that to occur. Most of the time your shipments would go straight on through, with no problem at all."

"I suppose you are ready to guarantee that," Lee suggested.

"I can't guarantee it," Mike said. "How can I guarantee the business practice of someone else's business? I can only guarantee that your cattle will arrive in Boise."

"Then the risk is ours to take," Lee said. "Gentlemen, I don't know about the rest of you, but I have no wish to take that risk."

Mike ran his hand through his hair, then he pulled out his gold nugget and fingered it for a moment. Finally he made up his mind, and he held up his hand to call for quiet.

"All right," he said. "I'll assume the risk."

"To what degree will you assume the risk?" Lee asked.

"I will pay the feeder-lot costs in Boise, should there be a delay in shipping the cattle on to Denver. But believe me, there really *is* no risk."

Lee smiled. "Then we should all come out ahead, shouldn't we?"

"Yes," Mike said.

"How many head can you handle?" Lee asked.

"I could handle five hundred with no difficulty," Mike said.

"All right," Lee said. "We'll have five hundred head of cattle at the loading pens Thursday morning. I suppose you would like to be paid then?"

"That would be nice," Mike said, thinking of the twelve hundred and fifty dollars.

"You'll have the money," Lee said. "But I shall expect your signature on a contract in which you agree to the feeder-lot charges, should any occur."

"I'll sign," Mike agreed.

"Flynn, we have a deal."

"Yahoo!" one of the cattlemen shouted, and the meeting then dissolved into groups of excited ranchers, discussing the unexpected but beneficial outcome of the meeting.

"A net of *thirty* dollars! Hot damn, that sounds good!"

"And we're going to keep the range land without having to buy it!"

"Yeah, but what about the squatters?"

"We've handled them up to now, we'll keep on handling them."

Sara came over to Mike and extended her hand. She was smiling. "Well," she said. "You worked that out pretty well."

"I hope so," Mike said. "I don't mind telling you, I've been wondering how the cowboys would react to my proposal."

"It all sounds so good," Sara said. "How could they have rejected you?"

"You're right, how could they?"

"Mr. Flynn, will you be going back to town now?" Sara asked.

"Yes," Mike said. "Would you like to ride along?"

"No, I'm here with my father and I'm not ready to go back just yet. But I thought I might get a statement from you, if you don't mind."

"A statement?"

"Yes. For the newspaper, remember? I'm part of the working press."

Mike laughed. "Yes, of course. I'd be glad to give you a statement."

"Perhaps if we went out on the front porch?" Sara suggested. "We would have less distraction."

"Good idea," Mike said.

Sara walked back through the house, now mixing and mingling with men and women, as the business meeting had ended and the socializing had started again. Sara noticed Jennie out of the corner of her eye, not socializing at all, but discussing with the other ranchers the logistics of the upcoming cattle shipment. Sara laughed.

"Something funny?"

"Not really," Sara said. "I was just noticing Jennie, mixing with the other ranchers. She's certainly not like any other woman I have ever known."

"Perhaps you should be more like her," Mike suggested.

"What do you mean?" Sara asked sharply. She was stung by Mike's remark, and her own reaction to it surprised her. Why should she care what he thinks about Jennie . . . or any other woman for that matter?

"Jennie is at least honest with herself," Mike said.

"And I am not?" Sara retorted. Even as she asked the question, she wondered at the answer. She found Mike Flynn an exceptionally attractive man, and yet she made every conscious effort to deny that.

Mike chuckled. "Only you can answer that question, Sara, girl. I'm not privy to your thoughts."

"Perhaps this interview isn't such a good idea after all," Sara suggested. "I can see that I'm just wasting my time. I'd better go back inside."

"Not until I have a chance to do this," Mike said. Then he took Sara in his arms and kissed her. Sara was surprised by his move, and at first, she was too shocked to resist. Then she began to struggle, but Mike's arms were too strong, and his lips too sweet.

Mike's kiss burned against her lips, spreading fire through her body, making her knees grow so weak that she had to lean into him to keep from falling. She felt the muscled hardness of his chest, the steel of his arms, and then, in a thrilling realization, she felt the impatient pressure of his manhood. The center of her womanly feelings boiled with a damp heat.

Finally, after what seemed an eternity, and yet far too soon, the kiss ended. Mike looked at her, his eyes penetrating deeply into hers.

"Please," Sara said quietly, now finding the strength to pull away from his embrace. "Please go now. Please, leave me."

"I'll go," Mike said. "But I won't leave you. I'll be a part of your memory now. The kiss we just shared will linger, on your lips and in your heart."

"Please," Sara said again, her voice barely audible. "Oh, won't you please just leave?"

Mike smiled at her, then turned and walked across the dark lawn to the hitching rail where he had tied his rented horse. Sara watched him go, and, as Mike Flynn had promised, she could still feel the heat of his kiss on her lips.

Chapter Ten

When the roosters crowed on Thursday morning, the sun, its disc blood red and not yet painful to the eyes, rested on the rim of McCauley Pass, turning the McCauley River into a flowing stream of red.

Sara heard the cock crow, but it did not awaken her, for she had lain awake for more than an hour in the predawn darkness, her mind heavy with the personal dilemma she faced.

There were two men in Sara's life now, and each of them seemed capable of arousing her passions to frightening heights of intensity. Her father had told her that such feelings were natural, and perhaps they were. . . .

What was wrong with her? she asked herself. What imperfection in her makeup gave her a body that responded so readily to men? First Mike, and then Lee, had caused her body to flare into the white-hot fire of desire. Then, with a frustrated sigh of self-condemnation, she recalled the brief moment with Professor Barnes. Even he had aroused her desires.

Perhaps such desires could be controlled, if they were directed toward one man, Sara thought. If she could convince herself that she was in love with the man who so enflamed her desires, and, equally as important, if she could believe that he loved her, then everything would be all right. But the question that bothered her now was, *which* man?

The best way to handle this, Sara thought, *is simply to go see Mike and Lee, one at a time, and talk to them.* She wouldn't come right out and ask them their intentions; that would be much too bold. But she had faith in her ability to determine, through subtle interrogation, their intentions. If one or the other showed signs of being moved by more than lust for her, then there would be room for further exploration.

Sara smiled. She had just applied all the principles of logic, as learned in her Principles of Logic class. Her professor would be very proud of her.

"I thought I would go over to the Star Hotel and speak with Mike before he leaves for Boise," Sara told her father after breakfast that morning.

"Oh?" her father replied. "What about?"

"To get material for a story," Sara said. "After all, that was quite a compromise he and the ranchers reached the other night. It will affect all our readers, and I think I should find out as much as I can."

"Do you really think it was a compromise, Ra?" Franklin asked.

"Certainly," Sara said. "Don't you?"

"No, I don't."

"Then what *was* it?" Sara asked, confused.

Franklin got up from the breakfast table and walked over to the cupboard. He picked up an envelope, then handed it to Sara.

"What is it?" she asked.

"It's a handbill," Franklin said. "I received it in the mail yesterday, along with a letter asking me to verify that the claims of the handbill are accurate."

Sara removed the handbill and opened it up, then gasped as she saw its contents.

The best
VALLEY FARMING LANDS
are for sale by
CASCADE RAILROAD LINE

Buy tickets to Butte Valley, Oregon, and the ticket cost will be applied to the purchase of the land. This is the best farming land in the world. It is available for settlers at only three dollars per acre, and your first year's crop will more than pay for the land. The land may be purchased over a ten-year period, with only a small down payment. HALF FARE to Families of Purchasers. LOW FREIGHT FARE on Household Goods and Farm Stock.

Contact Mike Flynn, Cascade Line, Butte Valley, Oregon.

"But I thought he was going to let the cattle-men use the range land," Sara said.

"If you will recall," Franklin said, "Mr. Flynn's exact words were," Franklin opened Sara's note tablet and read, " 'For the time being, I am willing to let things stay as they are.' In fact, as I recall, he even asked you if you were getting it all down."

"Yes," Sara said. "I do recall now. Why, that, that *liar*," she said.

"He didn't exactly lie," Franklin said. "He just didn't tell us the whole truth. For the time being, he is willing to let things stay as they are, but with the arrival of the first settlers, things will begin to change."

"Are you going to tell Lee?" Sara asked.

"Honey, I'm going to tell the entire valley," Franklin replied. "I'm running this handbill on the front page of today's paper. Now, do you still want to go over to the Star Hotel and speak with your Mr. Flynn?"

"Yes," Sara said. "Now more than ever."

Sara walked down the boardwalk toward the hotel. It was just two days until the big Fourth of July celebration, and already a banner was strung across the street. It swung gently in the morning breeze, and the sign in front of Dr. Conkling's Apothecary, to which the banner was attached, made a squeaking sound as she walked by. The banner read, *"Butte Valley wishes Happy Birthday to the U.S.A., July 4th, 1881."* Sara nodded politely to half a dozen greetings, then stepped into the lobby of the Star Hotel.

The desk clerk looked up and smiled as Sara entered.

"Good morning, Miss Landers. You haven't come for the advertising copy, have you? Your father picked that up two days ago."

"No, nothing like that, Mr. Peterson. I've come as a reporter, not an ad salesman. Which room is Mr. Flynn's?"

"Mr. Flynn is in room 208," Peterson said, without having to check the register.

"I'll just go on up, if you don't mind," Sara said, starting for the wide, carpeted staircase.

"I don't mind at all," Peterson said. He watched her as she climbed the stairs, and Sara felt his unabashed staring until she rounded the landing and passed out of his field of view.

Room 208 was at the far end of the hall. She walked down the red-carpeted hallway until she stood just outside the door. She knocked, waited for a few seconds, then knocked again.

"Mr. Flynn?"

"Just a minute," a muffled voice answered.

Sara stood there quietly until the door opened. Mike saw her, then he smiled broadly and pulled the door all the way open.

141

"Come in," he said. "Come on in. What a pleasant surprise."

"Yes," Sara said. "We both seem to be in the business of providing surprises, don't we? Only some of the surprises aren't so pleasant."

The smile left Mike's face, and he looked at Sara with a confused expression.

"What do you mean?" he asked. "What are you talking about?"

"I'm talking about the best farming land in the world," Sara said. "For sale, cheap, by the Cascade Railroad."

"Where did you hear about that?" Mike asked.

"There is no need for you to deny it, Mr. Flynn. I saw one of the handbills you have distributed. I must say that we could have done a better printing job, but the information is quite legible. Certainly legible enough to bring hundreds of settlers into this valley."

"I see," Mike said, quietly. "And you wouldn't want that to happen?"

"Mr. Flynn, this is a ranching valley," Sara said. "Our economy is based upon cattle. Without the range land the cattle ranchers will suffer, and when they suffer, the entire economy of the valley will suffer."

"That's where you're wrong," Mike said. "The best thing that could happen to this valley would be to diversify the economic base. Don't you see? If a few hundred more people come into the valley and began raising crops, their income would benefit everyone. The merchants would get their business, I would get their business, even the newspaper would have more readers and more advertising."

"And the ranchers?"

"They won't suffer," Mike said. "Perhaps they won't have the same stranglehold on the valley they have now, but they won't suffer."

"I . . . I wish I could believe you, Mike," Sara said, and her words were spoken with an intensity that surprised Mike. It also did not escape his notice that she called him Mike. "We need to talk," she said. "Not only about this, but about a few other things as well."

"Sara, I'd be only too happy to talk to you, girl, for I'm sure I could make you see my side of it." Mike stepped back and held his arm out, inviting her into his room. "Come on in."

Sara started in, then hesitated. What was she doing? She couldn't go into his room! If he kissed her again, if she lost control of her passions, there would be nothing to prevent her from . . . Sara felt a flame in her body, and she closed her eyes and put her hand on the doorframe, as if consciously holding herself out of the room.

Mike saw the discomfort Sara felt over entering the room, so he added, "Or perhaps you'd feel more comfortable in the restaurant. I haven't had my breakfast. Would you like to join me?"

"I've had breakfast, thank you," Sara said. "But we could talk as you eat, if you don't mind." She would be safe in the dining room, she knew. There she could speak of the most delicate matters without fear of losing control of the situation.

"I don't mind at all," Mike said. "Come along."

Just as Mike started to pull the door to, a woman called from the end of the hall at the top of the stairs.

"Mike, wait! I left something in your room this morning, and I want—" The woman saw Sara and she stopped. "Oh," she stammered. "Excuse me, Mike, I didn't realize you had company."

Sara looked at the woman. She was very pretty, though in a showy sort of way. Her hair was brown and her eyes were blue, but the most striking thing about her was her rouge. Sara had never seen that much rouge on a woman, especially at this hour of the morning. The woman also reeked of perfume.

"It's all right, Rosie," Mike said. "The room is unlocked. Go on in and look around."

"Thanks," Rosie said. She passed by with her eyes looking down, self-consciously, toward the carpet.

"Do you know Mrs. Mullens?" Sara asked.

"Do you?" Mike replied.

"Only by name, I'm afraid," Sara said. "I have never figured out exactly what she does. I know she works here at the hotel, perhaps as head housekeeper or something."

Mike chuckled. "Or something," he said.

"She called you by your first name."

"We've grown rather close," Mike suggested with a wry smile.

"Close? What do you mean, close?" Sara asked.

"Rosie and I spent the night together," Mike said.

Sara gasped.

"I'm sorry," Mike said. "I thought you realized that Mrs. Mullens was a prostitute."

"I realized no such thing," Sara said. "How *could* I know that? How would any *decent* person know that?"

"Oh, I see," Mike said. "And of course, being a decent person, you are totally blind to life all around you."

"I try and avoid coming in contact with the seamier aspects of life, yes," Sara said. "And so should you."

"And so should I?" Mike said, raising his voice. " 'N tell me, lassie, who gave you the callin' to tell me how to live my own life, now?" Mike's Irish brogue, intensified, with the increase of his Irish temper.

"Oh," Sara said. "Oh, I should have my head examined for coming over here. To think that I was going to talk to you, to measure your . . . ," she started to say, to measure his feeling about her, but she stopped. "To give you a chance to explain about the land," she said, instead. Tears spilled from her eyes.

"And so I did explain about the land," Mike said.

"And the woman you spent the night with," Sara said. "Can you explain her?"

"Now, wait a minute," Mike said. "What right do you have to tell me that any explanation is due?"

"Perhaps I have no right, sir," Sara said angrily, fighting back the tears. Her anger grew out of proportion to the event, because she was angry with her own, strange reaction to it. "But neither do you, sir, have a right to be offensive in my company."

"Madam, I would remind you that you came to my room of your own volition," Mike said coldly. "And you may leave the same way."

Sara looked toward Mike with eyes which were wet with tears of hurt, and snapping with the light of anger.

"Thank you for giving me your permission to withdraw," she said. "For that is exactly what I shall do."

Sara turned sharply on her heel and walked quickly and haughtily down the corridor, leaving Mike to stare at her as she walked away.

"I'm sorry, Mike," Rosie said, returning from Mike's room at that moment. "I had no idea she would be up here, or I would have waited."

"Ah, don't worry about it, Rosie," Mike said easily. "It doesn't mean anything."

"You name your train after her, and you say it doesn't *mean* anything?"

"Rosie, if Miss Landers is going to take me, she's going to have to take me as I am, and not as what she thinks I should be."

Rosie laughed aloud. "You know what? I think you're both crazy."

"How so?"

"You're crazy for believing you have a chance with her, and she's crazy for not giving you a chance."

"Rosie, m'girl," Mike said, laughing at her comment, "How'd you like to eat breakfast with me?"

"Sure," Rosie answered. "I'll get breakfast sent up and we can—"

"No, I mean in the dining room," Mike said. He laughed sheepishly. "I'm sorry, I don't have time for anything else."

Rosie looked shocked. "You would eat with me, in public?"

"Of course."

"You wouldn't be shamed by my presence?" Rosie asked.

"Rosie, m'girl, now you tell me how an Irish lad could ever be shamed by bein' seen with a colleen as pretty as yourself?" Mike asked, throwing a great deal of brogue into his voice.

"Michael, sure'n I'd consider it a great honor to eat breakfast with you," she said, imitating his brogue.

When Mike went down to the depot after breakfast, he saw that Butte Valley had started its Independence Day celebration early by making the loading of the train a gala event. In the spirit of the event, Sollie, Carl and Burke, had decorated the train in red, white, and blue bunting. The brass had been polished until it shined with blinding brightness. Twenty-five cattle cars, loaded with twenty head each, stretched out behind the engine, making a line from the depot, all the way to the western edge of town.

The cowboys who herded the cattle into the loading pens, were dressed in their best work clothes, and the entire town was turned out to watch. Sara's news had evidently not spread to the others, for no one mentioned the handbill, or the fact that new settlers would be coming into the valley.

Mike climbed up on the first cattle car and looked out over the crowd to see if he could see Sara, but she was nowhere around. Sollie opened the throttle and the train started forward. Mike began walking toward the back of the train, so that in effect he was remaining in the same place with respect to the crowd, though the train was pulling out from under him. When he reached the caboose he waved back at the crowd. He stayed there until the train was well out of town and starting up the grade for Butte Pass.

Mike watched the scenery slide by. It was beautiful country, but it was wild and rugged, with great mountains, rushing, untamed rivers, huge trees, and high, torrential cascades tumbling down sheer cliffs. It was the last remaining wilderness in America, and he was determined to be its master.

Which seemed a lot easier than the task of taming Sara Landers.

Chapter Eleven

===

Lee Coulter stood in the crowd with the others until the train carrying his cattle disappeared around the far curve of the track. Then, when only a pencil-thin strip of smoke told where the train was, he walked over to the Wells Fargo office, where he checked on the reply to the telegram he had dispatched the day before.

"Yes, sir, it's back," the operator said. He pulled a yellow envelope from a box and handed it to Lee.

"Thanks, Tim," Lee said, as he read the message. He smiled. "This is just what I wanted to hear."

"I was a little surprised you used the Wells Fargo line to send that message," Tim said. "It bein' railroad business, I'm sure Flynn would've sent the message for free."

"I had my reasons, Tim," Lee said. "I did have my reasons."

Lee stuck the message into his pocket, then walked down the boardwalk toward the *Valley Monitor* office. Franklin and Sara were both busy getting the day's newspaper set.

"I know you have a deadline," Lee said. "But I was still surprised that you two weren't down at the station, watching the train pull out."

"Hello, Lee," Franklin said.

"Professor, Sara," Lee said. "Sara, I came to see if you would go to the dance with me. You know, this Saturday it's going to be a big, outside affair, the Fourth of July and all that."

Sara looked up at Lee and smiled. "I would be *very* glad to go with you, Lee," she said.

"You would?" Lee answered, a little surprised by her easy acceptance of his invitation. He was then emboldened to go a little further. "Then perhaps you would also, that is, the two of you," he amended, "would have dinner with me that evening, at the Star Hotel?"

"Not me," Franklin said. "Have you forgotten that I have to cook the fish for the fish-fry that evening? Surely you wouldn't rather have dinner in the Star Hotel, than eat my fish?"

"I would," Sara said.

Both Franklin and Lee looked at Sara with surprise, then Sara went on, "I love your fish, Dad, really I do," she said. "But I think a nice, quiet, dinner after an entire day of celebration might be just the ticket. Lee, I hope you don't mind if just *I* accept your invitation?"

"Mind?" Lee said. He smiled broadly. "I can't think of anything more wonderful. In fact, it would be great!"

"Well, now, you don't have to go *that* far," Franklin said. "You'll make me feel as if I am an unwanted party here."

"Oh, no, Professor, I didn't mean anything like that, honest I didn't."

Franklin laughed. "I was just teasing. Oh, I hate to be the one to spoil your happy mood," he went on, "but I have something here that I think you should see."

Franklin handed the handbill to Lee. "What do you think of that?" he asked.

Lee read Mike's handbill, and then, to the surprise of both Franklin and Sara, he laughed out loud.

"Well, I must say, you are certainly taking this better than I thought you would," Sara said.

"It's wonderful," Lee said. "It just makes what I did all the more sweet."

"What you did? I don't understand," Sara said. "What did you do?"

"I just made certain arrangements which are going to make it most difficult for Mr. Flynn to hold onto his land, that's all."

"What do you mean?"

"Oh, nothing," Lee said, very mysteriously. "Let's just say I purchased some insurance in case something like this should develop. Now I can see that it was a most propitious move on my part."

"I'm glad to see you are taking it so well," Franklin said. "I just hope that Mr. Flynn takes the Polecat column as well."

"What do you mean?"

"Dad has written a rather blistering editorial against Mr. Flynn and his underhanded, sneaky tactics," Sara said.

"Good for you, Professor," Lee said. "And you, Sara, what do you think of the article?"

"I think it is time someone put Mr. Flynn in his place," Sara replied, with a surprising amount of bitterness.

Lee smiled broadly and rubbed his hands together. "Well, I'm glad to see you feel that way. And don't worry. Flynn is going to discover that he bit off more than he can chew when he came here. I'll see you Saturday," he said, waving goodbye, then walking back outside. He chuckled to himself. He was going to beat Flynn good, and it was going to be sweet. Oh, it was going to be sweet.

As the Sara Landers Special rolled into Boise the next day, Mike hopped down from the caboose while the train was still rolling, and walked across the station platform toward the freight and passenger office. The train continued to move slowly through the station yard toward the feeder-lots, for they would have to off-load the cattle there, then load them onto the cars for transshipment to Denver.

Mike looked over toward the spur tracks, expecting to see the cars he would need. He had wired ahead for them just before he left Butte Valley. They should have been here by now, unless there was some unexpected delay.

"Howdy, Mike," Eb said, as Mike stepped into the station. Eb was stamping freight manifests.

"Hello, Eb," Mike said.

"I see you brought your cattle."

"Yes," Mike said. "Listen, Eb, have you heard anything from the Denver and Missouri? They were supposed to have cars here to take my cattle on."

"I haven't heard a word since you wired me yesterday to order the cars," Eb said. "Would you like me to check on it?"

"Yes, would you? I'm going over to the hotel to take a bath and grab a nap. I'll be back in a couple of hours."

"I should have word by then," Eb promised.

"I'd like to think that the cars will be here by then," Mike said.

"Oh, by the way," Eb said. "Will you be ready to take some passengers Monday?"

"I've got passengers?"

"I'll say," Eb said. "There are about twenty immigrants wanting to settle your land."

"Really?"

"Yep. Your handbills seem to be doing the job. They've all paid cash for the land, too. I'm holding over six hundred dollars for you."

Mike smiled broadly. "That sounds good," he

said. "I'll be ready for them Monday. Oh, you won't forget the telegram?"

"I'll send it right now," Eb said, starting for the instrument.

"Thanks," Mike said.

Half an hour later, Mike was sitting in a large brass bathtub, smoking a cheroot and singing at the top of his lungs, while at the same time scrubbing his back with a long-handled brush. He dropped the brush on the floor behind him.

"Would you like me to get that for you?" a woman's voice asked.

"Laura, darlin', sure'n is it you?" Mike asked brightly.

"None other," Laura said, and she knelt down beside the tub and began to wash Mike's back with slow, sensuous strokes.

"Ah, it feels as if the angels themselves are dancin' on my back," Mike said. "Tell me, girl, what brings you here to my room?"

"I saw your train arrive," Laura said. "The Sara Landers Special."

"Ah, yes," Mike said. "I'm beginnin' to think, darlin', that I could have been more wise choosin' a name. Miss Landers and I certainly don't seem to be hitting it off all that well."

"Not like you and me, huh, lover?" Laura asked, looking at Mike with eyes smoky with the memory of the last time they had been together, the time just before Mike negotiated his loan.

"No, darlin', not like you and me," Mike agreed.

"I brought you luck then, didn't I?" Laura asked. She put her fingers on the gold nugget which, even now, hung from Mike's neck. "More luck than this did."

"Maybe you did at that," Mike admitted.

"Could you use a little more luck?" Laura asked, and her hand dipped down into the bathwater where, boldly, brazenly, she wrapped her long, skilled fingers around him.

Mike felt a charge of electricity go through him as her fingers made contact, and he was instantly receptive to her suggestion.

"A man can always use a little luck," he said, standing up, dripping water from his naked body, and from her arm and hand which had gone under, to grasp his manhood. "Besides, I can get a nap any time."

"I feel a little overdressed now," Laura said, and as she looked at him through those smoke-gray eyes, she began removing her clothes, pulling the dress off her shoulders, then pushing it down her body.

Mike watched with the anticipation of pleasure mounting, as he was treated to the sight of Laura's breasts, firm, well rounded, and tipped by red nipples which had known the caress of many lovers.

Laura folded her clothes carefully, with the relaxed practice of one who is well skilled in the art. Then she turned to face him. Her body was well lighted by the afternoon sun, and the tangle of hair at the junction of her legs shined in reflected light.

Mike grew impatient and pulled Laura to him, kissing her open mouth with his own, feeling her tongue darting against his. He eased her down onto his bed, then crawled on top of her.

Laura received him happily, wrapping her legs around him, meeting his lunges by pushing against him. She lost herself in the pleasure of the moment, until a few minutes later she could feel him jerking and thrusting in savage fury, spraying his seed into her and finally collapsing across her.

Later, as Mike slept, Laura put her hand over on him, feeling at rest that part of him which had so recently been vibrant and active. She had never met the woman, Sara Landers, but she wished she could. She wished she could tell Sara Landers how lucky she is to have the love of a man like this. She could never have anymore of him than this, she knew, but if there had been the slightest chance she would have taken it.

Life wasn't fair, she thought. She, who knew what a prize Mike was, could not have him. Sara, who didn't know, could have him for the taking.

"What do you *mean* there are no cars available for shipment to Denver?" Mike asked Eb, when he went back to check on his message.

"Here is the wire," Eb said.

158

"That's the Denver and Missouri. What about the others?" Mike asked.

"I checked with them all, Mike," Eb said. "The Denver and Missouri, the Northern Pacific, the Union Pacific. There are no cars available for at least two weeks."

Mike crushed the message, then threw it on the floor. That meant he would have to make arrangements to keep the cattle in feeder-lot pens at his own expense. At fifteen cents per day per animal, Mike didn't need a pencil to figure the arithmetic. If he really did have to wait two weeks before he got his cars, he would wind up losing money on the trip.

"Just as a matter of curiosity," Mike said, "do you have any idea who in the hell *needs* that many cars?"

"Let's see," Eb said. "I think one of the messages did mention it. Yes, here it is . . . the Coulter Cattle Company."

"The Coulter Cattle Company?" Mike said. He hit his fist in his hand. "Damn, I should have known! It's Lee Coulter! Well, Coulter, you may have struck the first blow, but I'll get in the last," he swore under his breath.

At the quilting booth, on the Fourth of July, Mrs. Corley Abel and Mrs. Fran Carter were finalists in the quilting bee. Mrs. Abel's entry was Irish Chain, designed and quilted by her in patches of red, white, green and gold. It was breathtakingly beautiful, but Mrs. Carter's Jacob's Ladder, done in shades of red from a bright cherry color to a muted wine, was just as beautiful.

The judges were having a very difficult time selecting the winner, and they looked out over the faces of the anxious crowd, composed of supporters of both women, and knew that whichever they selected, they would leave half the people disappointed. The judges were Sara Landers and Jennie Adams.

"What do you think?" Jennie asked.

"I think we should do what a judge would do in a court of law," Sara replied.

"What's that?" Jennie asked with a little laugh.

"We should go into chambers and take it under advisement."

"What's that mean?"

"That means let's get out of here where we can talk it over without everyone hanging on our every word," Sara said, and she pointed to the crowd of people.

"That's a good idea," Jennie said.

The two women excused themselves, telling the onlookers that they wished to discuss the final two quilting entries, and walked over to the gazebo which stood in the center of town. They bought a lemonade apiece, then sat there in the shade of the gazebo, drinking the cool, refreshing liquid while they watched the workers stringing the lanterns for the evening's dance.

"The dance will be held outside tonight," Jennie said.

"Yes," Sara said. "It will be very nice. Are you going?"

"I don't know," Jennie said, sighing. "I really don't enjoy them all that much."

"Why, Jennie Adams, how can you say such a thing? I saw you last week and you looked as if you were having a wonderful time."

"I don't know," Jennie said. "It seems odd to be racing against all those men in the horse race one minute, then cuddling up to them in a dance the next."

Sara laughed. "You'll never change, Jennie Adams."

"I guess you'll be going to the dance?" Jennie asked.

"Yes," Sara said. "I'm going with Lee."

"Is Mike Flynn going to be back in time?"

"I really don't know," Sara said. "Nor do I care," she added.

"Oh, oh," Jennie said.

"What does that mean?" Sara asked.

"Generally, when someone says 'I don't care' in that tone of voice, it covers up just how much they *do* care. What is it? Do you want to talk about it?"

Sara took a swallow of her lemonade before she went on. "I . . . I'm not sure you would understand," she said.

"Try me."

"I can't," Sara said. "It's too personal, and embarrassing."

"Sara, don't think that because I can ride, rope, and brand, that I don't know what it's like to be a woman," Jennie said. "Sometimes I wish I couldn't do all those things. None of the men seem to recognize me for what I am, and now my own best friend doesn't either."

"Oh, Jennie, I'm sorry," Sara apologized. "Of course I know that you have feelings like a woman, I didn't mean anything contrary to that. It's just that, well, I'm not all that proud of the feelings I've been having. And now I discover that with one of the men, I was really wrong."

"With Flynn?"

"Yes," Sara said.

"Do you feel this way because of the Polecat column, or is the Polecat column written because you feel this way?" Jennie asked.

"The Polecat column?"

"Your father was pretty harsh on Mike Flynn for opening up the land to settlers," Jennie said.

"Oh, that," Sara said. "Well, yes, that too, but . . ."

"Something more personal, right?" Jennie asked.

"Yes," Sara said. "Jennie, Thursday morning I went over to the hotel to see him. I was going to talk to him, to see just how he felt, to see if . . ." Sara paused, not wishing to go any further. "Well, anyway," she said. "When I got there, I discovered that he had spent the night with that Mullens woman. He admitted it, right to my face."

"Sara, I was honest with you when I told you that I had a woman's feelings," Jennie said.

"But being as I can work like a man, some few times the men around me forget that I'm a woman, and I hear them talking. Men are apt to sleep warm whenever they can. That's the difference between being a man and being a woman. Women probably have just as strong a need, but it's a bit easier for a man to do something about it."

"You . . . *you know about that need?*" Sara asked.

"Yes," Jennie said quietly. "I know about it."

"I'm glad," Sara said. "I'm glad we had this chance to talk." She laughed self-consciously. "I was beginning to think something was wrong with me, first with Mike and then with Lee. But now, I know what to do. I know that Mike Flynn is wrong, and Lee is right. I'm glad that I will be with Lee tonight."

"Are you . . . are you in love with Lee Coulter?" Jennie asked quietly.

"I don't know," Sara said. "But I think I am. I *must* be. I can't explain my feelings in any other way."

"He's a fine man, Sara," Jennie said seriously. "I don't think you could do any better."

Suddenly a firecracker exploded very close to the two young women, causing them to cry out in surprise. Two boys ran away from them, laughing at their great joke. Then both Sara and Jennie laughed. The firecracker changed the mood before Sara was able to look into Jennie's eyes, and see the torment of her soul.

"Well, I've got to get ready for the race,"

Jennie said. "You must decide between Mrs. Abel and Mrs. Carter."

"Oh no," Sara laughed. "Why must *I* be the one to decide?"

"Because," Jennie said, "you went away to college. That was supposed to make you smart."

"I certainly didn't learn anything in college which would make this an easy task," Sara said.

"I don't know what decision to make," Jennie said. "As far as I'm concerned, they are equal."

"That's it!" Sara said. "You've just solved the problem. We'll declare a tie!"

"I don't know," Jennie said. "Do you think the town fathers would come up with another ten dollars to give equal prize money?"

"They are either going to do that, or come up with two more judges," Sara said. "What do you say?"

"I say let's do it," Jennie replied.

When the two young women returned to the booth, they were besieged by the anxious supporters of the contestants.

"Who won?"

"Have you come to a decision?"

"It's the Irish Chain, right?"

"No, it's the Jacob's Ladder, the Jacob's Ladder," someone else called.

"Ladies," Sara said; then as she looked over the crowd she saw that there were a few men, including Lee Coulter, present as well. "And gentlemen. After a careful deliberation, my co-judge and I declare this contest to be a tie between Mrs. Abel and Mrs. Carter, and award each of the contestants the ten dollar first prize."

Everyone cheered and applauded, and even Mrs. Abel and Mrs. Carter, long-time competitors in the event, managed to smile and congratulate each other.

"Wait a minute!" Mr. Johnson called. Mr. Johnson was not only the banker, but also a member of the city council. "Where is the extra ten dollars going to come from? It wasn't allowed for in the city budget."

"I will donate ten dollars to the city," Lee Coulter said easily. "I agree with Miss Landers and Miss Adams, there is no way to determine which of these two marvelous quilts is more beautiful, and the ladies who worked on them should share equally the fullest benefits of their labor."

"Why, thank you, Mr. Coulter," Johnson said. "Ladies, that is just one more proof, as if such proof was needed, that Lee Coulter is one of the finest men in the valley. Let's all give him a hand."

The crowd applauded Lee, and Lee, holding up his hands modestly, smiled and waved at them as he worked his way through the handshakes and pats on the back until he reached Sara and Jennie.

"That was very nice of you, Lee," Jennie said. "You are really the hero in their eyes."

As Jennie spoke to Lee, the look in her eyes

would have indicated to the more observant, that he was just as big a hero to her.

"Ah, it was nothing," Lee said. "Besides, I'm counting on you to win the money back for me. I've bet on you to win."

Lee put his hand on Jennie's shoulder, as he would if he had been talking to one of his hands. But there was a strange sensation at the contact. She felt softer, and more vulnerable than Lee would have expected, and his hand on her was more exciting then she imagined. For a split second, they looked deep into each others eyes, trying to gauge their reaction, but each was overprotective of personal emotions, and the second slipped away so quickly, that it was almost as if it never happened.

"Oh, my," Jennie said. "I had nearly forgotten the race."

"Good luck, Jennie," Sara said. Sara had watched the reaction between Jennie and Lee, but she was even less able to analyze it than they had been.

"Come on," Lee said to Sara, as Jennie left for the race. "I have a place all picked out for us, down by the corner. We'll get to see them coming down the stretch, and we'll watch them cross the finish line."

"Here they come!" a man on the roof of the Millers' Emporium called. He was looking through binoculars toward the back road.

"Who's in front?"

"Johnny Purkee is in the lead," the man

called down. "Ed Farmingdale is second, and Morris Goodwin is third."

"Where's Jennie?" someone called up. "Do you see her?"

"No," the man with the binoculars said. "No I don't even . . . wait a minute, there she is, back in the pack. She's running about seventh."

There was a groan from the crowd, but one of the men called over to Lee.

"Get your money ready, Coulter. She's going to lose this one."

"The race isn't over yet," Sara called back.

"There's Purkee!" someone called. "They've rounded the final stretch."

"Get back! Get back, give 'im room!" someone called. One man ran across the street, carrying a small ribbon with him, then he held it up so that it made the finish line.

"Look at that!" someone else called. "Who's that on the black horse?"

"It's Jennie Adams!" another said.

"She's comin' up fast."

"She won't make it. She doesn't have a chance!"

"I don't know, look, she's already third and she's closing on . . . no, she got 'im. She's runnin' second now and she's chargin' Purkee!"

"Purkee works for you, Lee, can he hold her off?"

"I don't know," Lee said. "He's a fine rider, perhaps the best I have. But Jennie is awfully good too. Come on, Jennie!"

"Come on, Jennie!" Sara shouted, and soon

167

many others, except for those who, for financial reasons, were against her, also started shouting encouragement.

The horses entered the end of the street, Jennie and Purkee far out in front of the others. Both riders were bent low over their mounts, but were raised up from the saddles, holding themselves on with their knees. The horses' manes were flying, their nostrils distended, their muscles rippling, and their hooves drumming a thunder in the street.

The horses flashed by just in front of Sara and Lee, who saw, with a thrill, that Jennie had pulled in front of Purkee. Jennie's horse flashed across the ribbon, the winner.

Lee ran to congratulate Jennie, even before Jennie was dismounted. He left Sara's side so quickly, that she hadn't even anticipated it, and before she realized what was happening, she saw Lee pulling Jennie off her horse.

"Jennie, that was a magnificent ride!" Lee said. "I've never seen anything so exciting!"

Lee kissed Jennie, then, broke it off quickly, and as if to cover the embarrassment, he said; "I'm sure glad Purkee didn't win. I'd hate to have to give him a congratulatory kiss like that."

The others laughed, but Sara didn't. She remembered the look Lee and Jennie had exchanged earlier, and she felt a vague uneasiness.

"Sara, what do you think?" Lee called, taking her into the victory circle. "Isn't Jennie the greatest?"

"Yes," Sara said, and she meant it. Jennie was her dearest friend, and Lee's enthusiasm was just that, enthusiasm, and nothing more. Sara felt ashamed for her disquieting thoughts.

Chapter Twelve

When Sara and Lee walked into the lobby of the Star Hotel that evening, Sara noticed that the dining room was dark and deserted.

"Oh, Lee, I forgot," Sara said. "The dining room is always closed on the night of the Fourth. So many people eat at the fish-fry that they have no business."

"Don't worry about it," Lee said. "I have a surprise arranged."

"A surprise? What sort of a surprise?"

"We didn't want anyone anyway, remember? The whole idea was to have some time away from the crowd. Come this way."

Sara, who was a little confused now, took Lee's arm when he offered it, and walked up the broad, carpeted stairway with him to the second floor. There, Lee opened a door, then motioned for Sara to step inside.

The door opened to the Royal Suite. Sara had never seen it before, though she had heard that it was beautiful. It was so named because a Russian Count had once stayed there during a hunting trip to America.

Sara had been exposed to a measure of elegance while back east, but she was surprised to see that her own Butte Valley, Oregon, could boast of such a place as this.

The chandelier had been lighted, and it glowed in soft, golden light, with each of its hundreds of glass facets sparkling like diamonds. The furnishings of the room were in deep blue velvet, and the carpet a rich red wine. The table was covered with a beautiful damask cloth, and laid with china, silver, and crystal, all of which glistened in the soft light.

"I hope you like Beef Wellington," Lee said. "As a cattleman, I think any fine meal should include beef."

Lee assisted Sara into her chair, then sat across from her.

They ate slowly, leisurely, and the conversation, as Lee had said it would be, was one in which each of them learned about the other. Lee told of his "wild" days when he lived in San Francisco, and he told of his plans for the future. Sara told a few anecdotes from her school days, and finally, the meal was ended.

"Lee, I must say that this has been one of the most pleasant meals of my entire life," Sara said. And she meant it. The room, the wine, the atmosphere, but most of all, the languid pace of the meeting, combined to form a sensual setting which was pleasant without being threatening.

"If we were married we could have thousands of such meals," Lee said.

Sara couldn't have been more shocked if Lee had just slapped her! Here was the very thing she was looking for! If Lee cared enough about her to ask her to marry him, then surely the tumultuous desires she felt in his arms were not wrong.

"Married?" she replied. "Are you asking me to marry you?"

"Yes," Lee said. "Sara, I know you may think this is sudden. But I figure I need to work pretty fast. After all, I have Mike Flynn to consider."

"You do not have Mike Flynn to consider," Sara said. "Mike Flynn means nothing to me."

"Perhaps not," Lee said. "But I did see him kiss you on my front porch last Monday night."

"You . . . you *saw* that?" Sara gasped, putting her hand to her mouth.

"Yes," Lee said. "I didn't intend to see it. I was on the porch when you and Flynn came outside. I couldn't make my presence known without embarrassment. I wish now that I had."

"Lee, I'm sorry," Sara said. "I didn't want it to happen. He just grabbed me and kissed me, I don't know why."

173

Lee stood up and came around the table, then pulled Sara up from her chair. "I can't blame Mike Flynn for doing something I wanted to do," he said. "I couldn't blame any man for doing this," and he took her in his arms, pressing his lips to hers.

Sara felt as if a thousand butterfly wings were brushing against her lips. The kiss was fire and ice, brutalizingly sensual, yet delightfully tender. Her head began to spin. Then she felt Lee's tongue darting about, touching her mouth lightly, setting fire to her body, and suddenly, and without shame, she knew that she would be powerless to resist anything Lee asked of her tonight.

Finally the kiss ended. Then Lee, his eyes reflecting the golden light of the candles, poured a brandy for each of them, and handed a glass to Sara. She drank it, tasting the controlled fire of its fruit on the tip of her tongue, then feeling the spreading relaxation as the liquor began, almost instantly, to work.

"There is another room to this suite," Lee suggested.

Sara stood there for just a moment, then she closed her eyes and held the glass out toward him. She knew she should leave now. She should turn and walk through that door and fight down these feelings which, once more, threatened to overtake her. And yet, though her mind told her what she should do, her body dictated what she could do, and she was powerless to take a step. The spreading fires raced ahead, and a consuming desire rushed over her, as they continued to kiss passionately, his hands seeking to pleasure her.

Lee filled her glass a second time, and again she drank the liquid which had the effect of feeding fuel to her enflamed desire, while weakening her mental resolve against such action.

Without the power to resist, Sara followed Lee from the dining room into the bedroom. There, the covers of the bed were turned down, making the way even easier for her.

Lee began to undress Sara, doing it easily and skillfully with no awkwardness to impede the progress or give Sara more time to think. Before she was even fully cognizant of what was happening to her, she was nude.

Sara could feel the air of the room against her nudity, and it was a delightfully silken sensation, which further enflamed her passions, and she waited, anxiously now, for Lee to join her. She was surprised at her own ardor and her lack of embarrassment.

When Lee was also nude, he went to her and pulled her to him, kissing her again, but this time accenting the kiss with the full body to body contact of naked flesh against naked flesh. Sara opened her mouth hungrily on his, no longer attempting to resist, but taking it joyfully, submerging herself in the rapture of the moment.

"Lee," she whispered, as they lay on the bed. "I've never . . . I've never done this before."

Lee looked into her eyes, and she saw something almost like the thrill of conquest deep inside them. It puzzled her, but just for a second, because the other sensations continued unabated, and she reached for him, encircling her arms around his naked shoulders, just as in the dream, and pulled him down onto her.

At long last those rapturous desires Sara had kept buried were given their freedom, and she felt pleasure beyond compare as Lee made love to her. She was thrust to peaks of pleasure, bursting with all the fire and glory of the Fourth of July fireworks, which were even then exploding in the night sky outside their window.

Somehow, Sara felt as if she and the brilliant fireworks display outside were one and the same. They had not been set off by celebrants of the Fourth, but by her own intense passions, and she raced to the heavens with them.

Finally a shuddering moan of passion told her that Lee had joined her in this maelstrom of sensation, and she locked her arms around him and pulled him to her, giving him her own sweet body to spend his pleasure in.

They lay together for several moments afterward. Outside the rockets continued to burst, and the Roman candles continued to send up their stream of light and color. Sara was coming back down slowly from the passionate peaks she had attained, and she felt warm and glowing in the dark of the room.

Lee reached over and touched her, letting

his hand move protectively, possessively, over the most intimate parts of her body. Sara allowed it without question, and in so doing, realized that she had just given herself to him.

Now, she thought. Now there was some purpose and justification for all those feelings. Surely this wasn't wrong. Lee told her that he loved her, and wanted to marry her.

"Yes," she heard herself say in the dark of the room.

"Yes?" Lee asked, wondering what she meant.

"I will marry you," Sara said.

Chapter Thirteen

The outdoor dance was in full swing by the time Sara and Lee joined the celebrants, and such was the spirit of things that no one realized they were late.

"See," Lee said. "No one even missed us. We wouldn't even have had to come back if we didn't want to."

"But I wanted to," Sara said. "I hope you don't mind."

"No," Lee said, smiling. "I don't mind at all."

"Form your squares!" the dance caller shouted for the next dance, and Sara and Lee rushed onto the floor for the dance.

As the music played and the caller called, the dancers swung through the steps of the dances. None of the dancers was more popular than Jennie Adams. Although she had indicated to Sara, earlier, that she might not come to the dance, she had come, and the dress she was wearing now was in such contrast to the pants and shirt she had worn for the race that her femininity and beauty were all the more accented by it.

Gone now was the slight uneasiness Sara had felt about Jennie earlier, even though Jennie looked more beautiful tonight than Sara had ever seen her. The uneasiness was gone because Sara no longer felt doubt about Lee's feelings. Less than half an hour earlier she had been making love with Lee, and now she was on the dance floor with him.

As Sara moved through the dance sets, progressing from partner to partner, swinging and swaying with the steps and routines of the dance, she was still cognizant of the heavy dampness of her womb, the results of that love-making. The fact that she knew it, while the others suspected nothing, was very sensual to her. It was a rather delicious wickedness which she enjoyed, privately.

Suddenly the music and dance was interrupted by the sound of a train whistle, and everyone looked at each other in surprise. The train wasn't supposed to return until late the next afternoon, and yet, here it was on Saturday night. The whistle continued in a series of blasts which made the music inaudible, and several of the celebrating cowboys grew irritated by it.

"Someone needs to go down to the depot and

teach that train driver a few manners," Purkee slurred. Purkee was drunk, having gone immediately to whiskey to assuage his feelings over losing the race to a woman.

"Listen to that whistle," someone else said. "It doesn't normally sound like that. Do you suppose something's wrong?"

"I'm goin' down there," someone else said, and soon there was a general exodus from the dance floor to the train depot. By now, the train had arrived in town, and everyone could see it, the great yellow lantern wavering in the dark, the steamlike white tendrils of lace, and the sparks in the smoke, whipping up to scatter red stars among the blue.

"Hey!" someone called. "He's brought our cattle back!"

"What? What are you talking about?"

"Look on the train, dammit! Is them our cattle, or not?"

"I'll be damned! What did he do that for?"

The train stopped with a squeal of brakes, and Mike Flynn jumped down from the engine cab.

"Coulter!" Flynn called angrily. "Where is Coulter?"

"I'm right here," Lee said easily, moving forward from the crowd.

"Here are your cattle," Mike said. "And here is your money." He reached into his shirt pocket and took out an envelope, which he handed to Lee. "Count it, you'll see that it's all here."

"I think there's no need for that," Lee said.

"I said count it," Mike repeated, speaking very quietly in an attempt to control his anger. "From this moment on, Coulter, any dealings between us will have to be open. There is no trust left."

"Obviously," Lee replied. "Your promise to allow us to continue to use the range land is proof of that."

"Yeah, what about that, Flynn?" one of the other ranchers said. "Is the article in the *Valley Monitor* true? Are you opening the range land up for immigrants?"

Mike looked at Sara and his eyes snapped in anger. She returned his gaze with one just as angry.

"I was going to explain the situation to your—*reporter*," he said mockingly. "But she was unwilling to listen."

"Yeah? Well, suppose you explain the situation to us right now. Why did you tell us we could use the range land, if you knew you were going to settle it with squatters?"

"I was honest with you," Mike said. "I told you I had no intention of selling this land to you, and I also told you that you could continue to use it for the time being. It will be some time before the land is all settled."

"You expect us to share the land with the squatters?" someone asked.

"No," Mike said. "I don't intend to let you use any of the land now. Not since Mr. Coulter's little trick."

"What's he talking about, Lee?" one of the others asked.

"Yes, Lee, what trick is that?" Stump asked.

"No trick," Lee said. "When I discovered that Flynn intended to double-cross us, I just managed to work a little double cross of my own. I tied up all the cattle cars between Boise and Denver, so Mr. Flynn couldn't ship out the cattle we sent with him."

"Why did you do that?"

"Simple," Lee said. "Mr. Flynn had guaranteed our shipment. If he didn't have any cars, he would have to feed our cattle. If he had to feed our cattle, he would go broke, and if he went broke, the railroad would go out of business, thus causing those lands to be forfeited."

"Ha!" someone laughed. "That was pretty smart! Good thinking, Lee."

"As you can see, however, Mr. Flynn has reneged on his contract. He didn't deliver the cattle, and he didn't hold them for shipment. Instead, he brought them back to us."

"Yes," Mike said. "I brought them back. Now, if you would be so kind as to take your cattle off my train, gentlemen, I would appreciate it."

"Flynn, you aren't going to be so unsporting as to make these cowboys have to work during the dance, are you?" Lee asked. "I'm not certain they would appreciate that."

"You're damn right I don't appreciate it,"

Purkee said. "And I'm going to show you how much I don't appreciate it."

Purkee knocked Mike down with a sudden and unexpected blow. As Mike started to get up, Purkee still had the advantage since he was on his feet, and he clubbed Mike again.

Now the crowd became a part of it, and they started shouting encouragement to Purkee, screaming at him to finish Mike off.

Purkee smiled, and drew his fist back for one final, clubbing blow. But he was overconfident, and he took too long, and Mike was able to regain his feet before Purkee swung. This time Mike avoided the swing, and countered with a short, vicious chop with his left hand.

Purkee was stunned by the blow, but as Mike started to hit him a second time, he suddenly found himself jumped by half a dozen angry cowboys, anxious to defend Purkee, and Mike went down under the pummeling.

"Here!" Franklin shouted, moving into the melee. "You men stop this! Stop this at once!"

"Oh, Lee!" Sara said. "Oh, stop them, please! Dad will be hurt!"

"All right, that's enough!" Lee said, and when he called out, the men who had jumped Mike stepped back from him, leaving him sitting on the ground, holding his hand to a split lip.

"I'm sorry, Flynn," Lee said. "It seems that a few of the men have had too much to drink. I think you can understand that tonight would not be a good time to unload your train. They'll

184

do it tomorrow, even though tomorrow is Sunday. Is that fair enough?"

Mike pulled a handkerchief from his pocket and dabbed at the blood.

"I suppose it will have to be," he said. "And, Coulter?"

"Yes?"

"Get all the cattle off my land. All of them, do you understand? If you don't get them off, I'll get them off, and I promise you, you won't like the way I do it."

"I'm sure you are correct in that statement, Flynn," Lee said. "For the truth is, I don't like the way you do anything. And now, ladies and gentlemen, I propose that we not let this unpleasant episode spoil our party," Lee went on. "Let's get back to the dance."

"Yahoo!" one of the cowboys shouted. "We got the whole night ahead of us, boys!"

Gradually the crowd started back toward the dance floor, which had been constructed in the middle of the street. Then the music started and the dancing resumed. Mike walked over and sat on the station platform in the dark and watched the party from a distance.

Within fifteen minutes, the party was in such full swing again that anyone who was just arriving would have no knowledge of the fact it had ever been interrupted. Then Lee walked up to the band leader and asked him to call for attention so he could say a few words.

The band played a fanfare, then Lee stepped up onto their raised platform. He held his hands up to call for quiet, and everyone looked toward him.

"Ladies and gentlemen, this has been quite a day," he said.

Everyone laughed and someone shouted out: "Lee, you aren't going to make a speech, are you? You know the town's passed an ordinance against Fourth of July oratory!"

More laughter.

"No speeches, Tom," Lee said. "But a few words about a couple of beautiful women. Jennie, would you come up here, please?"

"Me?" Jennie said, looking surprised.

"Come on up here," Lee beckoned, and Jennie, with the help of a few pushes, came up to the platform.

"Look at this beautiful creature, would you?" Lee said. He put his arm around her. "Can you believe that someone this pretty, could ride Purkee into the ground?"

There was a loud guffaw from all the cowboys, and Purkee, who was standing near the punchbowl, turned his back and took another quick drink.

"I was mighty proud of Jennie today," Lee said. "And I don't mind telling any of you how special Jennie is to me. In fact, she is so special, that I wanted her right here, by my side, while I make this next announcement." Lee stretched his arm out toward Sara. "Sara, would you come up here, please?"

The crowd parted as Sara walked down to the platform, then stepped up onto it. Lee put his arm around Sara too, so that now he was in the middle of the two young women.

"Folks, I just had a talk with Professor Landers, and he has given us his blessing. I want you to know that Sara and I are going to be married."

There was an explosion of applause, cheers and hurrahs, then the men and women hurried to offer their congratulations and best wishes to the engaged couple. No one noticed Jennie, as she crept away from the others.

Mike's train crew was in no mood to join the Fourth of July celebrations, but they didn't want to stay back in the dark either.

"The Bull's Neck Saloon is open Mike. What say we go down there and have a few drinks?" Burke invited.

"You guys go on," Mike said. "I really don't feel like drinking now. When I drink in this condition I just get drunk."

"That's the idea," Burke said.

"No, thank you," Mike said. "You guys go on, get drunk if you want. But remember, we have to go back to Boise tomorrow to pick up our first load of immigrants on Monday."

"We'll be ready to go, Mike," Burke promised.

Mike watched the three men walk toward the saloon, then he went into the depot. The back room of the depot had been converted into a small apartment for his use. At first, he had thought the room would be too remote from the center of town and from people. Now, that remoteness was just what he wanted.

Mike lit a candle and pumped water into a basin. He took off his shirt and prepared to bathe the cuts and bruises on his face and body. That was when he noticed that his lucky nugget was missing. He shrugged nonchalantly. It hadn't brought him much luck lately, anyway.

Jennie heard Lee's announcement, and she was one of the first to offer her congratulations and best wishes. Then, as the others swelled around, she moved toward the edge of the group until she was alone. She started toward the gazebo where she and Sara had held their afternoon conversation, but she saw a small, dim light on in the depot. She didn't know what made her go in that direction, but a few moments later she found herself standing in the doorway, watching Mike wash his face.

"Does it hurt much?" she asked.

Mike looked over toward her and he grinned, a small, self-conscious grin.

"Only when I laugh," he said.

"I see you aren't laughing."

"No," Mike said. "There doesn't seem to be a great deal to laugh about."

"Did you hear the announcement?" Jennie asked.

"Yes."

Jennie walked over and took the washcloth from Mike's hand.

"Here," she said. "Let me help. You aren't doing a very good job of it."

Jennie started to wash what she thought was a spot of dirt, and Mike winced. She put her hand up to his face, touching it gently with her fingers, and she saw that it wasn't dirt, but a bruise.

"I'm sorry," she said quietly.

"You smell good," Mike said.

Jennie smiled. "You should have been around me after the race," she said. "I smelled like horse. I had to go get cleaned up or people really wouldn't know I was a woman."

"You look like a woman, you smell like a woman," Mike said. Slowly, he put his arms around her and pulled her to him, pressing her body against his. "You even feel like a woman. It is very obvious to me that you *are* a woman. Why can't Lee Coulter see that?"

Jennie gasped, and looked up at him.

"You know?" she asked. "You know how I feel about Lee Coulter?"

"Yes," Mike said. He brushed her hair back from her forehead and kissed her gently. "I know."

"We are alike, Mike Flynn," Jennie said quietly. "Each of us loves another, and they are in each other's arms, right now."

"As we are in each other's arms."

"Oh, Mike, why couldn't I have fallen in love with you, and you with me?" Jennie asked. She put her arms around his neck, and Mike kissed her, feeling her soft, resilient mouth against his

189

split lip. Then she surprised Mike with an intensity of response, which belied her normal, easygoing personality. She opened her mouth hungrily, and drew his tongue into her.

As they kissed, Mike gradually moved them toward the small cot beside the wall. His eager hands pulled at fastenings and buttons, until soon their clothes lay on the floor, while they lay on the cot, body against body, and kissed. Mike moved his hands slowly over Jennie's naked skin, along the gentle curve of her hips, and then to the mounds of her breasts.

Mike rubbed the palm of his hand across her nipples, feeling the small, hard texture of them, and Jennie writhed in pleasure and moaned into his mouth as their kiss deepened. Mike's hands continued their sensual exploration, moving across her belly, hips, thighs, and finally into that secret place where his fingers stroked gently.

Jennie lay back then and pulled Mike onto her, using him as a surrogate for the one she loved, but appreciating the full measure of pleasure they shared. For this moment, at least, they were as one, and neither Sara nor Lee existed for them.

As the members of St. Paul's passed through the front doors, Lee Coulter, who had come to church for the first time in longer than Father Percy could remember, excused himself from Sara and her father, telling them that he needed to get down to the depot to help with unloading the cattle.

"It's a wonder he didn't take them back to Boise with him when he left this morning," Sara said.

"He couldn't have done that," Lee said. "He would have been responsible for feeding them. As it is, they have sat over on the spur track without food and water for long enough. It would be cruel not to get them out on the range as quickly as I can."

"You will come for Sunday dinner?" Franklin asked.

"I wouldn't miss it, Professor," Lee said, smiling. "A man ought to know what kind of a cook he's marrying."

Father Percy wandered over to them just before Lee left. "You will be wanting to be married in the church, Lee?"

"I would like to be married at the ranch," Lee said. "But of course, I shall want you to perform the marriage rites."

"You'll need to come to church more often," Percy suggested.

"I will, Vicar, I promise you," Lee said.

When Lee reached the depot most of the cattle had already been off-loaded from the cars, which had been shunted off onto the spur track. The cowboys were herding the cattle through the center of town and out onto the range land.

"Them cows sure is thirsty," Purkee said, taking his hat off and wiping the sweat from his brow. "Fact is, I'm awful thirsty myself."

"I don't see how," Lee said, "after all the liquor you drank last night."

"Ain't that the truth?" Purkee agreed. "I never have understood why a man got so thirsty on the morning after drinking so much the night before. Here, Nelson, let me help you," he called out, as he saw a cowboy struggling to open one of the doors to another cattle car.

Lee watched the operation for a few minutes longer, then he turned and walked toward the Landers' house for Sunday dinner. Things seemed to be heading his way, now.

Chapter Fourteen

From the Polecat column, July 17th, 1881:

In but two short weeks, the valley has changed. Nearly one hundred families have arrived, placing a burden on the services provided by the valley, staking claims on land without regard to proper procedure, and in some cases, stealing cows, pigs, and chickens from the older, established valley residents.

Mr. Flynn may have had in mind the guarantee of business for his railroad by bringing in the immigrants, but so far it has had just the opposite effect. The ranchers have quite effectively boycotted his railroad, and the immigrants themselves seem bent upon driving everyone else away.

One has only to visit the depot to see the effects of such unrestricted travel. The air in the depot, and indeed on the train cars, is fetid and unhealthy. Pipes bearing strange-smelling tobaccos are lighted, meals of sausage, garlic, sauerkraut and dried fish are consumed, bodies and strange appearing costumes are unwashed, thus causing decent folk to seek alternate means of transport. Now while I I have no argument against the peoples and races of other countries, I can't help but inquire as to why the Germans, Slavics and Russians feel they can send the most undesirable of their species to our peaceful valley.

"Ra, the ranchers have called an emergency meeting this evening," Franklin said to Sara as he came back into the newspaper office. "I'm going to attend."

"Very well," Sara said. "Is there anything in particular you want me to do?"

"If you would finish setting the ad for Dr. Conkling's curative powders, we'll have all the ads set for next week's issue."

"I'll do it," she said.

Sara read the claims of the ad placed by Dr. Conkling. His powder, made from "Buffalo Tallow, combined with healing herbs and barks, would cure Rheumatism, Sciatica, Pulmonary, Kidney Difficulties, Malaria, Dyspepsia Liver, and all stomach afflictions.

Sara smiled. With so many wonderful cures around, one would think that the world would be free of all illness. How could people be so naive as to believe such wild claims? And yet, how were these wild claims any different from the claims made by Mike Flynn? He promised a utopia to the immigrants and rail service to the valley, but the valley couldn't use his rail service, and the immigrants were finding anything but a utopia.

The front door opened, and Sara looked up to see Mike Flynn.

"Hello, Sara," Mike said.

"Mr. Flynn," Sara responded coolly.

Mike had a rolled-up copy of the newspaper in his hand, and he laid it on the counter. "Is your father in?"

"No," Sara said. "Is there something I can do?"

"Not unless you want to take the responsibility for the articles that have been running about me."

"I *do* take that responsibility, Mr. Flynn," Sara said. "My father is the author of the Polecat column, but we are in accord on his opinions."

"I see," Mike said. He sighed. "Don't you feel you are being a bit unfair?"

"Not at all," Sara said.

"I guess your being engaged to Coulter has killed any chance of objectivity. He's bought you and your father."

"No, he has not!" Sara said, slamming the plate down so hard that some of the type popped out onto the floor. "My father has the courage of his convictions, and he writes what he believes."

"What about you?" Mike asked. "Do you have the courage of your convictions?"

"What do you mean?"

"Would you come with me out to the grant lands to meet some of the immigrants?"

"Why should I?"

"Why should you indeed?" Mike asked. "If your mind is already made up, why confuse it with the truth?"

"All right, Mr. Flynn," Sara said. "I *will* come with you."

"What?" Mike asked, surprised by Sara's statement. "Are you serious?"

"Yes, I'm serious. Why, aren't you? Are you afraid that the *truth*, as you put it, may not be all that different from the way my father perceives things now?"

"I'll go to the livery stable and saddle your horse for you," Mike said. "I'll be back in ten minutes."

"I'll be ready," Sara said. "Come to my house."

They rode west, following the McCauley River, and it rushed and splashed beside them as it swirled and broke into white water along its mad dash to the Willamette, and then the Columbia, to the sea. A large, brightly colored fish splashed, and Mike laughed.

"Oh, if I had a pole now, we'd have a nice fish dinner."

"You think you could catch him, do you?" Sara teased.

"Do you think I couldn't?"

"It takes a very special skill to catch fish from the McCauley."

"I intend to develop that skill," Mike said.

"When?"

"When my work is done."

"We'd all be better off if you would develop that skill now, and leave the work alone," Sara said.

"Who would be better off? The ranchers? Lee Coulter?"

"Yes," Sara said. "And the residents of the valley."

"Don't forget, the valley has some new residents now. What about them? Would they be better off if I just left? What would happen to them? And what about Penrake? Until I came along and gave him some legality, he was faced with herds of cows driven through his fields, fences and storage sheds being destroyed . . ."

"You gave Penrake legality?" Sara asked.

"Yes," Mike said. "He bought his land from me, why shouldn't I?"

"But he is nothing more than a common criminal," Sara said. "He came in here and squatted on the land, even *before* you made the offer. How can you justify that now?"

Mike laughed. "What do you think the *cattlemen* were doing, if they weren't squatting?" he asked. "They had no more legal right than Penrake."

"Just the same, Penrake has caused so much trouble for the valley," Sara said.

"No more than the valley has caused for him," Mike answered. He looked up at the tree-covered mountains that walled the valley, and at the rolling land of the valley floor. "It's so wild and so beautiful," he said. "It's a shame to try and hoard all this in a few greedy hands. After all, this is America—a land of opportunity for everyone."

Sara was beginning to regret having come on this journey with Mike. No matter what she said, he seemed to have the correct answer for it. When she was with Lee, or her father, or Stump Adams, or the other ranchers, it seemed right and just to want to deny the immigrants entry into the valley. But Mike was making her feel a sense of guilt over it. It was an unwelcome feeling.

They came across a small rise. Then, below them, they saw a very neat-looking house, barn, and livestock lot. It was much smaller than Lee's house, but it appeared to be as well cared for, and the front lawn literally burst with brightness as hundreds of flowers bloomed in colorful profusion.

As they approached the house a woman stood up from working in the garden, and she brushed her hair back from her eyes to look at the approaching riders.

"Hello, Mrs. Penrake!" Mike called, waving his arm.

The woman smiled broadly. "Ah, Mike, what

a pleasant surprise," she said. "You've come at a good time. I'm about to set the table for the noon meal."

"No, we couldn't put you out any," Mike said. "We've just stopped by for a look, and then we'll ride on."

"Nonsense, Arnold and Caleb will be comin' in from the field just any minute now. They wouldn't hear of you leavin' without takin' a bite with us." Mrs. Penrake smiled again. "I've made a nice blueberry pie."

"Say no more," Mike said. "I'd be a fool not to stick around for some of your blueberry pie."

"Young lady, if you're bent on trappin' this man, you better let me give you the recipe for my blueberry pie, for I've never known anyone set as much store by it as he does."

"I, uh, thank you for the thought," Sara said, blushing under the woman's mistaken conclusion.

"Mrs. Penrake, this is Miss Landers," Mike said. "Her father is Professor Landers, publisher of the *Valley Monitor*."

"Is that a newspaper?" Mrs. Penrake asked.

"Yes," Sara said. She and Mike had dismounted, and Mike was tying their horses to the hitching rail.

"Well, it's a good thing for a community to have a newspaper," Mrs. Penrake said. "We don't get to see one out here, but I think they are a good thing. Come on in. I see the men comin' in from the field now."

The inside of the house was as cheery as the

199

outside. It was spotlessly clean, with flowers scattered about in brightly colored bottles, which were passing as vases. Muslin curtains at the windows filled with the soft breeze, and the smell of freshly baked pie permeated the air.

"I put it on the windowsill to cool," Mrs. Penrake said. "I think it's about ready, don't you?" She held it under Mike's nose.

Mike sniffed appreciatively. "Uhmm, uhmm," he said, nodding his head and licking his lips. "Take it away, Mrs. Penrake, before I lose control of myself and eat it all, right now."

Mrs. Penrake laughed and set the pie on the stove.

"Mike!" Arnold Penrake said when he came into the house. "Mike, it's good to see you!"

"Hello, Mr. Penrake, Caleb," Mike said to the father and son.

Sara looked at Arnold Penrake. The last, and only, time she had ever seen him was the night of the dance, when he had attacked Lee with a pitchfork. How large and menacing he was that night, with eyes that flashed with the fires of hell. He was still as large, but now she felt no fear, for he was smiling in genuine friendship as he greeted Mike.

"Mr. Penrake, Mike brought a young lady to see us," Mrs. Penrake said. "I've invited them to eat."

"Fine, fine," Penrake said. "Any friend of Mike Flynn's is certainly a friend of mine, and you are welcome at our table, Miss. . ."

"Landers," Mike said.

"Landers?"

"She's the newspaper lady, Pop," Caleb said. "She 'n her pa are the ones been printin' all them stories about the settlers."

"Oh?" Arnold said.

"I've brought her out here to have a look," Mike said quickly. "I thought it was about time she saw both sides of the story."

"Yes," Arnold said. "That might be a good idea." The tone of Arnold's voice indicated that he didn't have much hope for a change in conditions, no matter what Sara saw of the settlers' side.

"How are things going?" Mike asked.

"We've had two fields destroyed," Arnold said.

"And the Kincaids had their barn burned," Caleb put in. "And Martin Kincaid was beat up, and had thirty chickens stole."

"Are they still tearing down the fences?"

"Quick as we can get them up," Arnold said. "We're having a meeting tonight, all the settlers, and we are going to organize. I don't intend to put up with this much more."

"Organize how?" Mike asked. "Mr. Penrake, you aren't planning anything like a vigilante committee, are you?"

"That's what *I* want to do," Caleb put in quickly. "And I know half a dozen others who would join me. Martin Kincaid, for one."

"That would be terribly foolish, Caleb," Mike said. "No one wins in a range war."

"All we are wanting to do with our organization is provide each other with aid, when such aid is needed," Arnold said. "And maybe if we organized, went to the government with one united voice, someone would listen to us."

"We can't go to the government with one voice," Caleb said. "Nearly half the immigrants don't even speak English."

"Caleb, there is no room in this household for bigotry," Mrs. Penrake scolded. "Don't forget, this entire country is made up of immigrants. It's a big valley, and there is room for everyone. Now, let us sit to the table. Arnold, you return thanks."

The food was simple but nourishing fare of fried pork chops, boiled potatoes, greens, and cornbread. Mike was obviously at home with them, laughing and talking as if he were a part of the family. Sara felt strangely reflective, and spent the entire meal dwelling on something Mrs. Penrake had said.

"Don't forget," Mrs. Penrake had said. *"This entire country is made up of immigrants."*

She was right. Sara had read essays in college extolling the virtues of a country made up of immigrants. Perhaps she and her father and the others weren't giving it a chance to work. And perhaps she, with her college education, could learn a lesson from Mrs. Penrake.

After dinner the pie was served, and it was every bit as good as Mike had promised it would be. Sara ate it, feeling guilty over the fact that she enjoyed it so. Shortly after the pie was served, Arnold and Caleb excused themselves, and returned to the fields for the afternoon. Mike and Sara used that as a cue to leave.

"Is Mr. Penrake quite the monster you had him pictured as?" Mike asked her.

"I must say that he was much more pleasant this time than he was the last time I saw him."

"Oh? And when was that?"

Sara told about the time Arnold Penrake had come to the dance, and started a fight.

"I know about that," Mike said. "He's never forgiven himself for doing that. But you must remember, he was a desperate man, pushed into a corner. Any creature will lash out under such circumstances."

"You like him, don't you?"

"Yes," Mike said. "The Penrakes are good people. Most of the immigrants are good people if you give them the chance," he added. "I'm sure they aren't all saints, but then what other group of people could make the claim that they were?"

Sara chuckled.

"What is it?"

"Mrs. Penrake. She called you Mike, yet she calls her own husband Mr. Penrake."

Mike laughed. "Well, I suppose I just look like a Mike, and he doesn't."

As they rode, the breeze intensified, carrying with it the feel and smell of impending rain. Over the mountains, great, billowing clouds darkened, then began to rumble with distant thunder.

"We'd better get a move on," Mike said. He urged his horse into a trot, and Sara's horse kept up with him. They moved at the increased rate for about three or four minutes, but then the rain started.

The rain fell in torrents, drenching them as thoroughly as if they were standing under one of the many mountain cascades.

"Sara, this way," Mike said, turning off the trail.

"What? Where are you going?"

"There's an abandoned house over this way. Come on, it'll get us out of this."

Sara followed him, barely able to see him through the driving rain, until finally a small, weather-beaten cottage loomed dimly in the distance.

"Hurry!" Mike called, urging his horse into a lope. Sara followed, urging her horse on faster, until at last they were there.

The roof of the cottage extended out to one side, and it was there, under the protection of the roof, that they tied their horses.

Mike took Sara's hand and led her around to the front door of the cottage. He pushed it open, then they went inside.

It was fairly dark inside, as the windows were dirty, but it was surprisingly dry. Sara looked around to take stock of the place that was providing them with shelter. She saw a rough-hewn bed, with a mattress made of cloth-covered straw, a table and two chairs, a chest, and a washstand. There was also a fireplace.

"Oh, a fireplace," Sara said. She shivered. "I wish we could have a fire."

"Ask, and ye shall receive," Mike said. He walked over to the woodbox and raised the lid. There were a couple of logs in the woodbox, and he took them out and tossed them into the fireplace.

"We'll need something for kindling," he said, and he looked around the room, then settled on the washstand. "This'll have to do." He smashed the washstand into small pieces, and, using them as tinder, got the fire started. A moment later, a dancing orange blaze began to warm the room.

Sara moved to stand before the fire, and she held her hands and arms out toward it, shivering as she did so. Mike looked at her, and saw that her dress was soaked clear through. It was so wet that it clung to every curve and crevice of her body, causing her nipples to stand out in bold relief.

Sara suddenly felt a heat in her body which wasn't caused by the fire, and she looked over to see Mike staring pointedly at her. She glanced down at herself and saw why he was staring so intently. Her breasts tingled then with the same sweet agony she had felt in the cab of the engine when he had massaged them.

Mike turned away, then walked over toward the bed. He took a blanket from the bed, then returned to Sara.

"You'd better get out of those clothes," he said.

"What?"

Mike held up the blanket. "You can wrap yourself in this," he said. "Hang your dress on this chair until it's dry. I'll step out front."

"You can't go out there," Sara said. "It's raining as hard now as it ever was."

"I'll stand under the eaves," Mike said.

"All right," Sara replied. She reached for the blanket. "Perhaps you are right. Perhaps I should get out of these wet things."

Mike turned and walked outside to stand under the eaves. He was aware of the fact that she was undressing behind him, and his blood raced and his pulse pounded as he thought of it, but he was determined to control his impulses. He wanted to go to her now, more than he had ever wanted any woman in the world. But he would not do so . . . unless she asked him. It was very important to Mike that Sara want it as much as he.

Though Mike was protected by the eaves, some of the water splashed on him, but he didn't really mind. Actually, he loved the rain. It blanketed all sight and sound and formed a curtain behind which his soul could exist in absolute solitude. Only those with whom he really wanted to share could penetrate it.

The door to the shack opened, but Mike didn't hear it. Not until Sara softly called his name did Mike know she was there.

* * *

As soon as Mike stepped outside, Sara began to strip out of her wet clothes. It felt very good to get out of the dress, not only for the discomfort of the wet cloth against her skin, but also because of the sensual feelings of being nude before a crackling fire.

Sara's skin was pink and glowing from the rain and the fire, from the flushed reaction to what was now a decidedly erotic situation. She wrapped herself in the blanket, feeling the rough texture of its material against her erect nipples. Then she stepped over to the door and opened it.

"Mike?" she called, when Mike didn't hear the door open.

"Oh," he said, turning toward her. "You're finished. May I come in now?"

"Certainly," Sara said.

Mike walked over to the fire and began to strip off his shirt.

"What . . . what are you doing?" Sara gasped. She had not been ready for the erotic reaction she felt on seeing his bare chest, with muscles rippling, and the thick mat of hair shining.

"I thought it would help a little if I at least dried my shirt," Mike said. He spread his shirt out on the hearth before the fire. "I hope you don't mind."

"No," Sara said in a tight, controlled voice. "No, I don't mind."

Now she felt such a heat in her body that the

blanket around her became almost unbearable. Her knees grew weak, and she felt a boiling dampness in the center of her being, which was so strong as to make her almost gasp for breath.

"Are you all right?" Mike asked.

"Yes," Sara said. And inexplicably she shivered, not from cold, for indeed she was burning up, but from desire; naked, wanton, desire. It was stronger now than all the yearnings and hungers she had ever felt.

"You are cold," Mike said, misreading the shiver, and he walked over to her as if to adjust the blanket. Instead, he opened it, and then he stood there, boldly and without shame. He looked at her body thus exposed, and Sara could feel the heat of his eyes as they drank in every feature.

"My God," Mike breathed quietly, reverently. "You are the most beautiful creature I have ever seen."

Sara's skin was smooth, and her breasts gently formed. Her nipples were proudly erect, and she felt a sense of pride in the effect she knew she was having on Mike.

Sara felt Mike's hand on her, as his arms enfolded her, and her body was pulled against his. His lips came down on hers.

Sara had never been kissed like this . . . not by Lee, not even by Mike in the engine cab. This kiss started far beyond where the other two kisses had left off.

Mike's tongue was fire and ice. The kiss was

tender yet savage, tentative yet eager, as frightening as a serpent, as sensual as a kitten.

Sara's knees gave way then, and she would have fallen had he not caught her and picked her up and carried her over to the bed, where he laid her gently down on the straw mattress. She floated on a languorous cloud of unreality. She watched as Make removed his trousers, feeling an ache that demanded to be satisfied.

Mike climbed into bed with her, and as his hands moved over her body, she trembled at their touch. She looked into his eyes and his intent was clear. When he entered her, she was flooded by such exquisite feeling that time and place were suspended. She gasped and clutched at him, digging her nails into his back. He responded by quickening his movements.

Sara began moving with him, and she knew that this was love as it should be. Nothing in her life had ever compared with this . . . not even the episode of passion and rapture she had shared with Lee. Then, there had been pleasant sensations, but this was ecstasy beyond compare. This was an exchange of souls, being, and essence. She felt what he felt—the hot surge of blood in his body, the tensing of his muscles—and she knew that he could feel as she did the aching hunger of her loins, the tingling at the bottom of her feet.

Sara felt a jolt of pleasure rack her body, spinning out like a pinwheel, sensitizing her from the souls of her feet to the scalp of her head. It was as if she were struck by a bolt of lightning, not once, but several times, and each time was as powerful as the time before.

From somewhere deep inside came a cry of passion and rapture Sara couldn't hold back, and then she felt Mike attain his own rapturous peak and she started all over again in a new burst of pleasure. Because she could still feel as he felt, she felt the bursting pulses of pleasure Mike experienced as he spent himself in her.

Sara came down slowly, floating like a feather, meeting new currents of pleasure and riding with them until they were exhausted, then moving on to another and still another, until it was several moments before everything had stilled. She lay in Mike's arms then, and listened to the rain outside. Finally, after several moments of silence, Mike spoke.

"You can't marry him, Sara," he said.

"The date is already set."

"But you don't love him. You can't love him. Not like you love me. And he can't love you as I love you."

"Do you love me, Mike?"

"Yes, oh, darling, more than you can ever know."

"Why couldn't you have told me earlier?" she asked.

"It doesn't matter now," Mike said. "I've told you, that's what's important. Go to Lee, tell him you're sorry, but you can't marry him."

"I can't do that," Sara said. She buried her

face in Mike's naked shoulder, and sobbed. "Oh, Mike, can't you see? I can't do that."

"No," Mike said. "I can't see." And he held the sobbing girl as he cursed the complexities that made life so difficult.

Chapter Fifteen

"Gentlemen," Lee said quietly and ominously, "I've called you here in secret, because I have something very serious to tell you."

"I know," Abel said. "Those damned foreign squatters have already cost me half my range land and a quarter of my water. They are squeezing me out of business."

"We're all hurting," one of the ranchers said. "But that's really no secret."

"The squatters are a problem, I agree," Lee said. "But it isn't the squatters I'm concerned about. Not right now, anyway. We have a problem which is much more serious."

"What is that?"

"Come out back with me," Lee invited. "There is something I want you to see."

The ranchers followed Lee out of the house

and into the barn, curious as to what Lee was going to show them.

"Professor, I especially want you to see this," he said. "For if the other ranchers concur, I want this incident publicized."

"Lee, what is it?" Stump asked. "What are you going to show us?"

"You'll see," Lee said mysteriously.

Once inside the barn, they walked back to a stall. This stall had been completely walled off and the door was barred shut, separating it from the other stalls and the rest of the barn.

"Purkee discovered it," Lee said. "He saw that this animal wasn't even bearing our brand. It was a ringer, run in on us by Mike Flynn."

Lee pulled the bar, then opened the door. Inside the stall, in the back corner, a single cow stood. The cow was drooling at the mouth, and as it moved around it limped noticeably.

"My God!" Stump exclaimed. He walked into the stall, then kneeled beside the animal and looked at its hooves. "Blisters!" he said. "This animal has hoof and mouth disease!"

The other ranchers drew back in revulsion.

"Look at the brand, Stump," Lee said.

Stump walked around to the animal's rump and looked at the mark which had been burned into its hide.

"It's a slash O," Stump said. "I don't recognize the brand."

"It's not any brand that I know," one of the other ranchers said.

"I don't think it's from the valley."

"In fact, gentlemen, it isn't even from the state," Lee said. "It's from a herd which was discovered at the feeder pen lots in Boise, and there it was condemned."

"But I don't understand," Carter said. "How did this animal get from Boise, Idaho, to our valley?"

"By train," Lee said simply.

"Train?"

"Think about it," Lee said. "Flynn reaches Boise, discovers that we know of his plan to sell off the range land, and, in anger, brings all the cows back home. Only he brings us a bonus cow. One cow with hoof and mouth disease. Don't you see? He hoped to infect all five hundred cows on the train, and those cows would in turn infect all the cattle in the valley. We would be wiped out."

"Wiped out? Oh, my God! What are we going to do?" Abel asked.

The other ranchers expressed the same shock and concern, but Lee held up his hand to calm them.

"His plan didn't work," Lee said.

"It didn't work? What do you mean it didn't work? Here is the proof that it did work," Carter said.

"Take it easy, boys," Lee said. "There is no chance for other cows to be infected by this one, as long as we keep this one separated."

"Yeah, but what about the beeves it's already been in contact with?"

"They can't be infected until the lesions ap-

215

pear, and we had a lucky break on this. Purkee saw that the count was off as soon as the cows came back, so he began to check the brands. When he found this strange brand, he pulled it out of the herd. The symptoms didn't start until it was already isolated."

"Well, thank God Flynn didn't pick an animal that was already infected," Carter said.

"No," Franklin said quietly. "What he did was worse. Much worse."

"Worse? What do you mean?"

"I was hoping you would realize that, Professor," Lee said. "Gentlemen," he explained, "it was worse, because Flynn sent us an animal in disguise. Don't you see? If he had chosen one of the animals that already showed signs of the disease, we would have caught it immediately. Oh, we would have had to destroy the five hundred cows we shipped to Boise, but our herds would have been saved. This way, by choosing an animal he knew had been infected, but was not yet showing the symptoms, there was a chance it would have sneaked through, been exposed to our herds in the valley, and everything would have been lost."

"That sneaky son of a bitch!" Abel said. "We've got to do something about him, Lee! Not only does he want to run us out of our range lands, he wants to get rid of us entirely."

"I say we pay the bastard a call," one of the other ranchers said. "Let's burn his damned depot and tear up his track."

"What good would that do?" Lee asked, as a

few of the other ranchers shouted their endorsement of the plan. "He would simply rebuild his depot and relay his track. No, we have to stop him for good."

"Do you have a plan?"

"Yes," Lee said. He looked at Professor Landers. "Professor, are you willing to print what you learned here tonight?"

"Absolutely," Franklin said.

Lee smiled. "Gentlemen, once this word gets out, Mike Flynn will never transport another cow for anyone. Public opinion will turn against him so strongly that he will be hard pressed to stay in business. And once Flynn is out of business, the squatters will be out too. Flynn is the prime mover. Without him, there will be no new settlers, and the ones who have already come will be forced to leave. What do you think, Professor? Do you agree with me?"

Franklin smiled. "Well, they say the pen is mightier than the sword. I suppose this is where we find out."

"Good," Lee said. "I can hardly wait until Thursday to read the story."

"You won't have to wait," Franklin said. "I'm going to the office right now. I'll print up an extra edition tonight, and I'll have it on the street by tomorrow morning. The sooner we get rid of Mr. Flynn, the better off this entire valley will be."

"You won't have any advertising to support this edition, will you?" Lee asked.

"I don't care. Sometimes service to a commu-

217

nity is the foremost requirement of a newspaper."

"I'm glad to hear you feel that way," Lee said. "It means a lot to me to know you are behind us as a matter of personal conviction." Lee rubbed his hands together and looked at the others. "Gentlemen, the situation is now in Professor Landers's hands, and I can think of no better hands to control our destiny."

"Hear, hear," one of the other ranchers said, and there was modest applause.

"What are you going to do with the infected animal, Lee?"

"I'm going to destroy it, then bury it in quicklime."

"Don't you think we should keep it as evidence?"

"No, I don't want to take the chance of infecting any other animals," Lee replied. "You've all seen it, you can act as witnesses if necessary. But after the story, I doubt that will be necessary at all."

"If there is going to be a story, I'd better get back to the office," Franklin said. "I'm going to have to set the plate up myself. I'm certain that Ra is already in bed by now."

The meeting broke up then, and Franklin rode reflectively back into town. He was shocked by his experience tonight. He would not have believed that Mike Flynn would be capable of such activity, if he had not seen the proof with his own eyes. Franklin had written some articles that were hostile to Flynn and his

218

operation, but only because he believed that the squatters were truly spoiling the good life of the valley. After all, he had left his teaching post and come west, just to enjoy the quality of life offered here, and now Flynn was going to change all that.

Those articles had been written in good faith, as a genuine expression of displeasure over the changes being wrought, though, and not as a personal attack against Mike Flynn. Until this evening Professor Landers had believed Mike Flynn to be, basically, a decent person. In fact, despite their differences, Franklin would have even admitted to liking Mike Flynn.

But no more. Flynn's cowardly act of introducing an infected animal to destroy the herds of the entire valley was a crime of unprecedented evil, and he was going to enjoy letting the world know.

Franklin went straight to the newspaper office. He wanted to write the story now, while his blood still boiled with anger. He hoped to capture some of that anger and transfer it to his readers.

Sara paced back and forth in the living room of the Landers home, waiting for her father to return. She wanted desperately to talk to him, to tell him about her day.

Perhaps she and her father were wrong in their relentless attack against the settlers. After all, if she could meet Arnold Penrake and come away with a changed opinion of the man who had been so frightening at the dance, then certainly she could change her opinion about the other settlers. Maybe there could be a peaceful solution after all.

But it wasn't only the settlers Sara wanted to discuss. She wanted to discuss Mike as well. The afternoon had lifted her to heights of rapture she had never dreamed possible, and she had never known such pleasure or joy. And yet, ever since that moment, she had felt only pain and confusion. She was convinced now that she loved Mike Flynn. But if that were so, what about Lee? Didn't she love him as well? She couldn't love both of them. What should she do?

"Oh, Dad, why are you late tonight, of all nights?" she asked aloud.

For the tenth time, she walked to the front window and peered down the dark street, hoping to see him riding up. That was when she saw a light in the newspaper office. The light had not been there before. That meant that her father, or someone, was there.

Sara turned down the lantern in the living room, then walked down the dark boardwalk to the other end of the street. She saw her father's horse just before she arrived, so the nervousness left her. For some reason he had come back to the newspaper office. Very well, she would just talk to him here.

When Sara stepped inside, her father had

just clamped a printer's plate onto the press, and was inking the drum.

"What are you doing?" she asked, surprised to see him working so industriously this late at night.

"Ra, wait until you hear," Franklin said. "Never in all my born days have I known anyone as capable of such an abominable act."

"Who?" Sara asked. "Dad, what are you talking about?"

"Read this," Franklin said, printing the first sheet, then handing it to her while the ink was still wet.

Sara read the story quickly, then her look of confusion turned to one of disbelief.

"Dad, you can't really believe Mike had anything to do with this?"

"Is it Mike again?" Franklin asked. He shook his head. "I'm sorry, Ra. But, yes, I have to believe what I have seen with my own eyes. I saw a cow with hoof and mouth disease, and I saw that the brand for that cow was the slash O. That is an Idaho brand. How else would that animal have come to the valley, if not aboard Mr. Flynn's train?"

Sara shook her head, and sobbed quietly. "He wouldn't do a thing like that," she said. "I know he wouldn't."

"Ra, darlin', he did do it," Franklin said. He took his daughter into his arms. "Ra, don't tell me that you think you are in love with Mr. Flynn?"

"I don't know," Sara said. "I . . . I thought I might be."

Franklin squeezed her gently as her tears increased.

"There, now, darling, you just go ahead and get it all cried out. You know, in the long run, it is probably good this happened."

"Good? How can you say something like this is good?" Sara wailed.

"Look at it like this," Franklin replied. "You are obviously having a hard time deciding you were right to tell Lee you would marry him. If you marry Lee, you would always wonder . . . *what if*? And if you had married the other fella, you would always feel a pang of remorse for having hurt Lee Coulter, who is one fine gentleman. Now, the decision has been made for you. You couldn't begin to harbor feelings for a scoundrel who would do something like this, could you?" Franklin pointed to the paper he had just printed.

"No," Sara said.

Franklin gave Sara his handkerchief. "Here," he said. He chuckled. "Who is going to supply you with handkerchiefs after I'm gone?"

Sara laughed through her tears. "Well, I hope I won't be needing them then."

"Oh?" Franklin teased. "You mean you won't even shed a few tears for my demise?"

"I didn't mean that," Sara said. "Of course I would. Anyway, I don't like to talk about such a thing."

"I must confess, it isn't my favorite subject either," Franklin said.

Sara looked at the paper again. "Why are you printing this now?" she asked.

"I'm getting out an extra," Franklin said. "I want to print a few hundred, so I can have them on the streets tomorrow."

"I'll stay and help you."

"No," Franklin said. "I'd rather you didn't. In the first place, you are too personally involved right now. The first law of journalism, you know, is objectivity. You have not been objective, and there is no sense in subjecting you to any more pain. I want you to go home and get a good night's sleep. Tomorrow things will look better."

"All right," Sara said quietly. "Don't work too long. You need your rest."

"I'll be all right," Franklin said. "In fact, I may just sleep here tonight."

Sara kissed her father, then took the first proof sheet with her and left. She didn't tell her father, but it was her intention to go directly to the depot, to see Mike Flynn. There, she was going to confront him with the fact that she knew what he had done.

The depot was dark, and the tracks deserted. The train was at the other end of the line, and not due back until the following day. Because of that, even the signal lights were dark.

Sara walked along the track for a small distance. It curved out of town, gleaming softly silver in the moonlight. Finally she reached the station platform, stepped onto it, then went inside the depot.

"Mr. Flynn," she called quietly.

"Yes," Mike's voice answered. "I'm in here, who is it?"

"Sara Landers."

A match was struck and a lantern lit, and Mike appeared in the door that led to his room. He was smiling broadly.

"Sara, m'darlin'," Mike said. "You've changed your mind and come back to me after all."

"No," Sara said coolly.

"No? But you are here, girl," Mike said. "That must mean something."

"It means that I now know you to be the lowest kind of a person," Sara said. "How could you do such a thing? How *could* you?"

Mike's face mirrored his confusion.

"Sara, girl, I have no idea what you are talking about. What thing did I do?"

"As if you didn't know about the infected steer," Sara said.

"Infected steer?"

"Are you going to deny that you brought back an infected animal from Idaho, hoping to spread disease through every herd in the valley?"

"Deny it? Of course I'm going to deny it. What are you saying, that I brought a sick animal here?"

"It's all here, in the paper that's coming out tomorrow," Sara said. "You put a cow with hoof and mouth disease in the train with the cows

224

Lee and the others shipped to Boise. You hoped the cow would infect the herds, but it was caught in time and your plan failed."

"You mean the herds aren't infected?"

"No," Sara said. "They are not infected, through no thanks to you."

"Thank God for that," Mike said, breathing a long, audible sigh. "But Sara, girl, you're wrong if you think I had anything to do with this." He reached out and put his hand on Sara's shoulder, but she twisted away from him.

"Don't *touch* me," she said. "To think that today I let you . . . we . . ." She put her hands to her face and began to cry.

"I'm sorry," Mike said quietly, and he drew his hand away. He looked at the paper. "When did this paper come out? I haven't seen it yet."

"It hasn't come out yet," Sara said. "It's coming out tomorrow."

"Then I've still got time to stop your father," Mike said. "Sara, these papers can't be circulated, don't you see? It would ruin everything. People would find me guilty just on the basis of this story."

"You won't stop him," Sara said. "He is convinced of your guilt, because he saw the infected cow. And if my father thinks you are guilty, then you are guilty."

"I've got to try," Mike said. "Your father is too well respected to be caught up in this. Don't you see what is happening, Sara? Your father is being used by Lee Coulter and the others to work a frame."

"No," Sara said resolutely. "My father isn't being used. He saw the animal with his own eyes, and there were more than a dozen other witnesses. You cannot dispute the facts, Mr. Flynn."

"Come with me," Mike said. "Come with me while I speak with your father. You can help me convince him that . . ."

"You want *me* to help *you*?" Sara said. She took a couple of steps back from him, and shook her head. "Now, it is coming clear to me. Lee isn't using my father, Mike Flynn. *You* are using me! At least, you tried to. You took me out to see the Penrakes today, then you. . . . you made love to me. . . . and all because you wanted to use me for your own nefarious schemes! Well it didn't work, sir! Do you hear me? It didn't work!"

Sara turned and ran from the depot, all the way back to her house. When she went inside she threw herself down on the bed and cried.

She must have cried herself to sleep. She opened her eyes and saw that she was lying on her bed, though she was still fully dressed. It was late, much later, because the flickering light from the lantern was out and she had not turned it out. That meant that the fuel had been exhausted.

What had awakened her? A noise? Yes, in her sleep, she had heard a loud noise, like the sudden peal of thunder. Now she could hear voices, shouting in excitement.

"It's the newspaper office!" one voice said clearly.

"The newspaper office is on fire!" another voice cried.

"Newspaper office?" Sara mumbled sleepily. She got up from the bed and walked over to the window. From the opposite end of the street, she could see a building burning. It was the newspaper office!

"Dad!" Sara called. "Dad, come quick, the office is on fire!"

Sara ran to her father's room and knocked on the door. When he didn't answer, she pushed the door open and stepped inside. His bed was empty, and hadn't been slept in.

"Dad?" she said, confused by the fact that he wasn't here. Then she remembered what he had said to her. He told her he might spend the night in the office.

"Dad!" she screamed, this time in fear. She ran through the house, out the front door and down the street toward the burning building. By now there were several dozen people there, and a bucket brigade had been formed.

"My dad is in there!" Sara shouted, starting toward the burning building.

"No!" somebody called, and a man who was near Sara grabbed her.

"You can't go in there, miss! You'd never come out alive!"

"But you don't understand! I *must* go in there!" Sara said, struggling to get out of the grip of the men who held her.

"I'm sorry, Miss Landers, there's nothing we can do," someone said.

Sara cried bitter tears as she watched the building burn. It created a glowing circle of light in the black of night. Just beyond the wavering flames, the people of the town were gathered in the darkness, watching in horror as the building collapsed in on itself. Finally the flames began to die, and gradually the men were able to approach the building.

Sara stood in fearful, almost painful silence, as the men probed through the rubble. Finally one of them called out something, and the others rushed to him. They stood around in a small group, looking toward the floor. Then one of them walked slowly over to Sara. It was the sheriff.

"Miss Landers," he started.

"You found him?"

"Yes," the sheriff said. "I'm sorry."

Sara felt dizzy, and she put her hand to her head. A man who was standing near her grabbed her and helped support her.

"I'll be all right," she finally managed to say.

"You want some water?"

"No," Sara said. "I'll be all right, believe me."

"The doc is here. Maybe he can give you something to help."

"What happened?" Sara asked. "How did the office catch fire?"

"It was blowed up," one of the men said.

"What?"

"It was blowed up. Someone come ridin' up

on a horse, throwed a bomb through the window, and the buildin' was blowed up. Me 'n Silbey seen it."

"Who would do something like that?" the sheriff asked.

"Mike Flynn," Sara blurted out. "He was upset because Dad was putting out a special edition telling how Mr. Flynn had introduced a diseased cow to the valley."

"Hey, sheriff," someone called. "Look at this. We found it in the dirt, right in front of the office."

"What is it?" the sheriff asked.

The man who called out walked over toward the sheriff, holding out a rawhide cord, with an object hanging from it.

"It's a gold nugget on a piece of rawhide," the man said. "Whoever throwed that bomb must've dropped it."

Sara gasped. "That belongs to Mike Flynn," she said.

"Miss Landers, are you positive?" the sheriff asked.

"Hell, sheriff, they's prob'ly a dozen people in this town could identify that thing for you," one of the men said. "That's what the railroad fella, Flynn, calls his good-luck piece."

"It ain't his good-luck piece no more," the sheriff said. "It's his bad-luck piece. Where's this fella live?"

"He's got a room over at the depot," someone answered. "But you don't expect him to be there, do you?"

"If he's not there, it'll give us a pretty good idea that he did do it, though, won't it?" the sheriff said. "Come on, let's get over there."

The sheriff, followed by an angry mob, hurried over to the depot. They yelled for Mike to come out, but no one answered the call. Finally, the sheriff and a couple of others went inside, but they came out a moment later empty handed.

"He's gone," the sheriff said.

"Well, I reckon that confirms it," another said.

"Let's find that son of a bitch, and when we do, we can get us a rope and string him up!"

"No!" Sara screamed.

The crowd looked toward Sara in surprise.

"No," she said again. "Please, if you did such a thing you would make a mockery of my father's life. Don't you see? He lived for law and order."

"The girl is right," the sheriff said. "We are civilized people here. There will be no lynch mobs as long as I'm the sheriff."

"Well, what do you aim to do, sheriff?"

"I aim to find Mr. Flynn," the sheriff said. "And once I find him, I'm going to arrest him. Then we'll get the judge in here, have us a trial, all legal and proper, and if we find him guilty, he will hang."

"What do you mean *if* we find him guilty?" someone shouted, and the others laughed. "You mean *when* we find him guilty, don't you?"

"Maybe so," the sheriff said. "But we have to

find him before we can do anything. Now, if any of you men want to ride in a posse, go get your horses and get back here in ten minutes. I'll deputize all of you and we can—"

"Wait a minute, sheriff," someone suddenly called. "There ain't no need for that."

"What? What are you talking about?"

"Look a'comin'."

They all looked in the direction indicated and saw, riding boldly toward them, Mike Flynn.

Chapter Sixteen

Mike Flynn lay on the bunk with his hands folded behind his head, looking at the wall of his jail cell. At some date in the past, an aspiring poet had been confined to these same quarters, and he left his record in the form of a poem.

Friend, here's a verse to
Help pass your day.
John Price Hampton
Once came this way.
I took some money
That didn't belong to me.
And now it'll be four long years
Before they see me free.

"Ah, John Price Hampton, m'boy, where are you now?" Mike asked under his breath.

"Did you say somethin' in there?" the sheriff called out. The sheriff was sitting at his desk out front. Mike was the only prisoner.

"I was wondering about John Price Hampton," Mike said. "He left his mark here on your cell wall. Where is he now?"

"He's dead," the sheriff said. "He tried to bust loose when they were takin' him to the pen. Let that be a lesson to you."

"I'll heed the lesson, Sheriff, believe me," Mike said.

The sheriff stood up from his desk, poured himself a cup of coffee and came over to stand near Mike's cell. "It might make it easier if you tell me what happened," he said, slurping his coffee noisily.

"I told you what happened," Mike said.

"Tell me again."

"I heard that Professor Landers was going to put out a special edition, accusing me of introducing hoof and mouth disease into the valley. I didn't want him to do that."

"I don't doubt that part of it," the sheriff said with a chuckle. "Not a bit. Folks in a cattle raisin' community don't take too well to anyone low enough to do somethin' like that."

"That's just it," Mike said. He sat up in bed. "Sheriff, I didn't bring a diseased cow into the valley. At least, not on purpose."

"But you could have, right?"

"I . . . I don't know," Mike said. "I don't

234

see how one of the condemned cows could have found its way onto the train. I certainly didn't put that cow on the train. That's why I went to talk to the professor, to get him to see my side of it."

"But he wouldn't listen?" the sheriff asked.

"No," Mike said. "He was convinced that I had done it, and he said that in his mind there was no difference between doing it purposely and doing it accidentally. He said that kind of negligence was criminal."

"He's right," the sheriff said. "What happened next?"

"I rode out to see Lee Coulter. I thought if I could talk to him, I might get an idea on where that cow came from. That's where I had been, when I came riding back to the depot."

"Lee Coulter says he never saw you," the sheriff said.

"He didn't see me," Mike said. "He wasn't there. None of the ranch hands were there either. The place was completely deserted."

"That's a tough break for you, isn't it?" the sheriff said. "If one person had been there, you would have an alibi. Now all you have is a motive—and proof that you were there at the newspaper office." The sheriff pulled out the nugget and cord.

"Sheriff, I *admit* that I was at the newspaper office," Mike said. "Earlier in the evening I went to see the professor to talk to him. But that doesn't prove anything," he added, pointing to the nugget. "I lost that a couple of weeks ago."

"You mean you lost it a couple of *days* ago, don't you?" the sheriff asked. "When you threw a bomb at the newspaper office?"

"I did not kill Professor Landers."

"I'll give you this," the sheriff said. "I don't think you *intended* to kill him. I think you just meant to put him out of business, and didn't realize he was sleeping in there. But it doesn't make any difference whether you intended to kill him or not. You are going to hang for it, as soon as you are found guilty."

"You speak as if I have already been tried," Mike said.

"As far as I'm concerned, mister, you are," the sheriff replied. "All we have to do now is wait for the judge."

"I hope the judge has a better view of justice than you do," Mike said.

The front door of the sheriff's office opened and Sara stepped into the room. It was the first time Mike had seen Sara since the night he was arrested, though he had asked repeatedly to see her on the day before. He stood up and walked to the bars, then wrapped his hands around them, as soon as she came inside.

"Sara!" he said. "Thank God you've come! I've got to talk to you!"

"Miss Landers," the sheriff said. "You don't have to come in here if you don't want to. I'm sure seein' this man will only serve to get you more upset. It's goin' to be bad enough at the trial."

"I'm all right," Sara said. She stared

236

pointedly at Mike. "Sheriff, would you excuse us, please? I would like to talk to Mr. Flynn in private."

"Well, I don't know," the sheriff said. "He's a dangerous man. It might not be such a good idea to let you stay in here alone with him."

"He's behind bars, sheriff," Sara said. "What can he do? Besides, he's obviously a coward. My father was killed by a bomb thrown in the night. Mr. Flynn has no bombs with him, does he?"

"No, of course not," the sheriff said. He sighed, then walked over to the rack to take his hat down and put it on. "I'll leave you with him, but you be careful, you hear me?" The sheriff turned to leave; then, just before he exited, he turned back to face Sara. "Listen, Miss Landers, you don't have it in mind to . . . to do somethin' foolish now, do you?"

"Mr. Flynn is as safe with me as I am with him," Sara said. "I am willing to wait and allow the law to take its course."

"Good, good," the sheriff said. "I sure wouldn't want to see you get into any kind of trouble, not on top of ever'thin' else that has happened to you."

The sheriff stepped outside and closed the door behind him and Sara moved over to the cell. As she stared at Mike, there was a hurt, accusing expression on her face which cut through to Mike's very soul.

"I wish you wouldn't stare at me like that," Mike finally said.

"How else should I stare at the man who murdered my father?" Sara asked.

"Sara, I know it's—"

"Don't call me Sara. My name is Landers. Landers, do you recognize it? It was the name of a good man."

"He *was* a good man," Mike said. "I can't begin to tell you how sorry I am this happened."

"I don't want your condolences," Sara said bitterly. "You aren't good enough to even mention his name."

Mike sighed. "I did not kill you father," he said. "I hoped you had come here to give me a chance to explain that to you, but evidently that is not the purpose of your visit."

"No, it isn't why I am here."

"Then why have you come?"

"I . . . I don't know," Sara said. Now her angry eyes filled with tears. "I hoped that, somehow, I could live with my shame if I came to see you, to tell you what I think of you now. I . . . I let you make love to me on the very day you were to kill my father. I can't help but feel that, somehow, I must share in the blame for his death."

"In that, at least, you are right," Mike said. "You do bear some of the blame for your father's death, and so do I, and so does everyone who has been a party to this whole series of misunderstandings which has brought so much hate."

The door opened again, and this time the sheriff had two people with him. One was a man Mike had never seen, and the other was Jennie Adams.

"I'm sorry to butt in on you like this, Miss Landers, after tellin' you I'd give you some privacy," the sheriff apologized. "But somethin' has come up. Somethin' important, and, if you want my way of thinkin', mighty mysterious." The sheriff looked pointedly at Jennie.

"Jennie, what is it?" Sara asked. "What are you doing here?"

"I've been with the judge," Jennie said, indicating the man with them. "I went to see him as soon as he arrived in town."

"Why?" Sara asked.

"Miss Landers, Miss Adams claims she was with Flynn on the night your father was killed."

"What?" Sara asked, shocked by the sheriff's words.

"That's right," Jennie said. "Mike Flynn couldn't have killed Professor Landers."

"How do you know?"

"We were together when I heard the bomb explosion," Jennie said quietly.

"Together? What do you mean, together? Where were you?"

"We were . . . *together*," Jennie said again.

Sara was confused for just a moment, then she gasped and put her hand to her mouth. "Jennie, you mean you were . . . you and he were . . ."

"This young lady is willing to testify that she

239

and the prisoner were in bed together at the time of the explosion," the judge said. "And as long as she is willing to testify to that, I can't authorize his further incarceration. I'm ordering you, Sheriff, to set this man free."

"Judge, there's somethin' mighty mysterious about all this," the sheriff said. "How come Flynn never said anythin' about it before now?"

"Perhaps Mr. Flynn didn't wish to compromise my reputation," Jennie said. "That is very noble of you, Mr. Flynn, and I thank you for it. But better that I have a besmirched reputation, than you be wrongly hanged."

"Let him out," the judge said again, and the sheriff opened the cell door, then swung it open.

Mike looked at Jennie, but Jennie wouldn't meet his gaze. Then he looked at Sara.

"I didn't kill your father," he said quietly.

"I . . . I *hate* you!" Sara sobbed. She looked at Jennie. "I hate both of you!" she turned and hurried through the door.

The sheriff returned Mike's wallet, but he kept the gold nugget.

"I'm going to have to keep this as evidence until the case is settled," he said.

"That's all right," Mike said. "I don't know that I ever want to see it again, anyway." He started for the door, then he stopped and looked back toward Jennie. She had neither spoken nor looked up since Sara's outburst. "May I walk you to your horse, Jennie?"

Jennie nodded her head and left the office quickly.

"All right," Mike said, as they stood beside Jennie's horse a moment later. "What is this? Why did you ruin your reputation and lie for me?"

"You didn't kill Professor Landers, did you?" Jennie asked.

"No, I didn't."

"Then don't look a gift horse in the mouth."

"But I don't understand," Mike said. "Surely there must have been another way you could have come to my aid? Do you think that loud-mouthed sheriff is going to keep quiet about all this? He'll drag your name through every gutter and saloon in the county."

"It was the only way I could be sure the judge and the sheriff would believe me," Jennie said. "They wouldn't think I would say such a thing, ruin my reputation, just to provide you with an alibi, if it was false."

"Then why did you?" Mike asked.

Jennie swung onto her horse, then looked down at Mike. Tears were flowing steadily down her face, though she had not sobbed aloud.

"Because I know who did do it," she said. She jerked the reins, turning her horse, then slapped her heels against his flank, urging him into a gallop, before Mike could reply.

The largest crowd ever to gather in one place in Butte Valley gathered for Franklin Landers's funeral that afternoon. There were so many people that they couldn't all be accommodated at St. Paul's Church, so the overflow stood around outside until the service was concluded, then they marched in solemn procession to the graveyard at the edge of town.

Ironically, the graveyard had a clear view of the depot, and Sara, dressed all in black, with a black hat and veil, could see a solitary figure standing on the station platform. She knew that it was Mike, free now, because of the testimony of Jennie Adams.

Sara had been torn with conflicting emotions ever since Jennie's startling revelation. If Jennie told the truth, that meant that Mike did not kill her father.

But it also meant that Mike had gone right to Jennie's bed on the same day he had sworn his love to Sara. He had made a fool of her.

If Jennie lied, then Mike did kill her father. But why would Jennie lie?

Sara looked toward Jennie. The two had not spoken during the funeral and, because word of what Jennie had told the sheriff spread like wildfire through the valley, she was ostracized by most of the other mourners as well.

Father Percy pulled at his collar, then stepped up to the open grave as the pine box was lowered into it. When the ropes were pulled away, the priest bent over and picked up a handful of dirt. He dropped it onto the coffin.

"In the sure and certain hope of the resurrection to eternal life through our Lord Jesus Christ, we commend to Almighty God our brother Franklin, and we commit his body to the ground, earth to earth, ashes to ashes, dust to dust. The Lord bless him and keep him, the Lord make his face to shine upon him and be gracious to him, the Lord lift up his countenance upon him and give him peace. Amen."

The mourners began leaving the cemetery and the gravedigger who had been sitting quietly on the other side of the pile of dirt, now came around and began filling in the grave. The dirt made a ringing sound as it left the shovel and a clumping sound as it fell on the box.

Sara had cried for three days, and now there were no tears left. There was just a terrible hollowness inside, and an ache in her heart which she knew could never be erased.

Mike walked back into the depot, and over to the counter. Burke was standing just on the other side of the counter, marking out sections of land on the large map of the valley.

"Where do you want to put the next group, Mike?" Burke asked.

Mike looked at the map. "Put them down here," he said, pointing to a section of the valley. "They will have water, and this is good, fertile land. Also, it's far enough from the ranchers that, for the time being at least, we might be able to avoid any further trouble."

"Good idea," Burke said. "In fact, that's

probably where I should have put young Penrake, but he insisted on going into Green River Canyon."

"What?" Mike asked, puzzled by the remark. "What are you talking about?"

"Martin Kincaid and Caleb Penrake came in here yesterday, while you were still in jail. They had the money to buy a piece of land, and they insisted on going into Green River Canyon. I tried to talk them out of it, but that was where they wanted to go."

"You didn't sell it to them, did you?"

"Well, yes," Burke answered. "Mike, it's already charted. I didn't think it would matter."

"Damn," Mike said. "Those two hotheads up there like that? They're right in the middle of cattle country."

"I'm sorry," Burke said. "I guess I made a mistake."

Mike looked at Burke and smiled. "Well, I guess I could welcome you to the territory," he said. "For there is no one around who has made more dumb mistakes than I have."

"Aren't we going to sell off any of this land?" Burke asked, pointing to the area that ran, like fingers, in between the cattle ranches of the valley.

"I'll sell it," Mike said. "But I didn't want to let that property go until the rest of the tracts were sold. That way, we never would have anyone stuck out by themselves. There would at least be safety in numbers."

244

"Mike, do you think Kincaid and Penrake are in danger?" Burke asked.

"Not if they're careful," Mike said. He studied the map for a moment and rubbed his chin. "But I'd be willing to bet my last dollar that they aren't being careful at all. In fact, I wouldn't be surprised if they didn't choose that particular piece of land because it *was* a challenge to the ranchers."

"You want me to find something wrong with the deed and run them out of there?" Burke asked.

"No," Mike said. He sighed. "Maybe they're right. Maybe the way to settle this thing is to challenge the cattlemen right off. At least young Kincaid and Penrake have the courage to go in there. I just hope they have common sense to go along with their courage."

"Bring that wire across the draw, Martin, and I'll nail it to this tree. That way we'll have it fenced off," Caleb said.

Caleb and Martin were working with a roll of barbed wire, fencing off the perimeters of their land. They were wearing denim trousers and jackets and heavy leather gloves, to protect them from the barbs that protruded from the heavy roll of wire in the back of the wagon.

Martin giggled as he brought a length of wire across the small gulley and handed it to Caleb.

"How many cows you think we have trapped in here?" he asked.

"About twenty or so, I'd say," Caleb replied. He cut the wire with a large pair of wire cutters, then wrapped a strand around the trunk of a fir tree and began hammering it into place. "Just enough to pay back some of the damage they've done."

"It ain't like we're stealin' either," Martin said. "After all, these cows come onto our own territory all by themselves. We didn't do nothin' to bring them here."

"But we're sure doin' somethin' to keep 'em here," Caleb said, laughing. He finished putting the wire up, then stood back and looked at it, reaching out to test the tension of the strands.

"We've got to do something," Martin said. "It's for sure no one else will. All the homesteaders are like a bunch of old women. They moan and groan ever'time some cowman runs over 'em, but they don't do nothin' about it."

"I've got an idea," Caleb said.

"What is it?" Martin asked. "If it's as good an idea as this, I'm all for it."

"Back before any of the rest of the folks come into the valley, when they was just us Penrakes and you Kincaids. and a couple more families, the cowmen put up signs, warning us off the graze land, remember? They told us they would destroy our crops, tear down our fences, and burn our buildin's and such."

"Yeah, I remember."

"Let's put up signs here, tellin' the cattlemen that we will kill any cow that wanders onto our land. We got that right."

"Yeah," Martin said. "Let's serve notice on them. We'll let them know that here's two homesteaders that won't be run off or buffaloed."

There was a low rumble of thunder in the mountains, and both men looked toward them, to see a rapidly building thunderhead.

"We'd better get out of this draw before the rains come," Caleb suggested.

"I'll get the tools," Martin replied.

Both men began to work quickly, picking up the tools and extra wire and throwing them in the back of the wagon. Then, just as they were ready to leave, there was the cracking sound of a bullet smashing through the side of the wagon, and the loud roar of a rifle shot.

"Hold it, boys!" a voice called from behind them.

Martin and Caleb froze in their tracks.

"Well, well, well, now look here, would you?" a taunting voice said. There was a sound of horse hooves on the rocks, and Martin and Caleb turned to see half a dozen riders approaching them slowly. All were armed with rifles, held out in plain sight, ready for use, should the need arise.

"You men are trespassin'," Martin said angrily.

The leader of the riders smiled, and looked at the others. The leather of his saddle squeaked as he twisted around toward them.

"Did you men hear that?" he asked. "These here fellas think we're trespassin'."

247

The armed riders laughed.

"Mister, this here is range land," the leader of the group said. "It always has been, and it always will be." He pointed his rifle toward the strands of wire which had been stretched across the draw. "Now you tell me what the hell that is for."

"It's to protect our property," Caleb said.

"To keep your damn cows out," Martin added.

One of the riders swung down from his horse and examined a cow pile. He looked up toward the leader of the group.

"Curly, I'll tell you the truth, it's looks to me like these fellas is tryin' to keep a few cows in. Look at this."

The one called Curly got off his horse and walked over to examine the cow pile. He looked toward Martin and Caleb.

"Is that right?" he finally asked. "Have you fellas stretched a little wire to keep some cows in?"

"Yes," Martin said defiantly. "There are a few head of cattle trapped in here, but we are going to keep them until we are paid for the damages you have done to our property."

Curly looked around, at the draw, the trees, and the rapidly climbing terrain to the mountains which formed the walls of the draw.

"Now, except for the devil's wire that you two galoots stretched across here, this here land is just the way God made it. What makes you think we done any damage?"

"We're talking about our families," Caleb said. "And the other homesteaders of the valley. They've had their crops ruined, their barns burned and their fences torn down."

"I see," Curly said. "Well, fellas, it's like this. When we do those things, I don't figure we are doin' any damage at all. I figure we are just puttin' things back the way God made 'em in the first place."

"Who made you God's avenging angels?" Caleb asked bitterly.

Curly smiled, and looked toward the others. "Hey, that's a good name, isn't it? Whyn't we call ourselves the Avengin' Angels?"

Everyone laughed, except Martin and Caleb. Then, after the laughter had died, the smile left Curly's face, and he pointed to the wagon.

"Slim, you 'n Poke take that wagon up to the overhang up there, and push it over. That ought to bust it up enough that they can't use it to haul any more barbed wire."

"What about the horses?" Slim asked.

"Spook 'em, 'n run 'em off," Curly said. "Maybe a walk back home would do these galoots some good."

It started to rain then, just a few drops at first, then a steady, heavy downpour. The armed riders began to pull their slickers out of the saddlebags.

"You two," Curly said. "Pull down that wire."

Two riders rode over to the fence, and threw ropes around the center pole. They pulled until

249

the pole snapped, and the wire popped out of the trees on each side of the draw. There was a cheer from the others when the fence came down.

Martin and Caleb stood helplessly in the rain, watching as the fence was pulled up and then, a moment later, as their wagon came crashing down over the edge of a nearby cliff. The wagon smashed and splintered into pieces as it hit.

"Now," Curly said, pointing his rifle at the two men. "Git outta them clothes."

"What?" Martin asked.

"I said shuck outta them clothes," Curly said. "I think a walk home in the rain is just what you need to cool you off."

Martin and Caleb hesitated for a moment, so Curly fired a shot, hitting the ground between them. The bullet kicked mud up on them, then careened off through the valley, whining as it did so.

"Get 'em off," Curly said menacingly.

Martin and Caleb glared angrily at the riders, but they took their clothes off. Curly picked them up.

"Now, we are going to ride on back and find our cows," he explained. "We'll leave these clothes wherever we find the cattle. You fellas are lucky. Normally, we hang cattle rustlers, right on the spot. And if we ever catch you with any more of our cows, we'll hang you."

Curly shouted to the others, and the cowboys rode off, sending back one last, defiant shout.

Martin and Caleb, naked and exposed to the rain and the elements, started walking back.

"I'm going to kill that son of a bitch," Caleb swore.

"Who?" Martin asked. "The one they call Curly?"

"No," Caleb answered. "I'm going to kill Lee Coulter. He's the one behind it all."

Chapter Seventeen

The fire that killed Professor Landers and burned the newspaper office also destroyed the printing press, type, paper, ink, woodcuts, and all the other equipment and materials stored in the building. Because of that, Butte Valley was without a newspaper for three weeks after the fire, and Sara Landers was without anything to keep her mind off what happened.

Lee tried several times to get Sara to set the date for their wedding, but he seemed unable to bring her out of the long periods of depression she suffered. The situation was further exacerbated by the fact that Sara and Jennie, once the best of friends, had now become estranged.

In fact, Lee's own relationship with Jennie had changed. He and Jennie had always had a close, easy friendship. Now Jennie was keeping her distance from him. Lee was puzzled by that. Why was she avoiding him? After all, he was the injured party, not Jennie. She had been the one to make love with another man.

Why had he thought that? As soon as the thought came to his mind, he dismissed it with a curious shrug. After all, it wasn't Jennie he was engaged to. It was Sara. Why should he care what Jennie did?

Fractured relationships seemed to abound in the valley after the fire. Sara and Jennie were estranged, Jennie and Lee were estranged but nowhere was there a wider gulf than that which separated Sara and Mike Flynn.

Mike had been cleared of her father's murder, at least as far as the law was concerned, but he was cleared at a terrible price. Both he and Jennie had suffered from the alibi Jennie provided for him, and now they were the butt of gossip all over the valley. Decent women turned their heads away from Jennie whenever they saw her, and they often crossed the street to avoid Mike, if they saw him approaching.

Mike tried several times to speak to Sara, to try to convince her of his innocence, but she wouldn't speak to him. She refused to answer his knock when he called at her house; she turned and walked away from his if he accosted her on the street. Finally the sheriff informed Mike that Sara had filed a complaint against him for harassment, and the sheriff told Mike that if he tried to speak to Sara again, he would be arrested and jailed. Mike took the hint.

One day, shortly after Mike was cautioned by the sheriff, another man knocked on Sara's door. He arrived in the middle of a late summer rainstorm brought on by a chinook wind. Sara wondered who would come to see her in the midst of such foul weather.

"My name is Harris, Miss Landers," the man said, when Sara opened the door. "I've brung you a printing press, plates, type, paper, ink, ever'thin' you need to get back in operation."

"What?" Sara gasped.

"Yes, ma'am, it's all out there on the wagon," the man said.

Sara looked around the man and saw a wagon standing in the street in front of her house. The back of the wagon consisted of lumps covered with a canvas cover. Ropes held the cover secure.

"Who are you?" Sara asked. "Where did you come from?"

"I told you, miss," the man said. "My name is Harris. Walter Harris. I'm a freight operator from Eugene. You know where Eugene is, don't you, ma'am? It's on the Willamette."

"Yes, of course I know Eugene," Sara said.

"Well, I come all the way here from Eugene carryin' this here load. It took me two days, so I hope there ain't no trouble with it."

"But . . . I don't understand," Sara said. She was confused. Why was this equipment being delivered? "You see, I didn't order any

255

such equipment. Indeed, I can't even pay for it."

"You don't have to pay nothin' for it, ma'am, it's already paid for," Harris replied. "Even the freight has been paid. All you got to tell me is where shall I put it?"

"Wait a minute," Sara said, suspiciously. "Who paid for it?"

"I don't know, ma'am," Harris said. "But maybe this will tell you. I'm supposed to give you this here letter."

Harris pulled an envelope from his inside pocket and handed it to Sara. It was damp, though it had remained dry enough to be legible.

"Please," Sara said, "come in."

"No, thankee, ma'am," Harris said. "I been out in it so long now that I don't even notice the rain. Besides, I'd just be gettin' your house all muddied up an' ever'thin'. What I'd really like to do is get this stuff delivered somewhere so's I could go into the saloon and get me somethin' to ward off the cold an' the wet, iffen you get my drift."

"Oh, uh, take it . . . take it to Miller's Emporium," Sara said. "He has a place in the back of his store which he offered to let me use, right after the fire. Of course, I didn't have anything to put there then, so I couldn't take him up on his kind offer."

"Yes'm," Harris said, tipping his hat. "Miller's Emporium. I'll get all this stuff unloaded there."

Sara opened the letter after Harris left.

Dear Miss Landers:

Words cannot express the sorrow we of the *Eugene Daily Register* felt, when we learned of the tragic death of our friend and colleague, Professor Landers.

Your father's death has left a void which cannot soon be filled. His voice has been stilled, his wisdom taken from us, and we all share in your loss.

It is enough that our state has lost the company of this great man, but we should not have to suffer the loss of the great newspaper he founded. Therefore, I beg of you to accept from an admirer of your father's, this gift of equipment which will allow you to publish the *Valley Monitor* again. You can understand that your benefactor wishes to remain anonymous, but this generous person and the admirers of the *Valley Monitor* hope you will accept.

Sincerely,

Tom Post,
Publisher

Tears came to her eyes as she read the letter. So, thanks to some unknown but very kind soul, her father's paper could continue! The *Valley Monitor* would be published again!

Sara threw on a coat, then ran joyfully, through the muddy street and the pouring rain to Miller's Emporium. It was the first moment of joy she had allowed herself since her father's death.

The small bell on the door of the shop tinkled as Sara pushed it open and stepped inside. Jake Miller was behind the counter, measuring material from a dark blue bolt of cloth. He looked up as Sara entered, then smiled broadly.

"Is it true, Sara? Are you going to publish the newspaper again?"

"I don't know, Mr. Miller. It depends on what you charge me for rent for your back room," Sara teased.

"For you, Sara, it will be a bargain, believe me," Miller said. "Mrs. Simmons, would you finish measuring your own cloth?" he asked. "I want to see the press with Sara."

"Yes, of course," Mrs. Simmons said. "But my arms aren't as long as yours, and I won't get as much cloth," she complained.

"You may have an extra arm's length," Miller said, and Mrs. Simmons, beaming happily, picked up the cloth, held her thumb under her chin, then extended it straight out, rolling off a length.

"She has arms as long as a giraffe's neck, that woman," Miller said under his breath as he went into the back room with Sara. "But no matter, I want to see the equipment which makes the newspaper."

"Oh!" Sara cried, as she looked at the equipment Harris was setting up for her. "Oh, it is beautiful!"

Sara walked over to the press and rested her hand lightly on the platten. She looked at the type cases and the rows of clean, never-before-used letters. Tears of happiness came to her eyes.

Miller put his hand on Sara's shoulder.

"I'm glad," he said. "I'm glad for you, and for the town, that we will have a newspaper again."

Sara took off her raincoat and hung it from a hook. "We won't have one unless I get to work," she said. "There's a lot to do to get the first paper out."

"Boss, I found another slaughtered steer," Purkee told Lee, at about the same time Sara was beginning to work on the paper.

"Where?"

"Down at the South Fork," Purkee said. "And it's on our land too, boss. I mean, this critter wasn't anywhere near the range land. Whoever kilt him come right onto our place 'n done it. And here's the strange part, boss. *They didn't even take no meat.*"

"What?" Lee asked, rising from his chair. He had been working on the ranch ledger when Purkee came to him with the news, but not until Purkee told him the last part of it did he really become upset. "They didn't take any meat?"

"Not so much as one steak," Purkee said.

"Damn!" Lee said, hitting his desk with his fist.

"Why you reckon someone'd go to all the trouble of sneakin' onto the ranch 'n killin' a steer, then not even take any meat from it?" Purkee asked. "It's pure bewilderin', if you ask me."

"It isn't bewildering at all," Lee said. "Whoever killed that cow did it from malice, not from need. It was some low-lifed squatter's way of getting at us."

"He couldn't of been very smart," Purkee said. "Hell, boss, he left tracks a blind man could follow."

Lee reached for his hat. "Take me to it, Purkee. Let's see if we can find him."

The rain continued to fall as the two horsemen rode through the rugged gulleys and draws that led down to the South Forks. Both men wore ponchos and had the brims of their hats turned down to keep the rain away, but they were soon soaked to the skin.

Finally Lee saw the animal, a mound of brown and red, as they approached. Two cougars were tearing at the meat, so intent on their unexpected feast that they didn't even notice the arrival of the men. Lee held out his hand, then slipped his rifle from his saddle holster.

"I'll take the one on the right," he said. "You take the one on the left. We'd better fire at the same time, or we'll spook 'em."

"I'll count three," Purkee said, pulling his own rifle from the holster.

Purkee counted quietly, then two rifles

roared as one. Both cats twisted around, then fell, twitching. When the two men rode up to the cow, Purkee finished off both cats with his pistol.

"Purkee, are you sure the cats didn't get to this animal?" Lee asked. "It's pretty well torn up."

Purkee pointed to the head of the steer.

"Not unless cougars have suddenly learned how to use guns," Purkee said. "This cow was shot through the head with a Winchester thirty-thirty."

"Yeah," Lee said. "I see what you mean."

"And there are the tracks," Purkee pointed out, indicating hoofprints which stretched out across a muddy field as deep as if the field were plowed.

"All right," Lee said. "Let's follow them."

Purkee and Lee started along the trail, riding at a fairly rapid gait. Finally they approached a box canyon.

"He went in here," Purkee said. "Come on, let's go take him out of there."

"Wait a minute," Lee cautioned. He pulled his horse up short.

"What's wrong?" Purkee said. "Come on, boss, he's in there. Don't you see the tracks?"

"Why is he in there?" Lee asked.

"Why? I don't know. Why did he kill the cow and not take the meat? 'Cause he's a dumb sodbuster, that's why."

"Maybe he's not as dumb as we think," Lee said.

"Why? What do you mean?"

"I think this fella, whoever he is, is trying to lead us into a trap. Look, that's a natural ambush."

"Yeah," Purkee said. "You're right."

"I'll tell you what. You circle on around that way, so you can come up behind those rocks. I'll go right on in. If there's anyone waiting, we'll know about it."

"All right," Purkee said. He looked toward the rocks that formed the natural fortress. "I'll get up there and wave. You don't start in until you see me."

Lee waited until Purkee was in position, and when he saw the cowboy wave, he started on into the narrow gorge, following the tracks.

"That's far enough, Coulter!" a voice suddenly called.

Lee stopped. From behind the rocks, a man stood up. Lee recognized him as Caleb Penrake.

"So," Lee said. "You're the one who killed my steer."

"That's right, Coulter," Caleb said. "I thought it would bring you around."

"Well you thought right," Lee said. He saw Purkee coming up slowly behind Caleb. "Does your dad know about this?"

"Leave my dad out of it," Caleb said. "I'm my own man."

"Yeah, I can see," Lee said. "Killing a dumb animal for no reason is a very manly thing to do."

"I didn't kill it for no reason," Caleb said. "I had a reason. I had a good reason."

"Would you mind telling me what that reason is?" Lee asked. Behind Caleb, Purkee drew closer.

"I wanted to get you in here," Caleb said.

"All right, you got me in here. Now, what do you intend to do with me?"

Caleb smiled, an evil smile, and he raised a pistol. "I aim to kill you, mister," he said.

Lee looked toward Purkee. Purkee was still too far away to be of any help, though he was moving steadily down the rocks toward Caleb. Lee felt his hair stand on end, and a nervous roll in the pit of his stomach.

"Why?" he asked. "Why do you want to kill me?" *Keep him talking,* Lee thought. *Anything to buy a little more time.*

Caleb laughed, a wild, demented laugh. "You ask me that? You have destroyed crops, burned barns, pulled down fences, beaten farmers, and you ask why I want to kill you?"

"Listen, son," Lee said.

Caleb cocked the pistol and pointed it at Lee. "Don't call me son!" he said. "Only my father can call me son!"

"I'm sorry," Lee said. "It's just that you're so young, and I see you making such a mistake."

"I'm not too young."

"How old are you? Eighteen, nineteen?"

"Twenty," Caleb answered.

"Caleb, you aren't going to live to see
263

twenty-one if you go through with this. You'll be caught, and you'll be hanged."

"I don't care," Caleb said. He took careful aim. "You'll be in hell before me."

Lee felt a sudden panic. He was about to be shot! He made a dive for a nearby rock just as Caleb's gun went off. He felt the bullet tear into his shoulder, and a searing pain like that of a branding iron pierced his flesh. He hit the ground, then rolled behind a rock.

"Penrake!" Purkee called, and Caleb, surprised by the shout from behind, turned around and fired wildly toward Purkee. Purkee was armed with a rifle, and thus had the advantage over Caleb. Purkee raised the rifle, took careful aim, and squeezed the trigger.

Lee heard the boom of the rifle, and then the echo returning from the canyon walls. Caleb pitched back, head down, and slid down the hill. His pistol bounced and clattered over the rocks, reaching the bottom before him.

Lee grabbed Caleb's pistol, then stood up and pointed it toward the young man, who came sliding and bouncing behind it. Finally Caleb's body stopped its slide and Lee walked over to it, still holding the pistol pointed toward it.

"No need for that," Purkee called from halfway up the side. He was working his way down methodically. "He's dead. I hit 'em plumb center."

Lee dropped to one knee and looked into

Caleb's face. His eyes were open, but opaque. His mouth was twisted grotesquely. There was a hole in his chest, and the rain-diluted blood washed away in bright red.

"You're right on that," Lee said. He dropped the pistol and clutched his shoulder.

"Are you all right, boss?" Purkee asked.

"Yeah," Lee said. "But it hurts like the blazes."

"Let me take a look at it," Purkee offered. He cut the hole in Lee's shirt wider and stared at it.

"How is it?" Lee asked.

"It's pretty deep. I'd better get you in town to a doctor."

"No!" Lee said.

"No? Boss, what are you talkin' about? That bullet's got to come out."

"Take me home," Lee said. "You can get a doctor to come out to Broken Lance. He can treat me there. I don't want Sara to know about this."

"What do you mean? She's goin' to find out, there's no way you can keep it from her. Anyway, why do you need to?"

"Sara has gone through enough lately. I don't want her to have to go through anything else. I don't know if she could take. it. Tell the doc I took a fall and I think my shoulder is busted. Then when he gets out to the ranch I can tell him the truth. I can also make certain word of this doesn't get around."

"All right," Purkee said. "You're the boss. What about this hombre? Are you going to just leave him here?"

Lee looked down at Caleb. The rain fell into his open eyes, but Caleb was beyond flinching.

"Tell the sheriff about him," Lee said. "Tell the sheriff to come see me, I'll give him the full story. Now, help me onto my horse."

The pain stopped shortly after Lee was on his horse, and numbness set in. The numbness was a blessing, because it allowed Lee to stay on his horse for the ride back. But it also brought on weakness, so that by the time they reached the house, Lee was only barely cognizant of what was going on around him.

Purkee put Lee in bed, then left to get the doctor. Lee passed out shortly after that, and didn't come to until he felt hands pulling and pushing and poking him.

"Oh," he moaned.

"Well," Doctor Teasdale said. "It's good to see that you're still alive."

"What are you doing?" Lee asked groggily.

"I'm cleaning your wound," Dr. Teasdale said. "I've already removed the bullet."

"You . . . you've already taken it out?"

"Yep," the doctor said. He picked up a red-soaked piece of gauze, and Lee saw the bullet, misshapen from its impact with his body. "A forty-four caliber, from the looks of it." He dropped the bullet with a clink into the pan of water. The water swirled red.

"Did . . . did Purkee tell you . . . ?" Lee started.

"That you wanted this whole business kept quiet?" the doctor replied. "Yes, he told me."

"Thanks, Doc."

"I don't agree with you," Doctor Teasdale said. "I think Sara Landers is a much stronger woman than you give her credit for."

"She's been through so much," Lee said.

"Well, that's kind of you to concern yourself so," Doctor Teasdale said. "But the truth is, you are goin' to need a little nursin', and she would be the perfect woman for the job."

"No," Lee said resolutely. "I don't want her out here yet. Maybe tomorrow."

"By tomorrow the worst of it will be over," Doctor Teasdale said. "Like as not, there was some infection set in. You'll be runnin' a fever tonight. Tonight is when you need a nurse."

"Not Sara," Lee said.

Doctor Teasdale sighed. "I thought you might be a mite obstinate. So I brought someone else to do the nursin' chores. That is, if you don't mind."

Lee felt himself growing dizzy again. "Yeah," he heard himself say. It sounded as if his voice were coming to him from a great distance . . . there was a hollowness to it. "Anyone is fine . . . as long . . . as it isn't . . . Sara," he finally managed, after a great effort.

"Good," Doctor Teasdale said. He turned toward the door. "You can come on in now," he called.

The door opened, and Lee, as if staring through a thick fog, looked to see who was coming in.

It was Jennie Adams.

Chapter Eighteen

Jennie sat in a chair beside Lee's bed while he slept. She kept a basin of water handy, and when he was feverish, she bathed his forehead with cool water to bring it down. When he got chilled, she put more covers on him. When he tossed restlessly, she took his hand and held it tenderly.

"Oh, Lee," she said quietly. "If only you knew why I told that lie about being with Mike on the night Landers was killed."

Jennie thought back to that fateful night, reconstructing the events in her mind.

"Are you absolutely certain it is hoof and mouth disease?" she had asked her father when he returned from the meeting Lee had conducted.

269

"Of course I'm sure," Stump replied. "The animal had blisters on its hooves, and it was foaming at the mouth. What other evidence do you need?"

"More evidence than that," Jennie replied. "There are diseases which look like hoof and mouth, but really aren't. I learned that from Dr. Tremain."

"Well, Dr. Tremain has been dead for two years now, and we only have our own wits to go on," Stump said. "My wits tell me it is hoof and mouth."

"I'm going to see for myself," Jennie said.

Jennie rode over to the Broken Lance Ranch. It was a pleasant ride. The rain had washed everything clean, and the stars twinkled brightly.

When Jennie reached Broken Lance, she was surprised to see that the house was totally dark. She knocked on the door, but got no answer. Even the bunkhouse was empty.

As Jennie thought about it, however, it seemed less strange, for surely Lee and the others were checking the herds closely, to make certain there were no other signs of the disease.

Jennie went out to the barn. She opened the stall, lit a lantern, and examined the sick animal closely. Its eyes were clear, and its nose clean. In fact, there seemed to be no soreness, nor foaming of the mouth, though her father had told her that there had been foaming when he saw it. The hooves were covered with blisters, though, and Jennie bent down to examine them more closely.

270

There was something strange about this. The blisters had an unusual pattern to them. She wished Dr. Tremain were still alive, or had lived long enough to allow her to complete the course in veterinary medicine she was taking from him.

"I wish you could talk," she said softly to the cow. She patted it on the head, and it nudged against her, as if grateful for some tender consideration.

Jennie sighed, and started to leave, when she saw something in the corner of the stall, covered by burlap bags. She walked over to look at it more closely, and saw that it was just a branding iron.

She laughed. *Lee will be wondering where this is, come branding time.* She picked it up, and as she did so, she heard a bottle clink. She laid the iron back down and flipped the burlap bag aside. Beneath the bag she saw a bottle of sulphuric acid.

"What in the world?" she asked aloud.

Jennie picked the bottle up and examined it. Now what would Lee want with sulphuric . . . Suddenly Jennie looked over toward the cow. Sulphuric acid! Sulphuric acid on the hooves would give the symptoms of hoof and mouth disease!

Jennie picked up the branding iron, and noticed then that the brand wasn't the Broken Lance brand at all. It was a slash Zero, the same brand as on the supposedly sick cow. Lee had faked the entire thing. *But why?*

Jennie went back to the house, then into the kitchen. She found some baking soda, took it back to the barn and made up a baking soda and water solution. She bathed the poor animal's hooves in the solution, hoping to give it some relief from the cruel pain it must be suffering from the acid.

Jennie had just finished when she heard horses arriving outside. She extinguished the lantern, poured out the baking soda solution, and left the stall, just as Lee and Purkee came into the barn. She stood in the shadows, unnoticed by either of them.

Purkee laughed. "Did all the boys look for other signs of the disease?"

"Yes," Lee said. "They and the other ranchers are all scared to death. They figure every other cow is infected."

"It worked fine, boss. You have everyone in the valley thinkin' Flynn brought that cow in here. He's gonna be 'bout the most unpopular man that ever set foot in Oregon."

"What about tonight, did it go all right?"

"It went fine," Purkee said. "This on top of the hoof 'n mouth will be about enough to get him run out on a rail. But I'll tell you one thing, the professor sure ain't gonna take to havin' his place burned down like that. I felt kinda bad doin' it."

"I'll build him a newer and bigger newspaper plant," Lee said. "Then he can print how Flynn was so upset by his exposure of the hoof and mouth disease that he bombed the newspaper

272

office. Don't worry about the professor, I'll take care of him. What about the gold nugget? Did you leave it there?"

"Right out front, boss, just like you said. They'll find it, and Flynn will get the blame."

"All right, only one more thing to do," Lee said. "You'd better take the steer out and shoot it, then bury it in quicklime."

"Seems a shame to shoot a healthy steer," Purkee said.

"Look at it this way," Lee said. "The poor critter has to be suffering from that acid. You'll be doing it a favor."

"Yeah," Purkee said. "I guess you're right."

Jennie waited until she could leave without being seen. Then she rode back home, sick at heart, and confused in her mind. When she learned that Professor Landers had been in the building when it burned, she knew that Lee's plan had backfired. It was going to go much further than he intended, because it would result in Mike Flynn being hanged for murder.

Jennie couldn't let Mike Flynn be hanged for a crime he didn't commit, but she couldn't save him at the expense of Lee's freedom. She knew that Lee and Purkee were unaware that the professor would be in the newspaper office. In fact, she had overheard Lee tell Purkee he would build a new office. That made the professor's death an accident. An accident for which Jennie thought neither man should have to suffer. Thus, she decided to provide Mike with an iron-clad, though costly, alibi.

"What time is it?" Lee asked.

The question startled Jennie, not only because it came in the middle of the night, after hours of silence, but also because his voice was clear and strong.

"I heard the hall clock strike three a short time ago," Jennie said.

"Why are you here?" Lee asked.

"You needed a nurse," Jennie answered simply.

"But why would you want to nurse me?" Lee asked. "I thought you were in Mike Flynn's camp."

"Oh, Lee, I . . ."

"You did let him make love to you, didn't you?" Lee interrupted.

"Yes," Jennie said, and as she spoke, a tear tracked quietly down her face.

"So that means you're in his camp. Do you love him?"

"No," Jennie answered.

"You don't love him?"

"No."

"Are you in the habit of letting men make love to you, even if you don't love them?" Lee asked.

"No."

"Then I don't understand. Why did you let Mike Flynn make love to you?"

"Why do you ask me that?" Jennie asked. "You have Sara, don't you?"

"Yes," Lee said. "I do have Sara."

"And you are going to marry her?"

274

"I am going to marry her."

Lee looked at Jennie for a long, quiet moment. Jennie held his gaze; then, because she knew she was letting him look too deep, all the way down to the scars on her soul, she broke off the gaze. She took the cloth from the basin and started to wipe Lee's forehead.

Lee reached up and took her hand in his and held it.

"Lee, no," Jennie whispered.

Lee put his other hand behind Jennie's head, then pulled her head down to his, her lips to his.

Jennie let out a low whimper; then, when his hand went to her breast, a warmth spread through her body, carrying her away with dizzying speed.

"Please, Lee," she said, finally breaking off the kiss. "Don't do this."

Lee began to unbutton Jennie's dress, and soon her breasts were exposed. She tried to turn away from him, but his hand slipped in under the dress, and her breast now blazed so hot that Jennie expected to see a mark branded there.

Lee moved over in the bed, then pulled Jennie down beside him. He tried to complete the job of removing her dress, but as his arm was bandaged, he couldn't do it.

"You'll have to help," he said.

"Oh, Lee, Lee," Jennie said. A sob escaped her lips, but whether it was a sob of protest or pleasure, she couldn't be sure, for all reason seemed to flee, as she divested herself of her clothes.

Lee tried to remove his sleeping gown, but he couldn't raise his arm to get it over his head.

"That's all right, darling," Jennie said. "You can keep it bunched up around your chest."

"No," Lee said. "No, I want nothing between us. Please help me."

Jennie sat up on the bed and leaned forward to remove Lee's sleeping gown. Her breasts swung down toward him, and one nipple brushed lightly across Lee's shoulder, sending pleasurable tingles throughout them both.

Gently, as tenderly as if she were caring for a baby, Jenny removed the gown, working it slowly over his wounded shoulder. Finally Lee was as naked as Jennie.

"Now," Lee said. "Lay beside me."

Willingly, Jennie stretched out on the bed beside him, feeling his muscled legs against her smooth limbs, his hairy chest against her resilient breasts, and the impatient, hard thrust of his manhood against her eager loins.

Lee tried to change positions then, to move over her, but as he did so a sudden spasm of pain seized him, and he winced and lay back down. Jennie saw him wince, and she rose up on one elbow to look at him with a worried expression on her face.

"Are you all right?" she asked.

"Yes," Lee said. He started to try again, but Jennie put her hand up to stop him.

"No," Jennie said. "You stay where you are. I'll come to you."

Jennie moved over Lee, acting as the director of the erotic dance they were doing. She positioned and guided and moved until she took him inside her. She could feel him below her, writhing in pleasure from the moment, thrusting up against her as she moved against him.

Jennie sat up, looking down at Lee's face, watching the pulse in his neck, and then she looked down across her own body, past her bouncing breasts, down her flat stomach, and finally to that golden juncture where they were one.

Jennie had been building toward the magic moment from the time Lee had first kissed her, and now it burst over her, moving through her body in wave after wave of pleasure, lifting her to such rapturous heights that it seemed impossible. It lasted for an eternity, and was over in an instant. Then, before it slipped away, she felt Lee shudder and heard him expel a long, pleasurable moan. She sat back, leaning on her hands, increasing the tension of the connection until at last his pleasure was spent. She looked down at him until his eyes opened, and then their souls were bared to each other.

"I love you, Lee," she said.

"I love you," Lee replied, and Jennie cried from the joy of hearing his words.

When the sheriff halted the wagon, he looked toward the Penrakes' house. In the back of the wagon, wrapped in canvas, lay the body of their son. This was not a moment he relished.

The wagon tilted under his weight when he stepped down, and as he started toward the house, the front door opened and Abner Penrake walked out onto the porch.

"Mornin', Sheriff," Abner said. He was rolling his shirtsleeves up, exposing massive forearms. "What can I do for you?"

"Mr. Penrake," the sheriff said. He paused, then took out his handkerchief and wiped his forehead. "I'm afraid I have some sad news to report."

"Sad news?" Penrake said. "What sort of sad news?"

"It's about your son," the sheriff said. He cleared his throat, then pointed to the wagon. "I have him here."

Abner looked toward the wagon and noticed, for the first time, the form under the canvas.

"Mrs. Penrake," Abner called.

Mrs. Penrake stepped to the front door of the house. She had a pleasant smile on her face, but as soon as she saw her husband's expression, she knew something was wrong.

"What is it, Mr. Penrake?" she asked.

"It's Caleb," Abner said, pointing to his covered form in the wagon.

"*Caleb!*" Mrs. Penrake screamed, and she ran to the wagon and began pulling at the canvas, crying and calling his name, over and over.

"What happened?" Abner asked.

"There was an accident," said the sheriff.

"An accident? What? Did he fall off a cliff or something?"

"Oh, Abner, our Caleb was shot!" Mrs. Penrake suddenly screamed, so distraught that for the first time in over twenty years of marriage she used her husband's Christian name. She had pulled the canvas back, and could see the bullet hole in his chest.

"What's that? Shot, you say?" Abner said. He moved quickly to the wagon, then looked down at the body of his son. He turned back toward the sheriff with anger on his face. "I thought you said it was an accident," he challenged.

"It was, Mr. Penrake," the sheriff replied.

"What kind of accident is it that would get a fella shot?" Abner demanded.

"The kind of accident when a man goes where he has no business going," the sheriff replied.

"What? Are you telling me someone shot my son because he was trespassing?"

"No," the sheriff said. "I'm not saying that at all. It really was an accident. You see, one of the ranchers was having some trouble with cougars. The cats were attacking their cattle. So a couple of men went out to hunt the cougars. They tracked them into a narrow gorge, then they shot both of them. They killed the cougars all right; fact is, I've got their hides down to the office as evidence. But your son was holed up in that draw, nobody knows why, and he caught a stray bullet."

"Where was the draw?" Abner asked.

279

"That's what I mean when I say he was where he had no business bein'. That draw was right there on the ranch."

"Which ranch?"

"Which ranch? Well, it don't really make any difference, does it? The point is, your boy is dead, and ever'body concerned is plumb sorry about it."

"Which ranch?" Abner demanded.

"All right, I'll tell you which ranch," the sheriff finally said. "But I'm warnin' you Mr. Penrake. You let this here matter lie, do you hear me? I've already investigated it, and I'm convinced it happened just like I told you it did."

"Which ranch?"

"The Broken Lance."

"That's Lee Coulter's place, ain't it?

"Yes."

"I might have known." Abner scooped Caleb's body up from the back of the wagon and started toward the house with it, carrying it as easily as he had when Caleb was a child.

"Mr. Penrake, I gotta ask you," the sheriff said. "What are you plannin' on doin'?"

"I'm plannin' on buryin' my boy," Abner replied without looking around.

"After that," the sheriff called out to him. The sheriff was standing alone now, for Mrs. Penrake had walked alongside her husband, holding Caleb's hand and crying. "After that, what are you plannin' on doin'?"

"My thanks, Sheriff, for bringin' the boy to me," Abner called back. Abner and his wife went inside the house and closed the door behind them.

The sheriff stood there for a moment. Then, with a sigh, he climbed onto the seat of the wagon, snapped the reins, and started back toward town.

The first issue of the *Valley Monitor* after the fire carried a blank white column, bordered in a heavy black line. At the top of the column beneath the title, *Polecat*, there was printed: *Franklin Stowe Landers*, 1832–1881.

It was a fitting tribute to her father, one which was much more appropriate than anything Sara could have written.

Sara also carried the story of the accidental shooting death of young Caleb Penrake. She remembered the meal she had eaten with the Penrake family, and she recalled the intensity of the young man. She felt a deep sympathy for the Penrakes, and she wrote the story with tender concern for their feelings, concluding with a genuine expression of sympathy.

Mike attended the funeral, along with more than two hundred other settlers. There was a general feeling that "one of their own" had been killed, and there was a large turn-out to lend support to the Penrake family.

"I'll tell you one thing," Martin Kincaid told Mike. "Caleb's gettin' kilt was no accident."

"How do you know?" Mike asked.

"I just know," Martin said. "He told me he was goin' out to Broken Lance to see Lee Coulter personally. If you want my thinkin' on it, Lee Coulter kilt him, an' he did it of a pure purpose."

"Martin, I know there are hard feelings between the ranchers and the farmers. But I don't think it has come *this* far," Mike said.

"Yes, it has," Martin said. "I know it for a fact."

"That kind of talk does no one any good," Mike cautioned. "You don't know it for a fact unless you actually watched it happen. Did you see it happen?"

"No," Martin said. "But I know Coulter kilt Caleb."

"How can you be so sure of such a thing?" Mike asked in desperation.

" 'Cause Caleb went up there to kill Coulter," Martin said.

"What? Why would he do such a thing? I mean, I know that Caleb was often a hothead about things, but I thought he would have more sense than to try something like that."

"You don't know what me 'n Caleb had to put up with that very day."

"Tell me about it."

"Me 'n Caleb was workin' some fence when a bunch of no-count cowboys jumped us. They were ornery cusses, every'one, 'n they jumped us and tore down the fence. Then they made us take off all our clothes 'n walk back nekkid."

"Was Coulter with them?"

"No," Martin said. He weren't with 'em. Fact is, we don't even know that it was Coulter's men. But Caleb said that Coulter was to blame just the same, 'cause all the cattle ranchers listened to what he had to say."

"Caleb was correct on that score," Mike said. "Coulter does call all the shots. But to go up there with the express purpose of killing Lee Coulter was a dumb thing to do."

"Yeah," the sheriff told Mike, when Mike went to see him after the funeral. "I know Caleb Penrake tried to kill Coulter. He slaughtered one of Lee's cows, and when Lee and Purkee went to investigate, Penrake jumped 'em, and took a shot at them. In fact, Lee got hit. He's at home now, recuperating from a bullet wound in the shoulder. Purkee got Caleb before Caleb could do any more damage."

"Then why did you tell Mr. Penrake that Caleb was shot by accident?" Mike asked.

"Mr. Flynn, do you want to see a range war out here?"

"No, of course not."

"Well, sir, that's just what you'd have if Penrake knew that Caleb was shot by Purkee, self-defense or no. I figured this was the easiest way to keep the lid on things, and if you got any concern about peace in this valley, you'll go along with it."

"I see your point, sheriff," Mike said. "I'll go along with it."

Chapter Nineteen

Article in the *Valley Monitor*:

CATTLEMEN TO DRIVE
HERDS TO PORTLAND

The Valley Cattlemen's Association announced this week, that they would unite their herds for one, massive drive to the Portland markets. Any unemployed cowboy who wishes to take temporary work in helping with the drive may apply to Lee Coulter of the Broken Lance Ranch. Mr. Coulter reports that this will be the biggest cattle drive in the history of the valley, and many extra hands will be required for a successful drive.

When asked why the cattlemen were driving their herds to Portland, rather than taking advantage of existing railroad service, the cattlemen replied that the railroad had adopted policies which were detrimental to the cattlemen's interest, and could not be used as a vehicle for shipping cattle. Mr. Flynn, of the Cascade Railroad, made no comment.

"So I made no comment, huh?" Mike said under his breath. "It's a little hard to make a comment when I'm not asked the question."

Mike was in the Bull's Neck Saloon, standing at the back end of the bar, having a drink. He had come in to think about the article which had appeared in this week's newspaper. He wasn't concerned about the loss of business from the cattlemen, because the farmers would soon be shipping their harvests to market and that would make the railroad survive.

Mike was concerned, though, about the continual worsening of the relationship between the railroad and the older, established inhabitants of the valley. For a railroad to survive in the long term, it had to have a good relationship with everyone, and the animosity which had developed between the settlers and the ranchers, and the ranchers and the railroad, was bad. That relationship would continue to deteriorate, as long as such articles continued to appear in the newspaper. And that responsibility, Mike laid squarely on Sara Landers.

It was late, and much of the early evening crowd in the Bull's Neck had already left. The only remaining customers were the serious drinkers, the drifters who had no other place to go, and the men who were waiting for their turn to visit one of the "soiled doves" of the establishment. Two of the latter were cowboys, standing at the opposite end of the bar from Mike. Mike knew them as Curly and Slim, and he knew also that they had been the ones who jumped Caleb and Martin.

"Hey, bartender," Curly called out. "Bartender did you happen to check Flynn's shoes?"

"Check his shoes?" the bartender replied.

"Yeah," Curly said. He held his nose. "Smells to me like he's been walking around in pigpens. Why don't you look at his shoes?"

"Is that right, Flynn?" Slim asked, laughing. "Have you been suckin' up to your pig-farmin' friends? You been playin' in their pigpens?"

"You know what he's been doin' in there, don't you?" Curly asked. He laughed. "He's been tryin' to find hisself a date for the Sat'y night dances. Some of them farmers' pigs is prettier'n some of their daughters."

Slim laughed. "Now that's a fact. That's truly a fact. Onliest thang is, Flynn, when you do that, you got to wipe your feet off when you come out. Most especial, iffen you are plannin' on comin' into a place where they's men tryin' to drink."

Mike drained the rest of his whiskey, left a coin on the bar and started to leave. He had no intention of becoming embroiled in an altercation with a couple of drunken cowboys.

"Hey, you ain't leavin', are you?" Curly asked.

"Yeah, he's leavin'," Slim said. "Didn't you read in the paper this week? Mr. Flynn don't like to make no comments. Ain't that right, Flynn? You don't like to make no comments?"

Mike tried to walk by them, but both of them stepped away from the bar and took up a position to block his exit.

"Now, you don't want to leave without makin' some kind of comment, do you?" Curly asked. He grinned broadly.

"Yeah," Slim said. "Tell us what you think about the big trail drive, why don't you?"

"Don't that seem a little strange to you, Flynn?" Curly asked. "What do you think about the ranchers driving their cows to Portland, when they could send 'em on your train?"

"It's the cattlemen's business," Mike said. "They can do what they wish with their own cows."

"Well, now, what do you think of that? He *can* talk," Slim said.

"If you gentlemen will excuse me, I'll be on my way," Mike said.

"Naw," Curly said. He smiled broadly, showing a mouthful of crooked, broken teeth. "Naw, we ain't gonna excuse you. We're gonna keep you aroun', and maybe have a little fun with you."

"If you keep me around, gentlemen, I assure you, you won't have any fun," Mike said.

"Oh, I think we will," Curly said, and he took a swing at Mike.

Mike had been braced for it, because he saw Curly tensing long before he actually swung. He was able to avoid Curly's wild swing easily. The swing left Curly off balance, and Mike counter-punched with a short, powerful blow, right into Curly's solar plexus.

Curly went down, gasping for breath, and Mike turned his attention to Slim, who was so surprised by the sudden turn of events that he hadn't even raised his fist. Mike drew his arm back to hit him.

"No, Flynn, no!" Slim said, raising his hands. "It was Curly that started the fight, not me."

Mike looked at Slim, cowering before him, and he let out a snort of disgust.

"Take care of your friend before he pukes on the floor," Mike said, walking out of the saloon.

Sara was sound asleep when a knocking on the front door finally seeped through to her senses. At first, the knocking was part of her dream, and she didn't know to wake up and see about it. But it continued beyond the dream, and finally she realized that someone was at the front door.

Sara sat up, fully awake now, and heard the knocking, loud and insistent. She reached for her robe.

"Just a minute," she called. "I'll be there in just a minute."

Sara walked boldly to the front door. It

never occurred to her that a woman living alone might be well advised to exercise caution when answering a strange knock in the middle of the night.

She opened the door, and there, standing on her front porch, illuminated only by the soft, silver light of the moon, was Mike Flynn.

"It's you!" Sara said. "How dare you come to my door in the middle of the night?"

"You've refused to see me in the middle of the day," Mike said.

"And I shall not see you now," Sara replied. She tried to close the door, but Mike caught it with his foot and held it open.

"Not this time, Sara," Mike said. "This time you are going to see me."

"Get out of here! Get out! Get out, or I will scream!"

"Sara, you must let me talk to you," Mike implored. "You *must!*"

Sara took a deep breath, as if she were going to scream, but Mike put his hand over her mouth.

"Promise me you won't scream," he said. "Promise you won't scream, and I'll remove my hand."

Sara shook her head no, defiantly, and she tried to bite his hand.

Mike looked at her for a moment; then he smiled. "I know a better way to stop you from screaming," he said, and he bent down to kiss her with hot, hungry lips.

Sara struggled against it, but Mike was persistent, and finally she felt herself giving up the struggle. His kiss burned through to her very core, and she grew dizzy from the sensations thus evoked. Mike's tongue forced its way past her lips, then inside, and she felt its sweet, thrilling pressure in her mouth.

Sara felt every muscle in her body grow weak, and she recalled all those other moments with Mike Flynn, in the engine cab, on Lee Coulter's front porch, in the deserted house in the rainstorm. What was there about this man that could move her so?

Finally the kiss ended, and Mike pulled his lips away. He continued to hold her, though, and her body trembled in his embrace.

"Sara, girl, I've been driven mad with desire for you from the moment we met. The afternoon we spent in that house on the range was the nearest I've ever come to heaven, and the time since, the closest I've been to hell. I must have you again—I *must!*"

Mike picked Sara up and carried her back into her bedroom. Sara was helpless . . . helpless before his virile strength and helpless before her own flaming passions. She wanted to cry out, to offer some protest, and yet the sounds which came from her lips were not sounds of protest, but of rapture.

Mike put Sara on her bed, then gently removed her robe and nightgown. She stretched out on the bed watching, waiting, as Mike took off his own clothes. When he lay on the bed beside her, his muscled body felt cool against her own fevered skin.

What am I doing? Sara thought. *Why am I letting this happen?* And yet, despite those still-born thoughts, she moved her body eagerly to allow Mike to continue his supplications to her desire. She tingled as his fingers trailed lightly across the nipples of her breasts, moved down the smooth skin of her stomach, and into the soft down at the juncture of her legs. Now all thoughts of protest, all ideas of resistance, even in the innermost recesses of her mind, were stilled. She welcomed Mike, in her mind and in her body, and she cried from the sheer joy of the moment, urging him to go on and on and on. No sense of guilt, no feeling of shame could extinguish the fires that raged within.

She pulled Mike to her, not surrendering to, but embracing the moment. There was a com-mingling of passion and emotion that made them as one, until finally a burst of pleasure, which exceeded all other pleasure, swept over her in wave after wave. Sara's whole body seemed to dissolve under the intensity of the sensation. The waves of ecstasy rippled through her body in such rapid succession that it was as if there were one long, sustained period of rapture. The feeling of pleasure was greatly multi-plied by the waves of delectation, one after the other. Even when it was all over, and they lay together side by side, Sara could still feel tiny tinglings of excitation as her enflamed senses slowly returned to normal.

And then Sara knew what she had done. She had been betrayed by her body, her mind poisoned by her own animal lusts. She stiffened.

Mike felt Sara stiffen, and he raised himself on one elbow and looked down at the girl by his side.

"What is it?" he asked. "What is wrong?"

"You ask me that?" Sara said. "My father is lying in his grave, and I am here . . . with you."

"Sara, you must believe by now that I had nothing to do with your father's death. My God, girl, you don't think I would be here with you like this if I were responsible?"

"I . . . I don't know what to believe," Sara said. "It's all so confusing. You were going to go see him, you told me yourself. You were upset by the article, and your nugget was found in front of the office."

"I lost the nugget long before that," Mike said. "In fact, I lost it on the night of the Independence Day celebration, when Coulter's men decided to celebrate with me."

"I wish I could believe that," Sara said.

"You can," Mike said simply. "Did you see the nugget around my neck anytime during the day, before your father was killed?"

"No," Sara answered. "But what does that prove?"

"If you'll think for a moment," Mike said, "it should prove a lot. After all, you had the opportunity to examine me closely that day."

Suddenly, Sara remembered the afternoon in

the deserted house, and the time when they made love. She had seen him totally undressed that afternoon, and he had not been wearing the nugget.

"Yes," Sara said. "Yes, I *do* remember. You didn't, Mike, you *weren't* wearing the nugget that afternoon."

"No, I wasn't," Mike said. "Nor was I wearing it that night."

"But if you weren't wearing it, how did it come to be in front of the newspaper office?"

"That's a good question," Mike said. "And it is one I can answer. It was placed there by whoever *did* bomb the newspaper office, so the blame would be shifted to me."

"But I don't understand," Sara said. "Who else would have a reason for bombing the newspaper office? You were the only one who stood to lose by my father's article."

"Precisely," Mike said. "I think whoever did it had no intention of harming your father. I'm sure they figured he would be safely home, in bed. All they wanted to do was make it look as if I had become so incensed by the article that I destroyed the newspaper office."

"Only they didn't count on Jennie coming forth to supply you with an alibi, proving that you had nothing to do with it," Sara said.

"No," Mike answered. "Nor did I, as the alibi she provided for me was false. We were not together on that night."

"What? Mike, what are you saying? Do you mean you *weren't* with Jennie?"

"No," Mike answered. "Sara, did you really believe I could go from your bed to hers? I told you that day, girl, that I love you. I couldn't have treated that love so lightly."

"Then why would Jennie *say* such a thing? She has ruined her reputation with that falsehood."

"I asked Jennie the same question," Mike said. "She told me that she knew I was innocent."

"Oh," Sara said. "Oh, Mike, how terrible that Jennie should believe you and I wouldn't."

"Don't feel too badly about it," Mike said. "Jennie knew that I was innocent, because she knows who did it."

"Jennie knows?"

"Yes."

"Who?" Sara asked. "Mike, who *did* bomb the newspaper office?"

"Who stands to gain the most by having me out of the way?"

"You aren't trying to convince me that Lee had anything to do with it, are you?"

"I didn't mention any names," Mike said.

"But you do mean Lee, don't you?" Sara asked.

"When I asked you who you thought stood to gain the most, whose name came to your mind?" Mike asked. "Am I wrong, or did you think of Lee?"

"Mike, that just isn't possible," Sara said. "Lee and his father were among my father's very best friends. George Coulter cosigned a

295

loan with my father, so he could build the office for the newspaper. Lee could never do such a thing."

"Perhaps he could never physically harm your father," Mike said. "But remember, also, that I don't think whoever did this, had any intention of harming anyone."

"You mean destroying the newspaper office wouldn't hurt Dad? Even if he had survived, he would never have gotten over the destruction of the paper. My father held the freedom of the press as dear as one of the Ten Commandments."

"I think Lee knew that, and was counting on it," Mike said. "Don't you see? He could step right in and rebuild the paper for your father, and your father would attack me in print from a platform of martyrdom, because I had attempted to stifle freedom of the press."

"I can't help but believe you are wrong," Sara said. "I know Lee wouldn't have done such a thing. I would bet my life on it."

"You *are* betting your life on it," Mike said.

"Are you trying to tell me that I am in danger?"

"Not an immediate physical danger," Mike said. "But you have your future to consider. After all, you are engaged to him, are you not?"

"Yes," Sara said.

"Do you still plan on going through with it?"

"Yes," Sara said quietly.

"What?" Mike asked. "Sara, you can't lie there in this bed with me after what we have just experienced, and tell me that you still plan to marry Lee Coulter?"

Now Sara felt naked. She had been totally unaware of her lack of clothes, because it had seemed natural and correct. But with the realization that she was engaged to Lee, she suddenly felt as if she were cheating. She felt cheap and deceitful, and she sat up and reached for her robe.

"Sara, you love me, girl. Didn't you tell me that you love me?"

"I told you that," Sara said quietly.

"Then how can you marry Lee Coulter? Tell me, girl, how *can* you?"

Sara sobbed. "I have to marry him, Mike, can't you see? If I don't, I'm denying everything my father ever stood for."

"No," Mike said angrily. "No, I *can't* see that." He got up and dressed quickly, while Sara, now covered with a robe, sat on the edge of the bed in which they had just made love.

"I wish you could understand," Sara said.

"I'm sorry," Mike said. "But I make no attempt to understand insanity. If you go through with this marriage, you are committing an act of lunacy, and you should have your head examined. But then, your actions and attitudes during the whole time I have known you seem to support that theory anyway. And God help me, woman, if I stay around you, I'll soon be as daft as you are. I'm leaving now, while I've still my wits about me."

"Mike, I'm sorry," Sara said. "I wish it didn't have to be like this."

"It doesn't have to be like this," Mike said. "You could—" He stopped when he noticed that Sara was shaking her head, while tears streamed down her cheeks. "Never mind," he said. "I'll go attend to my business, and you attend to yours. Goodbye, Miss Landers. And good luck."

Mike walked out of the bedroom without looking back. When Sara heard the front door close, she lay back on the bed, its sheets still musky from their love-making, and she cried bitter tears into her pillow.

Chapter Twenty

Jennie left the house with the first gray light of morning. The sun, still low in the east, sent long bars of light slashing through the tall fir trees, and the morning mist curled around the tops of the trees like wisps of smoke. She could feel the excitement of a cattle drive, before she could hear the sounds, and she could hear the crying and bawling of cattle, and the shouts and whistles of the wranglers, before she could actually see the herd.

More than twenty-five hundred head of cattle milled about on the high plateau of the Broken Lance Ranch. They represented the combined herds of half a dozen ranchers, all of whom had come together for the trail drive to Portland. When Jennie crested the last ridge she could see them. They were in a natural pen, bordered on the south by a sheer drop to the McCauley River, and on the east by the narrow draw from which the river emerged. Cowboys darted about on the north and west flanks, whistling and keeping the herd in check.

Jennie knew that this was the most critical time for the herd, for the cows had been thrown together and they were aware of different smells and feelings, and they would be nervous. The least thing could spook them, so the cowboys had to be very careful.

The chuckwagon was parked to one side of the herd, so Jennie rode toward it, keeping along the edge of the precipice so as not to spook the herd. She wanted to go down to the wagon to speak with the cook.

Jennie was familiar with chuckwagons, because her first round-up, as a little girl, had been as a cook's helper, and she had been fascinated by the honeycombs and cubbyholes of the chuck box. The chuck box sat at the rear of the wagon, with a hinged lid which let down onto a swinging leg to form a worktable. Here the cook stored his utensils and whatever food he might use during the day; such things as flour, sugar, dried fruit, coffee beans, pinto beans, tobacco, "medicinal" whiskey, and, when Jenny was a little girl, hard candy.

"Well, hello, Miss Jennie," the cook said, as Jennie got off her horse and helped herself to a cup of coffee from the pot which hung, percolating, over the fire. "Are you going on the trail drive with us?"

"No, Pete," Jennie said brightly. "I wish I could go. I remember when I was a little girl."

Pete laughed. "Yes, you thought the possibles drawer was made just for a little girl's candy, didn't you?"

"I sure did," Jennie said. "I guess those days are over now. I'm not a little girl any more."

"No ma'am, I guess you're not," Pete said, and as he looked at her, Jennie suddenly got the feeling that he was thinking of the stories which were circulating about her. Then he grew embarrassed, and coughed, and looked down.

"Pete, have you seen Lee this morning?" Jennie asked.

"Yes, ma'am, I seen 'im," Pete said. "Fact is, he said if anybody was lookin' for 'im, to have 'em wait, 'cause he was gonna come right back here after he rode around the herd to check on things."

"All right, fine, I'll wait here," Jennie said.

Despite the fact that Pete had just given an indication of the embarrassment and shame Jennie had been subjected to since providing an alibi for Mike, she was happy. She was happy because she had seen Lee several times since the night she had nursed him through his fever, and on each occasion they had made love. They had not only made love, they had told of their love for one another, and Jennie knew that they were going to be married. Lee had promised that he would tell Sara, and make a public announcement of their plans soon.

Jennie had just finished her coffee when Lee rode up. She tossed the last dregs out, and smiled at him.

"How is your shoulder holding out?" she asked. "Any problem with riding?"

"Not a bit," Lee said. He moved his arm around, demonstrating the mobility which had returned. "Thanks to some good nursing, recovery was complete."

Jennie looked over toward the cook, and when she saw he had started toward one of the other wagons, so that he was out of earshot, she spoke again.

"You haven't dropped by," she said. "I haven't seen you in several days."

"I've been busy," Lee replied. "It isn't easy getting a trail drive together."

"I understand," Jennie said. "I can wait. I was just wondering if you had spoken with Sara about us."

Lee walked over to pour himself a cup of coffee. He took a drink, slurping it to cool it.

Jennie waited for a long moment, and when he didn't answer, she spoke again.

"Lee, you are going to tell her, aren't you? You can't just let her hang like that. She's much too good a person to treat that way."

"Jennie," Lee said. "I've been giving this a lot of thought."

"You've been giving what a lot of thought?"

"This entire . . . situation," Lee said. He

pushed his hat back and sighed. "There are things you don't understand."

"Like what?"

"Like what is really between you and me," he said. "I'm afraid that you might have gotten the wrong idea over the last couple of weeks."

Jennie felt a sudden sinking sensation, and she had to close her eyes to keep her head from spinning. What was he saying?

"Lee, how can I have the wrong idea?" Jennie asked in a quiet, controlled voice.

"I'm afraid you were led to believe that . . . there was something more than friendship between us. But that simply isn't the case. We are friends, Jennie. We are very good friends."

"Friends?"

"Yes," Lee said. "We've always been friends, haven't we?"

"I see," Jennie said. "So, this is what it's like when you spend the night with one of the boys?"

"I don't mean that, Jennie, and you know it," Lee said.

"Then what *do* you mean?" Jennie asked. "What are you telling me, Lee?"

"I'm telling you that I am engaged to Sara Landers, and I intend to marry her."

"I see," Jennie said. "And it doesn't make any difference that you told me you loved me?"

"I know I have told you that, Jennie, but you must understand that . . ."

"You said it, Lee, and you meant it," Jennie

interrupted. She laughed, a small, desperate laugh. "There are certain times when you cannot fool a woman, and you and I have shared those times. When you told me you loved me, you meant it."

"All right, perhaps I did mean it," Lee admitted.

Jennie heaved a big sigh, and ran her hand through her hair. "Oh, Lee, you frightened me so," she said. "You shouldn't say such things. I was afraid you . . ."

"But I *am* going to marry Sara," Lee said again, holding up his hand to stop Jennie before she went any further.

"You can't," Jennie said in a small voice. Tears began to slide down her face, and she shook her head back and forth, as if unable to believe what she was hearing. "Lee, you can't mean that you are going to marry Sara."

"I'm sorry," Lee said quietly.

"You're sorry?"

"Yes."

"But how can you do this? Didn't you just admit that you meant it when you told me you loved me? All the plans we made, didn't you mean them?"

"I do love you, Jennie," Lee said. "And the plans we made . . . while I was making them, I meant them."

"Then if you love me and I love you, why are you going through with your marriage to Sara? How can you?"

"Because I need her."

"You *need* her?"

"Jennie, Sara is the publisher of the only newspaper in the valley," Lee said. "It is a paper that is respected throughout the state. You know we're going to need such support if we're going to be successful in turning back the squatters."

"Let me get this straight," Jennie said. "You are marrying Sara not because you love her, but because you need her. Is that right?"

"Please, Jennie, try to understand."

"You're talking to the wrong person, Lee, if you want me to understand," Jennie said. "The person you should be talking to is Sara. How are you going to make *her* understand that you don't love her, you just need her? Is that fair to her?"

"Jennie, I'm in the middle of a range war here," Lee said. "I'm trying to save our land and our cattle. You love this land and the ranchers' way of life as much as I do and you know it. Can't you see that what I'm doing, I'm doing for both of us? I'm trying to preserve what we have."

"Don't use that reasoning with me, Lee Coulter," Jennie said. She looked at Lee with ill-concealed disgust. "I don't know which of us should be most disgusted with you, Sara or me."

"Jennie, you aren't giving me a chance," Lee pleaded.

"Perhaps I'm not," Jennie said. "But then,

you didn't give Professor Landers much of a chance either, did you?"

"What?" Lee asked in a shocked, quiet voice. "What did you just say?"

"I know you are responsible for the bombing of the newspaper office," Jennie said.

"Jennie, I didn't do that," Lee said. "What are you saying?"

"No, you didn't do it," Jennie said. "Purkee did it. But you were responsible."

"How . . . how long have you known?" Lee asked.

"I've known from the night it happened," Jennie said. "Why do you think I told the sheriff I was with Mike Flynn that night?"

"You mean . . . you mean you weren't?"

"No," Jennie said.

"But you told me you had slept with him."

"And so I have," Jennie said. "But not on that night. I merely told the sheriff that to keep Mike from being hanged for something he didn't do."

"Jennie, there is something you need to know," Lee said weakly. "I really had no intention of hurting the professor. I didn't know he would be in the office. I just wanted to get the valley further enflamed against Flynn."

"I know," Jennie said. "I know you didn't intend for the professor to be hurt. But you were playing with fire, Lee. You started playing with it the moment you forced blisters on that steer's hooves with acid."

"You know about that too?"

306

"Yes," Jennie said. "I came out here to see you that night, right after Dad came back and told me about the steer with hoof and mouth. I wanted a chance to look at the animal. I thought I might be able to set your mind at ease. Then I discovered that you *wanted* people to think it was hoof and mouth disease. You wanted it so badly that you faked it."

"How did you discover it?"

"In the first place, the blisters on the hooves didn't look as they should," Jennie said. "Then I found the branding iron and the acid. Shortly after that, you and Purkee came into the barn, and I overheard the two of you talking."

"Oh, my God!" Lee moaned. "You've known about this all this time."

"Yes."

"And yet . . . and yet you've remained quiet about it. You even lied to find a way to save Flynn from hanging, without compromising me."

"Yes," Jennie said. She sighed. "I did it because I thought I loved you."

"You *thought* you loved me?"

"I was wrong," Jennie said.

"Jennie, wait," Lee said. "Don't you see how you've just proven my point? You covered up the bombing because in truth you knew that you stood to benefit as much as I by Flynn being discredited."

"What?" Jennie asked angrily. "How can you say such a thing?"

"Because it is true," Lee said. "And you can

307

also see the validity of my marrying Sara. But just because I marry her, things needn't change between us."

"What do you mean, things needn't change between us?"

"I mean, Sara and I might be married, but you and I could still be lovers," Lee said. He reached for Jennie, but she avoided his touch.

"No," she said coldly. "We can never be lovers, or even friends again. I don't know how I could ever have been so foolish as to think that you were worthy of any woman's love."

She swung up onto her horse, and, with tears stinging her eyes, started back around the herd toward her own home.

"How long do we have 'afore one of these thangs goes off, once we light 'em?" a tall, rawboned young man asked Martin Kincaid.

Martin pointed to the fuse on the end of the stick of dynamite the man was holding.

"If you light it out on the end like you're supposed to, you'll have about seven seconds."

"Seven seconds? Is that all? That ain't very long when you're aholdin' onter dynamite," one of the others said.

"Listen," Martin said angrily. "Do you want to get even with those bastards for killin' Caleb, or don't you?"

"Well, yes, of course we do," another answered.

"Then don't be such a yellow-belly, and listen to me," Martin said.

Martin was talking to half a dozen young men, all between the ages of sixteen and twenty. They were sons of settlers, and they felt the animosity of the ranchers and the community very keenly. They also felt a strong awareness of Caleb's untimely death, and it was to avenge that death that they had gathered here, in the same draw where Caleb had been killed.

"Are we gonna try and kill the cattle with dynamite?"

"No," Martin said. "Some cattle may be killed, but if so, why then that's just a part of it 'n it can't be helped."

"Go over the plan one more time."

Martin sighed. "All right, but pay attention this time. Now, out there, all the ranchers who are going to drive their cows up to Portland have got 'em put together in one herd."

"They sure is a bunch of 'em," someone said, looking out from the draw over the high plateau where the cattle had congregated.

"There are more than two thousand," Martin said. "I know that for a fact."

"Whew," someone whistled. "That's a lot of beef eatin'."

The others laughed, but Martin regained their attention. He held up a few sticks of dynamite.

"These here sticks of dynamite are our weapons. We light one, throw it, light another, throw it, then light another and throw it. We got to do it all in six seconds, see, because the first one is going to go off in seven seconds, and we've got to be out of there."

"Are we each going to have three?"

"No," Martin said. "I could only come up with fifteen sticks, so some will have two. You won't have any problem. It's them with three that'll have a problem. But now look at the fuse. You have to make sure you light it here, out on the end, for it has to have that long to burn for seven seconds. Iffen you light it here, or here," he touched the middle of the fuse, and then the part of the fuse nearest the stick itself, "it'll go off pretty fast."

"Boom!" one of the young men shouted, and the others laughed nervously.

"Now, this here ain't no laughin' matter," Martin said seriously.

"Come on, Martin, you're asoundin' like a cap'n in the army. We ain't no army."

"Yes," Martin said seriously. "Yes, we are an army. Don't you see? We got us a real, live war goin' on here. It's us agin' the ranchers, 'n iffen we don' win, they are gonna run us right off this land 'n back to Ohio or Missouri or wherever we all come from. We got to fight to keep aholt of what's rightly our'n."

"Martin's right," one of the others said. "We got us a real war goin' on here."

"Wow, then Martin *is* like a cap'n, ain't he?"

"Yes," Martin said. "And when your cap'n talks, the rest of you got to pay attention."

"We know what we got to do," one of the

310

others said. "Let's jes' git on our horses 'n go on down there and do it."

"All right," Martin said. "Let's do it. Remember, throw them as far as you can, light another an' then throw it. But don't throw 'em at each other. Throw 'em out in the herd."

Martin and the other young men mounted their horses, though in two cases, the mounts weren't horses but mules, and rode out toward the herd.

Jennie was riding at breakneck speed. Her eyes were burning with tears. How could she have been such a fool as to protect Lee? How could she have been such a fool as to love him? She had to go to Sara, to tell Sara what kind of man she was going to marry. *Please, dear God, let Sara listen!*

Suddenly there were a series of stomach-jarring explosions, one right after another. The herd of cattle, nervous anyway, reacted immediately. Twenty-five hundred animals started a mad, panic-stricken stampede, heading straight for Jennie.

Jennie had been so startled by the explosions that for an instant she forgot about the herd. Then, when she perceived her danger, it was too late. The herd was thundering toward her, and she had nowhere to go but the sheer drop of more than two hundred feet. She did the only thing she could do, and that was to try to ride right through the thundering stampede, hoping the cows would open a path for her.

Jennie might have made it, had she been astride a pony which was trained to work cattle. But this morning she had chosen to ride a horse that had been bred for speed, rather than work, and the horse was terrified of the onrushing cows. He wanted to depend on his one, proven commodity, speed, to get him out of the danger, because he didn't know of the drop-off behind him. As a result, instead of a finely coordinated effort of horse and rider to escape the danger, it became a battle between them. The horse tried to obey its own instincts, and failed to respond to Jennie's directions. It fell in the middle of the herd, and Jennie was thrown beneath the flashing hooves.

Jennie's last conscious thought was of Sara. Who would warn her about Lee now?

Chapter
Twenty-One

For the third time in as many weeks, the cemetery was the scene of an emotional funeral. This time it was for Jennie Adams, and the mourners bewailed not only her death, but the senseless slaughter of more than four hundred cattle, also killed in the stampede.

Jennie had always been a popular figure in the valley, and no one who attended the funeral could look at her coffin without thinking of the vivacious young girl whose brilliant ride had won the Fourth of July race just a short time before. Forgotten now was the fact that she had so recently been the object of their scorn, and women who had snubbed her just a few days before now wept openly and un-ashamedly.

Mike attended the funeral, even though he realized that his presence would be unwelcome. He didn't care what they thought. He had come for Jennie.

No one spoke to Mike during the service. Several glared at him with ill-concealed hostility, and Sara avoided his glance every time he looked in her direction.

After the funeral, Mike walked up to Stump Adams to extend his condolences.

"Why are you here?" Stump asked Mike.

"I am here to pay my respects to your daughter, Mr. Adams," Mike said. "I thought she was a wonderful young woman."

"You speak of respect?" Stump replied. "How can you speak of respect? The entire valley knows how you treat respect. You ruined my little Jennie's reputation."

"Mr. Adams, I'm sorry you feel that way," Mike said.

"How do you expect me to feel?" Stump replied angrily.

Sara saw the two men speaking and she came over to speak to them.

"Mr. Adams, if there is anything any of us can do," Sara said.

"Anything at all," Lee added. Lee was right behind Sara. "You just ask us."

"There is nothing anyone can do," Stump said. "Nothing."

Sara looked around the cemetery with a confused look on her face. "Lee, where are Purkee and the other cowboys?"

"What?" Lee answered.

"Purkee, Curly, Slim, and the others. Surely they would come to Jennie's funeral. They thought so much of her."

"I guess they just had something else to do," Lee said noncommittally.

"Something else to do?" Mike asked. "Coulter, what are you saying?"

"I'm saying that the men had something else to do today, and they couldn't make it to Jennie's funeral."

"Mr. Adams, do *you* know what Coulter is talking about?" Mike asked Stump.

"No," Stump said. "But it must be important for them to be absent."

"Lee, what is it?" Sara asked. "Where are they?"

Lee sighed. "Well, you might as well know," he said. "Slim recognized one of the riders who stampeded the cattle as Martin Kincaid. So Purkee took some men out to Kincaid's cabin. They are going to bring him in."

"Bring him in?" Mike asked. "Bring him in, or lynch him? Coulter, if anything happens to Kincaid, his blood will be on your hands."

"No, Flynn, his blood will be on *your* hands," Stump said. "As is the blood of everyone else who has died in this range war."

"There will be no range war," Mike said. "Not if everyone keeps their heads. Mr. Adams,

315

the ranchers respect you. Talk to them, urge them to remain calm."

"And who will urge the farmers to remain calm?" Stump asked.

"You can," Sara said to Mike. "The farmers will listen to you."

"Not if the Kincaid boy is lynched," Mike said.

"Lee, go out there," Sara said. "Go out and see that nothing happens."

"I'll go with you," Mike said. "Maybe we can stop this thing before it goes any further."

"There's only one way to really stop it," Lee said. "You started it, when you opened up a peaceful valley to immigrants, outsiders who have no respect for the rights or property of others, people who have no appreciation for what we have built here. Now the only way we can have peace is for you to stop selling land to the immigrants."

"That has nothing to do with whether or not Kincaid is lynched by that mob you sent out there," Mike said. "Now, are you going to go out there and stop them, or not?"

"Please go, Lee," Sara urged.

"All right," Lee said. "I'll go out there, Flynn. But I can't promise you that I'll be able to do anything. The men were pretty riled up about Jennie's murder."

Slim Tucker drained the last of his bottle and threw it against the rocks. The bottle smashed with a tinkling crash, and the pieces of glass

316

flashed in the noonday sun as they scattered across the ground. He scratched his crotch and belched as he stared across the open space toward the small log cabin.

"Well, what the hell?" Slim said. He belched again.

"What are you getting so antsy about?" Curly asked. "Sit down and take it easy. He has to come out sometime."

"I don't want to wait for the son of a bitch to come out. I wanna kill the bastard now."

"We're gonna kill 'im," Purkee said. "I'm just tryin' to figure on the best way to do it, that's all.

"Wait a minute," Curly said. "Purkee, you said we was gonna take 'im in to the sheriff. You didn't say nothin' 'bout killin' 'im."

"Sure, we're gonna take 'im in," Purkee said. "If he'll go peaceful. But if he ain't willin' to go peaceful, then we're gonna take 'im in anyway. And it don't much seem like he wants to go in peaceful, now, does it?"

"I don't intend to be any party to a lynchin'," Curly said.

"It's too bad we don't have no dynamite," Purkee mused. "Iffen we had us a little dynamite we could blast 'im outta there."

"Hell, I don' need no dynamite," Slim said. "He's jus' a damn pig-farmer. I can get 'im outta there by myself."

"Yeah? And just how do you intend to do that?" Purkee asked.

"Watch," Slim said. Slim pulled his pistol

317

and started running toward the log cabin, blazing away.

"Slim!" Curly shouted. "Slim, come back here, you damn fool!"

Slim ran all the way to the front porch, firing his six-shooter at the house. There was no answering fire, and when Slim reached the front porch, he turned around and shouted back to the others who were holed up in the rocks.

"See! I told you there was nothin' to it! Now come on, let's pull this chicken liver outta here and hang 'im!"

At that moment the front door of the cabin opened, and Martin Kincaid stepped out, holding a shotgun levelled toward Slim.

"Slim, look out!" Curly called.

At Curly's warning shout, Slim turned back toward the door. The smile of triumph on his face changed to a look of surprise, then fear, as the shotgun roared.

Slim's chest and stomach turned red as the load of buckshot exposed his insides. The charge of the shotgun knocked Slim back against the supporting post of the porch roof, and the impact tore the post away, bringing the roof crashing down. Slim fell back onto the ground, writhing in agony.

"Slim!" Curly called, and he stood up to go after his friend, but Purkee grabbed him and pulled him back down.

"You want to wind up the same way?" he asked. "Get down, get out of his line of fire."

"But Slim's out there!"

Curly watched in horror as Slim kicked and twitched a few times, then lay still.

"Damn you!" Curly called, and his voice returned in an angry, accusing echo. Everyone thought Curly was swearing at Kincaid, but he added, "Damn you, Slim! You fool! What did you do that for?"

"Andy," Purkee called to one of the other men. "Did you bring the kerosene?"

"Yeah," Andy said. "I brought it."

"I was gonna burn a couple of fields," Purkee said. "But I got me a better idea."

"What you want me to do with it?"

"You think you can get down there and splash it on the side of the house?" Purkee asked. "Me 'n the other boys could start firin', 'n that way Kincaid'd have to keep his head down."

"Yeah," Andy said. "I can do it."

"We'll burn the bastard out," Purkee said.

Andy took the kerosene and a box of matches, then started toward the cabin, running in a bent-over position, keeping low, behind a ridge line.

"When he gets there, start firin' at the front of the house," Purkee told the others. "But be careful you don't hit Andy."

A moment later Andy popped up behind the ridge, and when he did, Purkee gave the signal to the others to open fire.

Nearly a dozen guns began firing, and the sound of the gun shots rolled back from the walls of the nearby canyon like thunder. It had the desired effect, and Martin Kincaid kept his head down, so he didn't see Andy splash kerosene onto the side of the cabin and strike a match. When Andy ran back to the ridge, the entire side of the cabin was enveloped in flame.

"Now," Purkee said, after the firing ceased. "All we have to do is wait. He'll be out in a minute and we'll have him."

"Give him a chance to surrender," Curly said.

"Slim was your friend, not mine," Purkee said. "I figured you'd want the first shot."

"I want to do it legal," Curly said.

The cowboys held their guns anxiously and looked at the cabin, watching for any sign of Kincaid. The flames climbed the wall and leaped to the roof of the cabin. The shake shingles caught fire quickly, and the fire soon spread to the front wall, and then to the other side, so that the entire cabin was one roaring inferno. Flames and smoke boiled high into the sky, but still Martin Kincaid did not appear.

"Where is he?" the cowboys asked.

"How can he stay in there?"

"Why don't he come out?"

The flames roared and cracked, and even from their vantage point, the cowboys were driven back by the heat.

Martin Kincaid did not appear.

"Hey, Purkee, they's a couple of riders comin'," one of the cowboys called.

Purkee stood up and looked at the approaching riders.

"One of 'em is Mr. Coulter," Purkee said. "I can tell by the way he's sittin' his horse."

"Who's the other fella?"

"It's Flynn," someone else said.

"Flynn? What's he doin' here?"

"I reckon we're about to find out," Purkee said matter-of-factly.

Mike and Lee dismounted when they reached the group of men, and Mike looked toward the burning cabin.

"What's that?" he asked. "What's going on here?"

"That's Kincaid's cabin," Purkee said. "We set it afire to try 'n get him to come out."

"Try?" Mike said, looking at Purkee quickly. "What do you mean, try?"

"Just what I said, mister, try," Purkee said. "He didn't come out."

"You mean he's still in there?"

"Yep."

"Damnit, Coulter, your men burned him *alive*," Mike swore angrily.

"We didn't intend to burn him," Purkee said. "We was jus' tryin' to get him to come out. He stayed in there of his own accord."

"Besides, the son of a bitch kilt Slim," one of the other cowboys said.

"To say nothin' of killin' Miss Jennie," Purkee added. "If you want my way of thinkin', he got his just reward."

Mike walked toward the blazing cabin, but he couldn't get too far before he hit a blistering wall of heat. He stood there, watching as the

321

house began to fall in on itself, and he felt sick at heart. Maybe Lee was right. Maybe he was responsible for all of this.

"Get them out of here, Coulter," Mike said quietly.

"You men go on back to the ranch," Lee said.

"If you don't mind, Mr. Coulter," Curly said. "I'd like to stay till I can get Slim's body back."

"That might not be such a good idea," Lee said. "The squatters are sure to see the smoke. When they do, they'll come over here, and if they find you, it wouldn't go good for you. You'd better come with us."

"I'm not leavin' Slim's body here for the vultures," Curly said. "And that means the critters who walk on two legs as well as the critters that fly."

"I'll stay," Mike offered. "I'll get his body for you."

"You'll stay?" Curly asked. "What for? I don't see you as carin' much about Slim, one way or the other."

"I didn't want to see him killed," Mike said. "Nor did I want to see Martin, or Jennie, or Caleb, or the professor killed. And I especially don't want to see anyone else killed. I'll stay."

"Why, I . . . I appreciate that, Flynn," Curly said.

"Will you be able to handle the squatters if they come?" Lee asked.

"I don't know," Mike said. "Maybe I can convince them that Slim and Martin killed each other. If it'll stop the range war, it'll be worth the try."

"There's only one way to really stop it," Lee said. "And I told you what that was."

"I know," Mike replied. He paused for a moment, then drew a deep breath. "That's why I'm not going to sell any more of the range land. I'm stopping the immigration."

"Are you serious?" Lee asked.

"Yes," Mike said quietly. "Call it a wedding present for you and Sara, if you like. You won, Coulter."

Chapter Twenty-Two

Headlines in the *Valley Monitor:*

RANGE WAR ENDS!

Peace Comes to the Valley
Unsold Range Land to be used
for grazing

After a terrible series of killings, violence and wanton destruction, the range war which has set farmer against rancher and neighbor against neighbor has come to an end. It was ended when Mike Flynn, President of the Cascade Railroad, and Lee Coulter, President of the Valley River Cattlemen's Association, reached a compromise.

Lee Coulter has stated that the ranchers will

honor the claims of those immigrants who are already settled, and Mike Flynn has agreed to sell no more land. This newspaper commends both gentlemen for their diplomacy, and prays that the peace thus effected shall be a lasting one.

On page four of the *Valley Monitor*, there was another article of great importance. It was in the Society column, and it told of the upcoming marriage of Sara Landers and Lee Coulter. A large wedding party was to be held at the Broken Lance Ranch, and every resident of the valley was invited.

When the newspapers were fresh off the press and still smelled of the ink, Sara took one copy over to the depot to give to Mike. As the paper contained her wedding announcement, she thought it would be better if she gave it to Mike in person.

The depot was much quieter than it had been in the past. Whereas it had been fairly bustling with the arrival of new immigrants and their belongings, the cessation of selling the land had brought a halt to the railroad business. Now the depot was empty, and only two boxes of freight sat on the loading platform. Sara didn't know whether it was freight which had already arrived and was awaiting claim, or freight which was to be shipped out. The fact that there were only two boxes somehow made the depot look less busy than if there were no boxes at all.

Burke was inside, but Mike wasn't around. Sara stood on the depot floor, holding the copy of the paper she was going to give Mike, and looked around. She saw the clock, the same one she had seen put on the wall on the day she had helped clean up the place for the meeting Mike had conducted to announce the introduction of rail service to the valley. That seemed like so long ago, though in reality it was but two months past.

"Hello, Miss Landers," Burke said. "Is there anything I can do for you?"

"Is Mr. Flynn around?" Sara asked.

"Yes, ma'am," Burke said. "He's out workin' on the engine."

"Oh? Is there something wrong with it?" Sara asked anxiously.

"Nothing bad," Burke said. "A few adjustments that have to be made. Now that we aren't so busy, we'll be able to get it back in shape. Not that it matters any," he added.

"What do you mean, not that it matters?" Sara asked.

"Simple," Burke said. "With no immigrant travel, we have no business. And there haven't been enough immigrants moving in to provide steady business so we'll go under."

"But no, must you?" Sara asked. "The railroad could mean so much to the valley."

"All it's meant so far is trouble," Burke said. "If you ask me, I wish they was some way we could take up the track 'n lay it somewhere else. It's not like that printin' press Mike bought for you. You can go anywhere with it. We're stuck here."

"What?" Sara asked, shocked by Burke's offhand comment. "What did you just say?"

"I said we're stuck here."

"No, I mean about the printing press. Did you say that *Mr. Flynn* bought it?"

"Yes, ma'am," Burke said. "He got it from a fella over in Eugene."

"Are you sure?"

"I can show you the invoice if you want, Miss Landers," Burke said.

"No, that's quite all right," Sara replied.

"I thought you knew."

"No, I had no idea."

Burke chuckled. "Well, if you know Mike Flynn like I know 'im, you wouldn't be none surprised by that. He's always doin' one good turn or another without takin' any of the credit for it. Why, you take these here immigrants, now. He's done loaned money to more'n half of 'em, 'n believe me, Miss Landers, he don' have any money to loan. It's jus' that he does things like that 'cause he's a man with a heart that's good as gold."

"I think I'd like to walk out to the engine to talk to him," Sara said. "Do you think he would mind if I did?"

"Mind? Miss Landers, the store he sets by you, he'd welcome a visit from you anytime, 'n you can mark my words on that."

"Where is the engine?"

Burke smiled. "Well now, you can't miss it,"

he said. "All you gotta do is follow the track. It's down to the west end of the terminal."

"Thanks," Sara said.

She left the depot and walked along the tracks toward the engine. It was sitting, naked and alone, at the end of the track, next to the bumper. There were no cars attached to it, and it looked much as it had on the day she had ridden in the engine cab with Mike.

Sara heard a clanking sound as she approached, and when she got there she saw a pair of legs protruding from beneath the engine, from between the two large driver wheels.

"Carl, is that you?" a voice asked. Sara recognized the voice as Mike's. "Hand me the spanner wrench, will you?"

There was an open tool box on the ground, and Sara looked inside. She had no idea which wrench was a spanner, but she picked up the first tool her hand touched and passed it beneath the engine to him.

"No," Mike said. "The spanner wrench."

"I don't know what a spanner wrench is," Sara said.

"Sara! Is that you?" Mike said, and as he started out from under the engine he bumped his head. "Ouch!"

"Are you all right?"

"Yes," Mike said, rubbing his head gingerly. He sat up and smiled at Sara. "What brings you here?"

"I thought I would deliver you a copy of the paper," Sara said.

"Well now," Mike replied, smiling broadly. "Now that's what I call service. It isn't everyone who gets the paper personally delivered by the publisher, is it?"

"No," Sara said. "But then, everyone didn't buy the equipment for me. You did."

"How did you find out?" Mike asked. "I told Post that it was to be kept a secret."

"Mr. Post didn't tell me," Sara said.

"Who did?"

"Never mind," Sara replied. "You did buy the equipment, didn't you? I'm in business because of you."

"You are in business because the *Valley Monitor* is a good newspaper."

"Do you really think so?"

"Of course I do. If I didn't, I wouldn't say so."

"There have been articles printed in the paper which upset you," Sara said.

"Yes."

"And yet you were willing to put the paper back in business. Don't you think that looks a little suspicious?"

"What do you mean?"

"Maybe you were trying to ease your conscience for having destroyed the paper in the first place."

Mike sighed. "Sara, you can't still believe that?"

"I don't know what I believe," Sara said. "I will tell you this. Whether you destroyed the newspaper office or not, I don't believe you in-

330

tended to hurt Dad . . . any more than you intended to hurt Jennie."

"I see," Mike said dryly. "And you've come to tell me all this in the spirit of compromise, have you?"

"Yes," Sara said. "Oh, Mike, I want us to be friends, if that is possible."

"How can you be friends with someone you could believe would do such things?" Mike asked.

"Because I don't think you intended for anyone to be hurt," Sara said. "I think you just wanted to . . ."

"That's nonsense, Sara and you know it," Mike interrupted. "Why don't you tell the truth?"

"And just what do you perceive the truth to be?" Sara flared hotly.

"The truth, Miss Landers, is that you are in love with me," Mike said. "You are in love with me and you are trying to ease your own conscience."

"That isn't true," Sara insisted.

"What part of it is untrue?" Mike asked. "The part about easing your conscience, or the part about your being in love with me?"

"I'm going to marry Lee," Sara said. She looked down at the paper she was holding, then she added, quietly, "In fact, that's why I'm delivering the paper to you. It's in the paper this week, and I thought I should tell you about it before you read it."

"Most decent of you," Mike said sarcastically.

"Mike, please!" Sara said. "Must you make this so hard for me?"

"If I could, Sara, girl, I would make it *impossible* for you," Mike said. "You have no business marrying Lee Coulter."

"I'm going to marry him this Saturday," Sara said.

"Saturday? That's day after tomorrow!"

"Yes."

"Sara, you can't marry him," Mike said.

"Won't you at least extend your best wishes?" Sara asked.

Mike looked at Sara, and all the pain he had ever suffered seemed reflected on his face at that moment. For an instant, that look alone was enough to make Sara change her mind, and yet, she couldn't. Not now. Things had gone too far. Then the look on Mike's face changed, and a door seemed to close in his eyes.

"Best wishes," he said quietly. He pulled a spanner wrench from the toolbox and lay back down beneath the engine. A second later, she heard the sound of him working.

Sara stood there, looking down at his legs, wondering why tears were streaming down her face. Then, after a long moment, she laid the newspaper in the toolbox, and turned and walked slowly back to the center of town. Her mind was made up. She would have to put Mike Flynn behind her, now and forever.

Lee and his foreman were riding along the shores of McCauley Lake at McCauley Pass. The lake, 6,000 feet high, was the source of water for the McCauley River, which ran through Butte Valley.

It was cool at this elevation, even at this time of the year, and horses and men alike left vapor clouds as they breathed. There were still banks of snow clinging to the rocks and in the shadows as a reminder of the 160-inch base that had accumulated during the previous winter.

The river trailed out behind the riders, cascading in wild, rushing white water, tumbling and roaring its way down to the valley floor, behind and below them. From up here the entire valley was visible; the town a neat collection of houses and stores, the ranches, large even from this perspective, and the farms neat and orderly, with the fields of crops making checkerboard squares.

"There," Purkee said, pointing to a rock overhang. "That's what I was talkin' about. Iffen a body was to bring that thing down into the river channel, why the water'd have to flow through the old Green River Bed."

"There is no riverbed for the Green River anymore," Lee said. "The water only went there during flood stage, and since the dam, there's no way for it to get through."

"But, iffen the dam was to be broke at about the same time them rocks was dropped in the McCauley Channel, what then?" Purkee asked.

Lee studied the lake for a while, then twisted in his saddle and looked down toward the valley. The Green River bed used to run right through the part of the valley which was now occupied by the farmers. He grinned.

"It would cut a new riverbed," he said.

"Right smack dab through the center of ever' pig farmer in the valley," Purkee said.

"With their crops flooded, they'd have no reason to stay," Lee said. "How soon can you get it done?"

"You gettin' married Sat'y, ain't you?" Purkee asked.

"Yes," Lee said.

Purkee smiled. "I can give it to you as a weddin' present," he said.

Chapter
Twenty-Three

The main house at Broken Lance Ranch might have been the most popular night club in San Francisco, for all its laughter and gaiety. Lee was throwing a party to celebrate his wedding to Sara, and there were guests from all over the state. Nearly every resident of town and nearly every rancher was there. Only the farmers were conspicuous by their absence.

The party began at one o'clock in the afternoon and was to continue until four, at which time the marriage ceremony would be performed. It was now nearly four, and the party had been going on all afternoon. There were more people than the house could accommodate, so many had moved out onto the lawn, where they continued to celebrate.

Music spilled out from the house, played not by one of the bands which ordinarily performed for the Saturday night dances, but by a full orchestra, hired by Lee just for the occasion.

Tables were piled with glazed hams, roast

duck and chicken, and fruits and vegetables of every color and texture. On the lawn two steer halves were spitted, and they turned slowly over open fires.

Liquid refreshment shared honors with all the food, for there were several bars established, one in the parlor, one in the dining room, and one in the main hall. If anyone had a thirst, no matter where they were, they were but a moment away from satisfying their need.

"Hey, Lee!" one of the ranchers called. "I just saw the parson arrive. This business is getting serious!"

The rancher's comment was greeted with laughter, and Father Percy pinkened with embarrassment when he walked into the middle of such a celebration.

"Are you all ready, vicar?" Lee asked.

Father Percy pulled at his collar with his finger and looked around the house, as the party continued in full force, totally unaware of his presence.

"Yes," he said. "I can't help but feel, however, that the marriage vows would have been better served in church."

"Surely the Lord wouldn't mind a man celebrating his wedding?" Lee challenged.

"The celebration is in order," Father Percy said. "But the sacrament of marriage should not turn into a—a drunken revelry."

"I'll get them quiet before the wedding," Lee said. "You can count on that."

"Where is Sara?" Father Percy asked.

"She's in the guest room, getting ready for the ceremony," Lee said, pointing upstairs. "I haven't seen her since she arrived, early this morning."

"I'll have a few words with her, if you don't mind."

"Have all the words you want, parson," Lee said. "But tell her that it's nearly time. We must be married by four."

Father Percy chuckled. "Oh, surely there's no precise timetable."

"Yes, there is," Lee said. "I have an announcement to make at exactly four o'clock, and then I want to be married."

"Very well, I shall tell her."

Sara sat at the dresser, critically examining the reflection that stared back at her. Not one blonde hair was out of place. Her brown eyes were cool and appraising, her complexion smooth. And yet, there was something wrong.

"I'm just nervous," she said to herself. "I once heard that all brides are nervous, just before they are married."

Sara got up from the dresser and walked over to the window. She looked out at the party-goers who were celebrating on the lawn below her. Then she looked back toward town. She could make out the church steeple and the roof of the hotel. But she couldn't quite see the depot. It was just beyond the hotel. Perhaps if she stood on a chair, she could see the roofline.

Suddenly Sara blushed. What was she doing? She was trying to see the depot because her mind was on Mike Flynn. But how could that be? She was about to be married. Surely she wouldn't think of another man on her wedding day! And yet, she had only to close her eyes, and she could see him. With a little imagination she could almost *feel* him; the burning touch of his lips, the tender caress of his hands, the . . .

A knock on the door interrupted Sara's musings and startled her back to reality. The palms of her hands were sweating, and her skin was flushed. There was another knock.

"Sara, it's me, Father Percy."

"You can come in," Sara said.

Percy stepped into the room, and as he looked at Sara in her wedding gown, he smiled.

"My, my, my," he said. "Never have I performed a ceremony for a more beautiful bride."

"Thank you," Sara said.

"It is such a shame that your father can't be here to see you like this. He would have been so proud."

"My father thought a great deal of Lee," Sara said. "I hope he is happy about this . . . that is, if a spirit can be happy."

"Of course a spirit can be happy, child," Father Percy said. "After all, isn't that the hope of Christianity?"

"I suppose so," Sara said.

"What is it, Sara? You seem strangely pensive."

"Do I? I'm sorry, I guess it's just nervousness. Aren't all brides nervous?"

"Nervous, yes," Father Percy said. "Pensive, no. Sara, are you absolutely certain that you want to do this?"

"Of course I am," Sara said quickly. "What makes you think I'm not?"

"I don't know," Father Percy said. "Maybe it's just a feeling I have."

"Anyway, it's too late to be having second thoughts now," Sara said. "I'm about to be married."

"It's not too late yet," Father Percy said. "After the ceremony, it will be too late."

There was another knock on the door, and Mrs. Carter called out.

"Sara, honey, it's time. Is the parson in there?"

Father Percy looked at Sara, and Sara took a deep breath, then nodded at him. "I'm ready," she said quietly.

"We're coming now," Father Percy called back.

Sara waited for Father Percy to go downstairs. Then she picked up her bouquet and went down the stairs. At the foot of the stairs she looked into the parlor. The parlor had been filled with chairs, though an aisle had been left in the middle to allow her to walk through to the front.

"There she is," someone whispered.

"Oh, isn't she lovely?" one of the women said quietly.

The orchestra began playing the Wedding March, and Sara moved gracefully down the center aisle toward Father Percy and Lee. She moved into position to the right of Lee.

"Dearly beloved," Father Percy began. "We have come together—"

Suddenly the house shook with the sound of distant explosions, and there was a buzz of curiosity among the people.

"Don't be alarmed," Lee said, turning toward them and holding his hands up. "Don't be alarmed, that was just Purkee." He smiled broadly. "He just stopped up the McCauley, and blew the Green River dam."

"What?" Stump shouted. "What the hell did he want to do a crazy thing like that for?"

Lee pointed through the window toward the settlers' farms. "Just to take care of a little unfinished business," he said. "By tonight, every field these damned squatters have planted will be under water. They'll be ruined."

"Lee!" Sara said. "You did that?"

"Yes," Lee said proudly. "After tonight, this valley will be just like it was in the days before the immigrants arrived. They will all go home, believe me."

"Don't you understand?" Sara asked. "This *is* their home."

Lee laughed weakly. "Honey, that's no way for a rancher's wife to act."

"You're right," Sara said. "It is no way for a rancher's wife to act. Thank God, I'm not a rancher's wife. Father Percy, did you bring your buggy?"

"Yes, I did, child."

"How quickly can you get me into town?"

"I can have you there in under five minutes," Father Percy said, snapping the prayerbook closed.

"You can't walk out on me!" Lee said as Sara started toward the door. "Do you hear me? You can't walk out on me!"

"Watch me!" Sara said, and, angrily, she tossed the bouquet back over her shoulder.

True to his word, Father Percy had Sara in town in less than five minutes. She directed him to the depot, and when the buggy stopped, she hopped out and ran inside with her veil and train streaming out behind her.

"Mike!" she called. "Mike, are you here?"

Mike stepped out of his room and looked at Sara in total shock.

"My God, girl, what are you doin' here?" he asked.

"There's no time for all that now," she said. "Purkee's blown the Green River dam. All the farmers are going to be flooded out!"

"What?"

"The Green River bed runs through the land the farmers have been settling. That land is all going to be under water soon. We've got to warn them. They may be in danger."

"Damn!" Mike swore. "Burke, Burke, get out here!"

When Burke appeared, also shocked by

341

Sara's appearance, Mike told him what Sara said. "Get Carl," he said. "We've got to warn Penrake and the others."

The sound of hoofbeats made them look outside, and Curly swung down from his horse, almost before the animal had stopped running. He came inside.

"You!" Mike said, stepping toward him. "Is this the way the cattlemen honor their agreements?"

"Now hold on, Flynn," Curly said, holding up his hand. "I didn't have nothin' to do with this. Nothin' at all, 'n neither did Mr. Adams, nor any of the other ranchers. It was all Coulter's doin'."

"Well, whoever's doin' it was, it's too late now," Mike said. "The damage is done. We've got to get the farmers out of there."

"We can save their crops," Curly said.

"What?" Mike asked.

"We can save their crops," Curly said again. "If we can get enough people 'n enough shovels, we can close in Indian Chute. That way the water can't get into the old river bed."

"Yes!" Sara said excitedly. "Mike, that will work. Oh, but—it would take so many people."

"Well," Curly said, smiling broadly, "if Flynn can get the pig farmers to pitch in, I guess there'll be enough. Look outside at what's comin'."

Mike and Sara walked over to the door and Sara gasped. There were more than forty men approaching the depot, all carrying shovels, axes, and handsaws. There were cowboys and ranchers, and even some of the clerks and merchants from the town. Most were still in their suits, having just come from the party.

"Curly, isn't Indian Chutes close to Butte Pass?" Mike asked.

"Yes, no more'n a quarter of a mile away."

"Carl, make up the train," Mike said. "Burke, you round up the farmers. Tell them to get to the track and we'll pick 'em up. Come on, we'll take the train to Butte Pass!"

While Carl and Burke went about their jobs, Mike went out front and told the gathering men what he had in mind. They let out a cheer, and headed for the cars.

Carl had the engine backed up and connected to the cars in a few moments. Mike climbed up into the engine cab, then reached down and helped Sara up behind him.

"Does it look familiar?" he asked her, smiling broadly.

"It looks wonderful," Sara said.

Carl opened the throttle and the engine started, jerking the line of cars until the entire train was in motion. The steam puffed and roared, and the train began moving at a pretty good clip.

"Blow the whistle," Mike said to Sara, pointing toward the whistle cord. "We need to let the farmers know we're coming."

"I get to blow the whistle?"

"That you do, Miss Landers," Mike said. "Or is it Mrs. Coulter?"

"It is not Mrs. Coulter," Sara said resolutely. "And it never will be!" She punctuated her comment by pulling hard on the whistle cord, and the whistle called out to everyone that the train was in motion.

All along the track, farmers met the train, so that by the time it reached Butte Pass, it was full of people, farmers and their wives and children, ranchers and their hands.

"All right," Mike called to them. "We've got to close in Indian Chute. If we can, that will force the water back into the lake, and it'll cut its way through to the McCauley channel."

The water had already began to flow through Indian Chute by the time they started working, and they had to stand knee deep and shovel mud. They worked side by side, farmer and rancher, digging in the mud, piling up a hasty dam. A couple of times they nearly had it stopped, only to see a large, mud wall collapse, and they had to start over again.

"Mr. Penrake!" Curly suddenly shouted. "Mr. Penrake, look out!"

Curly had seen a boulder loosened by the water start to tumble toward Penrake, and only his timely shout prevented Penrake from being seriously injured. Penrake managed to jump aside just in time.

"Thank you, young man," Penrake said gratefully, after the boulder crashed into the mud right where he had been standing.

"That's all right," Curly answered, embarrassed.

The others had seen the close call as well. Then Mike got an idea.

"Men, we're going about this all wrong," he said. "Let's get up there and loosen as many rocks as we can. If we can get them to fall into the chute, they'll hold better than the mud."

At Mike's suggestion the workers clambered up the side of the hill and began working. After about thirty minutes of labor, the rocks started to slide down. They fell slowly at first, then faster and faster until the chute was completely dammed up. There was a loud cheer of victory.

Mike looked over at Sara. She was still in her wedding dress, and it was black with mud. She saw him looking at her, then she looked down at herself and moaned.

"Oh," she said. "Oh, I look awful."

Mike smiled. "No you don't," he said. "You look beautiful. In fact, I've never seen you look more beautiful."

"Mike," Carl said. "I think someone should go over to McCauley Pass and blow the dam that Purkee put across the river channel."

"That's a good idea," Mike said. "Would you do it?"

"I'll go with you," Curly offered.

"Me too," one of the squatters put in.

"I'll go," Carl said. "But who will help you drive the engine? You've got to get these people back to town."

Mike looked over at Sara. "I've got someone in mind," he said. "Someone with experience, if she'll take the job."

"I'll take the job," Sara said.

Mike walked over to her and took her hands in his. "I ought to warn you," he said. "This is a job with a lifetime commitment. Will you still take it?"

"I'll take it," Sara replied.

"Well?" Burke shouted. "Are you just going to stand there, or are you going to kiss her?"

"I'm going to kiss her," Mike said, and he pulled her to him, pressing his lips against hers. The crowd cheered in lusty approval—but Sara heard only the pounding of her own heart.